THE STORY OF AMERICA.
THE NOVELS OF J. L. REASONER...

RIVERS OF GOLD

Based on dramatic true events, the riveting story of the ultimate American dream: the 1849 California Gold Rush...

THE HEALER'S ROAD

In America's darkest hour, one family of doctors had the courage to heal a nation that was wounded by war...

HEALER'S CALLING

In a world where few women were allowed to become doctors, one woman dared to follow her dream...

Available from Berkley Books

Also by J. L. Reasoner

RIVERS OF GOLD
THE HEALER'S ROAD
HEALER'S CALLING

COSSACK
THREE
PONIES

J. L. REASONER

BERKLEY BOOKS, NEW YORK

COSSACK THREE PONIES

A Berkley Book / published by arrangement with
the author

PRINTING HISTORY
Berkley edition / February 1997

The Putnam Berkley World Wide Web site address is
http://www.berkley.com/berkley

ISBN: 0-425-15666-4

BERKLEY®
Berkley Books are published by The Berkley Publishing Group,
200 Madison Avenue, New York, New York 10016.
BERKLEY and the "B" design
are trademarks belonging to Berkley Publishing Corporation.

PRINTED IN THE UNITED STATES OF AMERICA

10 9 8 7 6 5 4 3 2 1

FOR DAVID WINKLER,
WHO PROVIDED BOTH THE IDEA
AND THE ENCOURAGEMENT

PROLOGUE

CLIMBS HIGH, CHIEF OF THE
River band of the Crows, walked from his lodge and gazed
around the village of his people. The winter had been hard,
and everywhere he looked, he saw the results of the long,
cold moons. There were fewer old ones, because some had
voluntarily starved to death so that the rest of the band
would have more food. And some of the children born the
previous autumn had not survived the winter, either. Gaunt
dogs who seemed to carry the knowledge of their ultimate
fate in their burning eyes slunk from lodge to lodge, searching for any forgotten morsel of food. Many members of the
band were gaunt, too.

But a warm breeze was blowing over the plains, and
Climbs High felt its encouraging touch on his face as it ruffled the feathers of his tall headdress. Spring was coming,
and with the spring would come the buffalo, and the hunt
would be a good one. Plenty of meat would fill the bellies
of the Crow children, and the people would be happy. But
only if the spirits allowed this to come to pass.

The wife of Climbs High, a young woman called Grass
Waving in the Wind, stepped up beside her husband and
rested a hand on his arm. Behind her was their son, a young
boy known for the time being as Rabbit's Hind Foot. He

would have a different name when he grew to manhood and became the chief of this Crow band, following in his father's footsteps.

"What are you thinking, Climbs High?" Grass asked quietly and somewhat tentatively. She knew her husband to be a man who did not share his thoughts readily.

But today the Crow chief was in an expansive mood. "A vision came to me during the night," he said to his wife. "It told me this will be a good year for our people, but only if we are able to please the spirits."

"How can we do that?"

"I must speak of this with the shaman to know for certain, but I believe it is time we strike once again against our enemies the Blackfeet. This will please the spirits, and they will look in favor on us."

"Then it is to be war?" Grass Waving in the Wind would accept anything her husband told her, of course; such was the way of their people. But she hoped, in her heart, that this year would not bring war with the Blackfeet.

"The boy," Climbs High said with a grunt. "It is time for us to take the boy again."

Grass knew he was not talking about their son. "You mean the grandson of Buffalo's Back Fat?"

Climbs High nodded, a look of savage anticipation appearing on his face. "This time when we steal him, the Blackfeet will not steal him back. The boy will become one of us, or he will be our slave. Either way, he will not become the chief of the Blackfeet when his grandfather dies."

Grass nodded in acceptance of his decision. This would not be the first time the Crows had kidnapped the Blackfoot boy from his people, but each time in the past, Buffalo's Back Fat and the other warriors of the Piegan Blackfoot band had rescued him. Grass knew that the memory of those past failures gnawed at Climbs High, and she thought that perhaps it was not the spirits speaking to her husband so much as it was his own thirst for vengeance. Either way, it would not matter. Climbs High had made up his mind.

Now all that was left to do was wait for the proper time to strike.

1

THE HEAVY BLAST OF EXPLOD-
ing black powder filled the crisp air of Montana Territory.
Spread over the rolling hills, almost as far as the eye could
see, a herd of buffalo grazed, great shaggy humpbacked
beasts of brown and black, the bulls sporting short horns
that curved wickedly like sabers. As the sound of the shot
echoed across the hills, one of the buffalo suddenly
lurched forward a step. The creature shook its head as if
mightily puzzled by what had just happened to it, then its
front legs folded underneath it. The buffalo fell forward,
its muzzle scraping the dirt and grass of the prairie. A low,
plaintive rumble sounded from deep within its body.

Slowly, the buffalo rolled onto its side and died.

"Hurrah! An excellent shot, Count Orlov! I daresay none
of these unwashed frontiersmen could have done better."

Count Frederick Orlov lowered the long-barreled flintlock rifle he held, a tendril of gray smoke curling from its
muzzle. A man in his very vital middle years, Frederick's
features were tanned by long exposure to the sun and wind.
He sported a closely trimmed mustache that was shot
through with gray, just like the thick shock of hair under his
fur cap. A satisfied smile stretched across his face as his
dark eyes regarded the kill.

The rest of the buffalo ignored the shot that had felled one of their number. According to the guides the hunting party had hired in St. Louis, these creatures had small, primitive brains and had not yet figured out the connection between the loud explosion, the stench of burned powder, and the death that usually followed almost instantly. Often dozens of the beasts could be felled before the rest of the herd began to realize they were in danger. Then they were likely to stampede.

Frederick turned toward his companions. A good-sized group stood on the hilltop with him, many of them dressed in clothes expensive enough to have outfitted a whole troop of American soldiers—such as the ones who waited down-slope, near the bank of the Missouri River and the riverboat tied up there. The men wore capes and high black boots and astrakhan hats. The women were garbed in fine gowns and had fur stoles wrapped around them to protect them from the slight chill that was still in the spring air. The berib-boned bonnets of the younger women were a splash of bright color in a landscape of browns and greens and grays. Several of the women applauded Frederick as he lowered the butt of the rifle to the ground and struck a pose: the great hunter. All that was lacking was the carcass of the buffalo at his feet.

Still smiling, Frederick asked, "And what did you think of my shot, Alena?"

An attractive young woman, some fifteen or sixteen years old, pushed back a strand of the long red hair that the wind had blown into her face. "It was fine, Frederick," she answered with a noticeable lack of enthusiasm.

The count's eyes narrowed, and the line of his jaw tight-ened slightly. He had not missed the young woman's tone. But before he could say anything else, the other members of the party crowded around to congratulate him, his fellow noblemen slapping him on the back, the women showering compliments. Frederick accepted the accolades as his due. After all, he had led the group here into the American wilderness on this journey of exploration and adventure.

The young woman called Alena was not the only one in

the party who was looking at the Russian aristocrat with something like disfavor. Indeed, some of the American soldiers were gazing at him with outright hostility, although they wiped such emotions off their faces every time the young lieutenant in command of the troop glanced their way. Less discreet were two men wearing fringed buckskins and broad-brimmed felt hats, each with an eagle feather stuck in the band. The older man, who had a full white beard, glared at Frederick. The younger man had shoulder-length dark hair and a drooping mustache, and it was clear that he did not care for the Russian aristocrat any more than his partner did.

The final members of the party were a small group of tall, muscular men in red coats and fur caps, armed with flintlocks and sabers. They were Cossacks, soldiers from the Russian frontier who were a natural choice to accompany Count Orlov and his companions on this expedition. One of them, a massive, broad-shouldered man with a neatly trimmed dark beard, met Alena's eyes as she looked past the group congratulating Frederick. A sympathetic expression appeared on the Cossack's face, but only for an instant. Then his features were once again set in firm, unreadable lines.

Frederick allowed the others to fawn over him for a few moments longer, then walked down the hill to speak to the American officer in charge of the troop. "You'll have your men skin the beast, Lieutenant O'Neal?" he asked. The words were more of a command than a request. "I shall want the head and horns as a trophy."

"Of course, sir," O'Neal replied. "what about the rest of the carcass?"

Frederick shrugged. "Leave it to rot, I suppose."

Flies were already starting to buzz around the head of the slain buffalo. Their hum could be heard, even at a distance, in the thin, high-country air.

The riverboat was still tied up at the bank of the Missouri, where it had been since afternoon when Count Frederick Orlov had first spotted the buffalo herd and decided to take a shot at one of the animals. The boat's captain, a veteran of many trips up and down the river known as the Big Muddy, refused to travel at night. The broad, slow-moving stream with its sometimes hidden sandbars was treacherous enough even in broad daylight, the captain said. A man would be risking his boat's hull to try it at night.

The buffalo Frederick had shot that afternoon was the first kill of the trip, and the celebration of that feat was still in progress. On the forward deck, Frederick and his friends were passing around a bottle of the finest Russian vodka, a reminder of home, and lustily singing folk songs at the top of their lungs. It was enough to wake the dead, Zephaniah Crawford thought as he stood at the railing of the boat, as far away from the Russians as he could get. He and his friend Titus had a jug of their own, but it didn't have anything in it made from potatoes, that was for sure. Zephaniah took the jug from Titus, tilted it to his mouth, and took a swig of good old American corn squeezin's.

He lowered the jug, licked drops of whiskey off the thick white mustache that hung down over his mouth, and said, "That's mighty good. I just wish it'd drown out the sound o' them Rooshans singin'."

"I don't reckon even a whole wolf pack could do that," Titus said. He glanced toward the celebrating group at the other end of the riverboat. "A wolf pack—that's what *they* are, Zeph."

Zephaniah sighed and combed his fingers through the tangles of his beard. "I reckon you're right, boy."

He looked toward the snowcapped mountains looming up in the distance. The moon was nearly full tonight, and as the silvery illumination washed down over the peaks, the snow and ice shone brilliantly. Not for nothing had the Indians dubbed them the Shining Mountains.

It had been twenty years since Zephaniah had first set eyes on those craggy heights. He had come west from Pennsylvania with the first wave of fur trappers venturing into the Rockies, drawn by the lure of easy money and freedom. Behind him he had left a farm that had never been successful, a wife who had long since grown tired of him, and a passel of kids. There had been nights when he'd felt guilty about abandoning them, sure enough, but the guilt eased whenever he looked at the mountains and the prairie and saw wildflowers waving in the breeze and smelled the clean scent of pines. Some men were meant for home and hearth. Others were destined for a lonelier, wilder existence. Zephaniah knew where he belonged.

A footstep behind them made both mountain men turn their heads. A large figure loomed up out of the shadows, and a voice asked in accented English, "Do you mind if I join you?"

Zephaniah grinned. "Suit yourself, Viktor."

The Cossack had taken off his fur cap, but even without it he was still more than a head taller than Zephaniah and Titus. His red coat hung open, revealing a hip-length shirt of heavy, light-colored linen, drawn tight by a broad black belt. As he leaned on the railing next to Zephaniah, he reached into one of the pockets of his coat and pulled out a pipe.

Zephaniah took a pouch of tobacco from his belt. "Let me fill that up for you, Viktor," he offered.

"I am much in your debt."

"Not hardly. It's just some 'baccy."

When all three men had their pipes going, Viktor gazed off toward the mountains. "This land reminds me of the steppes of my home," he said after a moment.

"So I've heard," Zephaniah said. "Ain't never been to Roosha, and 'tain't likely I'll ever go. I'm pretty fiddle-footed, but not *that* fiddle-footed."

"Fiddle-footed . . ." Viktor repeated. "This means you are restless?"

"Yep. That's sure 'nough what it means."

Viktor nodded. "Then I, too, am fiddle-footed. Most of my countrymen are."

Zephaniah knew Viktor was talking about the other Cossacks. They considered themselves Russians, but there was a big difference between them and noblemen such as Count Orlov. Zephaniah knew that much after only a couple of weeks spent with the party of visitors.

If all the Russians were like Viktor Dorochenko, Zephaniah reflected, they wouldn't be such a bad bunch. But Viktor seemed to be something of an exception.

Titus leaned forward and extended the jug past Zephaniah. "Have yourself a nip there, Viktor," he said.

Viktor took the jug and nodded. "My thanks, Titus. I
hope I am not interrupting your discussion."

"Nope. Me and Zeph was just talkin' about how that
Count Orlov fella don't know buffler chips from Sunday
breakfast."

"Titus!" Zephaniah said with a frown. "That gent is Viktor's boss, and you ain't got no call to talk about him that
way."

"But he wanted to let all that meat rot! You'd think they
never et buffler steak over there in Roosha." Titus smacked
his lips. "I sure enjoyed fryin' up a mess of it for supper
tonight."

Viktor was frowning as well, but in deep thought. Finally, his expression cleared and he nodded. "Ah! Buffalo
chips from Sunday breakfast—now I understand." He lifted
the jug to his mouth and tilted his head back. When he had
lowered the jug and wiped the back of his other hand across
his mouth, he nodded again and went on, "You are right,
friend Titus."

Zephaniah kept his voice pitched low so it wouldn't
travel. "I didn't figger you could talk about them aristocrats
like that."

Viktor glanced disdainfully over his shoulder at the
group on the far end of the deck. Their singing had gotten
louder and more slurred. "What Count Orlov does not hear
will not hurt him . . . or me."

The three men smoked in silence for a moment, then
Viktor continued, "Your Indians, they hunt buffalo, do they
not?"

"They ain't *our* Indians. They don't belong to nobody
but themselves, or maybe the Great Spirit." Zephaniah
scratched at a flea that had taken refuge in his beard. "But
they hunt buffalo, all right. Depend on the critters for just
about everything they got, in fact. You never saw some-

body use up a thing all the way down to nothin' the way an Injun uses a buffalo carcass."

"They eat ever'thing that's fit to eat in a buffler," Titus said, "and some things that really ain't, as far as I'm concerned. They use the hides to make robes when they leave the hair on, and when they strip it off and tan the hides by rubbin' the brains on 'em, they can make clothes and lodge skins. They use the bones for tools." He grinned broadly. "I've picked my teeth more'n once with a sharpened buffler bone."

Viktor nodded. "As always, I appreciate the way you are teaching me about this land. I have much to learn."

"I ain't sure why you're so interested," Titus said. "Shoot, once this here expedition is over, you'll be headin' back to Roosha with all the other folks."

"True, but I would still learn all that I can. It is important to know things."

Titus took another nip from the jug. "What I'd like to know is how did a pretty little gal like that Miss Alena wind up fixin' to marry an old fella like the count. That don't hardly seem right somehow."

In a warning tone, Zephaniah said, "That ain't none of our business, Titus."

Viktor answered anyway. "They are betrothed," he said heavily. "The marriage has been arranged by the families. Nothing more can be said or done about it. When we return to Russia, Alena will become the count's bride."

"Still don't seem right—" Titus began.

"Tell us some more 'bout the Cossacks, Viktor," Zephaniah cut in, deliberately changing the subject. "Sounds to me like you boys take to the wild lonesome over there in Roosha just like me and Titus do to this high country over here."

"Wild lonesome," Viktor repeated with a nod. "Yes, that is what our land is like."

The celebration at the other end of the boat hit a lull at that moment, as the last strains of another drunken song died away. From a distance, the howl of a wolf came floating over the prairie. Zephaniah and Titus looked at each other and chuckled.

Viktor seemed to be caught up in his own thoughts and didn't notice their reaction. He said, "Tonight, I miss Mother Russia more than ever. I almost wish the count and his friends had never come to your country to hunt the buffalo and see the Indians. But if they had not . . ." A grin spread across his normally stern face. "Then I would not have met my new friends Titus and Zephaniah."

Titus raised the jug. "Here's to the frontier, boys, no matter what country it's in!"

"Aye," Viktor said as he took the whiskey. "Here is to the frontier. . . ."

2

DROPLETS OF WATER SPARKLED in the sunlight like a silver curtain. The paddle wheel of the steamer kicked up the spray as it churned through the waters of the Missouri River. The riverboat, with the name *Prairie Flower* painted on its side, was a stern-wheeler, not as wide as the side-wheelers that commonly plied the Mississippi. While it was true that the riverbed of the Missouri was both shallow and wide, there were places where the channel of the river itself was rather narrow. A stern-wheeler stood a better chance of being able to navigate through those places.

Smoke rose from the vessel's stack, and the roar of its engine could be heard for a long way. Alena dipped her head and tried to shut out the noise, concentrating instead on the sounds that came from the instrument in her hands. Her fingers plucked at the strings of the balalaika, searching for the notes she wanted. Small creases appeared in her forehead as she struggled with the music. Finally, she sighed, shook her head, and lowered the balalaika to her lap.

Alena sat on a crate that had been placed on the deck. Beside her, an older woman perched on another crate with her back rigidly upright. The woman had placed a small, embroidered pillow underneath her, but it was obvious she still considered the seat to be quite uncomfortable. She looked over at Alena and said, "You should not become impatient. It takes time to master any skill."

Alena ignored the words of encouragement. Her green eyes scanned the horizon on both sides of the river as she asked nervously, "Do you think we will see any Indians today, Aunt Zora?"

Her aunt snorted, a sound that was perhaps unladylike but certainly emphatic. "I hope not! These so-called civilized Americans are barbaric enough. I do not know why Frederick and his friends were so excited about visiting America. They should be back in Mother Russia, helping our beloved Czar Nicholas protect the empire."

"I think Nicholas will be able to manage without them for a short time, Aunt Zora." Alena's gaze still searched the prairie, dreading and yet halfway anticipating a glimpse of bronzed skin and painted face. There was nothing there, of course, only endless grass and an occasional small animal. "I have heard that when these American Indians capture white women, they make them their wives."

Zora waved a hand in dismissal of such an obviously absurd idea. "Dorochenko and his Cossacks will not allow any harm to come to us. Twenty years ago, when that mad Frenchman Bonaparte came to our land, Dorochenko was one of the valiant defenders who sent him crawling back to France! The Cossacks may be almost as barbaric as these Americans, but they are great fighters."

"That *was* twenty years ago," Alena pointed out.

"Viktor Dorochenko is more of a man now than he was then!" Zora gestured demandingly at the balalaika. "You must practice."

Alena made a face and plucked idly at the strings. She thought about her aunt's words, especially her comments about Viktor Dorochenko. It was true that the Cossack was an impressive physical specimen. Alena knew him as well to be intelligent, not at all the ignorant country bumpkin that nobles such as Frederick who spent most of their time in Moscow or St. Petersburg would have one believe about all Cossacks. Alena glanced at Zora. Her aunt had sounded almost admiring of Dorochenko. Zora was only in early middle age and was still a handsome woman despite the threads of gray in her hair. Was it possible that she and the Cossack . . . ?

No, Alena decided, that was definitely impossible. Zora would never violate aristocratic social and moral codes by dallying with a commoner, and a Cossack at that, no matter how ruggedly attractive such a man might be. Still, it was an intriguing notion.

"Alena! The balalaika!" Zora's words broke into Alena's musings.

"I do not know why I must play this thing. I am no good at it."

"A young lady should play a musical instrument. There was no way we could bring a harpsichord on this riverboat, was there?"

Alena strummed the strings of the balalaika. "I suppose not." She began to play again, once more concentrating on the intricate movements of her fingers. Music flowed from the instrument, and this time the notes were true, the melody sweet and melancholy at the same time.

Behind the two women, Viktor Dorochenko emerged from a companionway, stopping when he heard the music. Alena's back was to him, but her head was uncovered and he could see the smooth fall of her thick red hair. The music was lovely, reminiscent of his homeland along the Don River. As he listened, the expression on his face softened.

After a moment he squared his shoulders, turned, and forced himself to walk back down the companionway steps.

The landscape seemed to be unchanging. The river wound its way through the endless prairie between low bluffs. In the distance to the west, the Rocky Mountains rose majestically. Viktor knew logically that they were drawing closer to the peaks, but it was difficult to tell that from looking at them. They seemed as far away as ever.

The riverboat was bound for Fort Union, an outpost of

the American army deep in this territory called Montana. From there, the group would travel on by wagon and horseback, penetrating deeper into the wilderness than any party of Russian dignitaries had ever journeyed before. The route, as well as all the other plans for this expedition, had been worked out during months of discussion between the American government and representatives of the czar. The Americans had welcomed their foreign guests with a round of parties in Washington. Viktor had been thoroughly bored with all of this. He had hated the long sea voyage that had brought them to this country, too. The trip had started to become interesting only when they headed west again, through mountain passes and along mighty rivers and across the vast expanse of what was coming to be called the Great American Desert. The prairie was not really a desert, of course; plant life was abundant, as were animals. As Viktor had said to Zephaniah and Titus, the terrain reminded him greatly of the steppes.

He stood at the railing and watched the riverbanks move slowly past. A brisk wind blew, making Viktor glad he was wearing thick trousers, a linen shirt called a *rubashka,* and a fur-lined, sleeveless jacket known as a *sarafan* underneath the red coat. To someone who had lived through many Russian winters, a spring day such as this seemed almost balmy, of course, but Viktor had to admit, if only to himself, that he was not as young as he had once been. His bones ached if they grew too chilled.

While the party was traveling on the riverboat, there was little for him to do. He and his fellow Cossacks had come along to protect the nobles, and the American soldiers had accompanied the group for the same purpose. There was no danger here on the river, though, at least none that flintlock and saber could ward off. The biggest worry at the moment was the boat getting stuck on one of the many sandbars that dotted the river.

Frederick and his friends were all at the forward railing of the *Prairie Flower,* using spyglasses to study the landscape—as well as to look for something to shoot at. Viktor

was not surprised when an excited shout suddenly went up
from one of the men.

"Look there! Are those reindeer?"

Frederick turned, looking for Zephaniah and Titus. He
gestured curtly to the two mountain men, who were loung-
ing on a couple of crates. "Come here and tell us what
those animals are," he commanded.

Viktor watched as Zephaniah and Titus exchanged a
glance, then placed their hands on their knees and re-
signedly stood up. They went forward, and Zephaniah
asked, "What critters are you talkin' about, Count?"

Viktor was certain Zephaniah had asked the question
solely to annoy Frederick. The eyes of the old, buckskin-
clad man were quite sharp, and Viktor felt sure they had already spotted the animals running swiftly and gracefully
along a ridge that paralleled the river. Viktor had noticed
them moments earlier, discerning them easily with the
naked eye before any of the spyglass-wielding noblemen
had done so.

Frederick pointed at the herd and said icily, "*Those* animals."

"Oh, them critters. Why didn't you say so?" Zephaniah
tugged at his beard. "Them's antelope."

"Can we shoot them?"

Zephaniah shrugged. "That's up to you."

"Antelope steak ain't too bad," Titus added. "They're a
mite harder to bring down than buffler, though. Critters are
fast, and they spook easy."

"Good," Frederick said. "Then they shall be a challenge." He turned his head and called, "Lieutenant
O'Neal!"

The American officer stepped up to Frederick and
saluted smartly. "What can I do for you, Count?"

"Have the captain of this vessel put in to shore immediately. We are going to shoot those antelope." Frederick
waved casually at the animals on the ridge, which had come
to a halt and were peering down curiously at the riverboat.

O'Neal sent a trooper to relay the orders to the captain in
the wheelhouse. The *Prairie Flower* edged toward the

shore. Zephaniah suggested, "Better get that engine shut off as soon as possible. Them antelope ain't goin' to hang around a long time with all that chuffin' and blowin' goin' on."

Within a few minutes the prow of the riverboat was nudging the bank where the river had cut a channel next to the shore. The captain called down to the engine room on the speaking tube, and a moment later the engine fell silent. The paddle wheel slowed to a halt.

"Bring the guns and the shooting stands," Frederick said to his majordomo. The servant nodded and hurried belowdecks, taking two more men with him from the small party of servants that had accompanied the expedition.

Viktor and the other Cossacks watched, along with Zephaniah and Titus, as half a dozen shooting stands were set up on the bank of the river. The antelope were still looking on, too, no doubt curious about the scurrying movements of the humans.

"They ain't runnin' off 'cause they're used to bein' hunted by Injuns," Zephaniah explained in a low voice to Viktor. "They know we ain't close enough to be shootin' arrows at 'em. They don't know enough about guns to be scared."

"They will learn, when enough of them have been killed," Viktor said.

"They sure will," Zephaniah agreed.

As the noblemen took their places, resting long-barreled flintlocks on the shooting stands to steady their aim, Frederick told them, "We must all fire together. The antelope will bolt once the shooting begins. Is this not correct?"

Zephaniah and Titus both nodded from the deck of the riverboat. "They'll take off for the tall and uncut, all right," Titus said.

"Each man should choose a different target," Frederick went on. He looked around. "Sasha! Do you not want to shoot?"

One of the noblemen, younger than the others, still stood on the deck. He shook his head and called, "You go ahead, Frederick."

A frown of disapproval appeared for a second on Frederick's forehead. It was clear what he thought of his younger brother's decision not to participate in the shooting. But that was not unusual, Viktor mused as he watched the exchange. In the twenty-five years of Sasha Orlov's life, he had done little to please his demanding older brother.

The count turned back to his own rifle and placed his cheek against the smooth wood of the stock as he began lining up his shot. The other men did the same. Along the railing of the boat, the female members of the party congregated, ready to applaud the efforts of their men. Alena and her aunt Zora were among them, Viktor saw, but also as usual, Alena did not seem particularly interested in the spectacle that was about to take place.

"Do you all have your targets?" Frederick asked his fellow hunters. A murmured chorus of assent came back from then. He continued, "Then on my command . . . *Fire!*"

A deafening volley rang out, and smoke poured from the barrels of the flintlocks, leaving a thick haze in the air to be slowly shredded and carried away by the lazy breeze. Viktor gripped the railing and leaned forward, scanning the ridge where the herd of antelope had stood an instant earlier. As the mountain men had warned, the uninjured members of the herd had fled at the sound of the shots, vanishing in the blink of an eye. But four of the antelope had been left behind on the ground. One lay still, perhaps killed instantly by the heavy lead ball that had struck it. The other three, however, were thrashing around and making noises of pain. One of the antelope tried to struggle to its feet and collapsed in a quivering heap. Viktor saw blood spray from its nostrils as it fell.

Zephaniah spat over the railing into the river. "Come on, Titus," he said. "Let's go put those critters out of their misery."

"Stop!" Frederick commanded as the two men in buckskins leaped agilely from the deck to the riverbank. "My friends and I will deliver the finishing shots ourselves. It is our right."

"Go ahead, then," Zephaniah said. "Get it done."

Frederick glared at the curt tone of the old man, but he did not pause to reprimand Zephaniah or argue with him. Instead he said to his servant, "Bring me my pistols."

The other aristocrats issued the same order to their servants, and a few minutes later the party of noblemen started up the hill toward the wounded antelope. Since it was obvious the riverboat was going to be here for a while, the women began to go ashore as well, although they discreetly turned their eyes away from the grisly task the men were about to carry out.

Alena had not watched the shooting at all, Viktor had noticed. She had kept her eyes downcast the entire time. She left the boat now, prodded along by her aunt.

3

ALENA TRIED NOT TO THINK about what was going to happen up there atop the ridge. A part of her waited for the shots that would signify the deaths of those beautiful creatures, but for the most part she was able to force those thoughts out of her head. The other women, the wives and daughters of the noblemen who had accompanied Frederick on this journey, chattered happily among themselves. Alena almost wished she could join in their talk, could accept her fate as easily and carelessly as they did their own.

It would do no good to brood about it, or to try to talk to Aunt Zora. Nothing could be done.

"Good day to you, Alena. I trust you are enjoying yourself?"

The man's voice made her glance up in surprise. Sasha, Frederick's younger brother, stood there in front of her, shuffling his booted feet rather awkwardly. He was taller and more slender than Frederick, and his face was clean-shaven. From the way he stood with his right hand behind his back, Alena knew he was concealing something from her.

She shrugged in answer to his question. In truth, she was definitely *not* enjoying herself, but it would accomplish nothing to admit that to Sasha.

He brought his hand from behind his back, revealing a bunch of wildflowers that were beautiful in their profusion of color. He extended the makeshift bouquet toward her and said, "I picked these for you."

Alena looked at him in surprise, her attention finally caught by this gesture. "Why?"

"I . . . I thought you might like them."

Alena took the flowers and smiled. "That is sweet of you." She buried her nose in the blooms and inhaled deeply. "They're lovely," she said as she lifted her head again.

Up on the ridge, pistol shots began to crack. Alena flinched a little, and she noticed that Sasha did so as well.

"Why are you not up there with your brother?" she asked.

It was Sasha's turn to shrug. "A man grows tired of shooting animals," he said.

Tired, as well, of being under the thumb of an older brother, Alena thought.

"Well," she said, "thank you for the flowers."

Sasha nodded and turned away, clearly embarrassed just to be talking to her. He walked along the riverbank, his gaze directed toward the ground.

Alena smelled the flowers again, then turned toward her aunt. Zora stood nearby, frowning. Obviously, she was not pleased about something.

"Sasha is very sweet, isn't he?" Alena said.

Zora snapped, "Sasha is nothing but a love-struck boy who wishes he was his brother Frederick. You know how he feels about you. A blind man could see it in his eyes."

Alena felt her face growing warm as she dropped her gaze toward the ground. "He . . . he is my friend. That is all."

Zora made a noise of disbelief. Alena did not glance up at her, unwilling to meet the glare of disapproval that was sure to be on Zora's face. Her aunt thought the impending marriage between Alena and Count Frederick Orlov was the best thing that had happened to the family in years, perhaps decades. She would be displeased to hear of Alena's reservations about the arrangement, but no more displeased than Alena's mother and father back in Russia would have been. They were counting on her.

She could not let them down, any of them . . . no matter what it might cost her.

Slowly, Viktor followed the count and the other noblemen down from the ridge. The four wounded antelope had been finished off with pistol shots to their heads. Viktor had seen plenty of bloodshed and death in his life. Violence was like meat and drink to Cossacks. But the killing of the animals still bothered him for some reason, especially the casual way Frederick and the others turned their backs on the creatures they had killed. It would not have been so bad if they had paused for a moment to reflect on the lives they had just ended.

It fell to Zephaniah and Titus to do that. Viktor saw the way Zephaniah laid a callused, gnarled hand on the flank of one of the dead antelope. There was a moment of communication, almost as if Zephaniah were trying to make the departed spirit of the animal understand why it had died. Then the old frontiersman sighed and got to work skinning the animal. Titus was busy with a similar task.

Frederick had ordered Viktor and some of the other Cossacks to accompany them up the slope, and Viktor would have gone even without that order. It was his job to protect these aristocrats, and he intended to fulfill his mission. While Frederick and his friends had been dispatching the wounded antelope, Viktor had stood nearby, all his senses alert, his eyes searching the surrounding terrain. He had been able to see quite a distance from the ridge. There had been no sign of any threat. He had spotted a dark smudge on the western horizon that might have been another herd of buffalo, but he did not point it out and no one else seemed to notice it.

Frederick and his friends were talking loudly and laughing heartily, as if killing the antelope had lifted their spirits. When they reached the riverboat, they walked across the plank gangway that had been put in place by several of the boat's crewmen to make it easier for the Russians to board and disembark. Frederick turned toward the nearest companionway, no doubt intending to climb the steps to the next deck, where the salon was located. He and his companions would be eager to break out the vodka once more.

As Frederick reached the steps, one of the crew, climbing from belowdecks, appeared on the landing. The American tried to get out of the way, but Frederick never slowed or even gave any indication that he saw the man. The two of them jostled together. Viktor saw what was happening but was not close enough to prevent it.

As Frederick jerked back from the crewman, his jovial mood vanished immediately. "Be careful, you lout!" he said, glowering at the crewman.

The American looked startled. "What did you say, mister?"

"I told you to watch where you are going, you great clumsy oaf!" Frederick raged. Behind him, the other noblemen were also glaring at the crewman who had dared to offend their leader. Frederick added, "And you will address me as Count Orlov."

Viktor watched the face of the crewman closely. He saw the anger in the man's eyes and knew it was justified, at least according to the way these Americans thought. They were an independent people, slow to anger but unwilling to suffer mistreatment at the hands of those they considered no better than themselves. They had lived under the British monarchy for a time, Viktor recalled from his study of their history, but they had thrown it off by going to war.

Still, the crewman was able to control his temper, and he stepped back to give Frederick even more room to climb the steps. Viktor relaxed slightly. What had looked like an ugly confrontation had been avoided.

But as Frederick brushed past the man with his face set in cold, haughty lines, the American could not resist muttering, "Count Asshole is more like it."

Viktor heard the words clearly, and he had no doubt that Frederick had, too. So had the other noblemen. Frederick could not let such an insult pass. His face flushed with rage as he stopped, jerked around, and slapped the crewman across the face. Viktor saw the count's arm raise, saw the blow flash forward, but there was nothing he could do to stop it. There was a sharp crack as Frederick's palm met the crewman's cheek.

"You son of a she-wolf!" the American howled. The muscles in his shoulders bunched, and his right fist flew toward Frederick's face.

Viktor was already moving before the man even started to throw the punch. Reaching the American, Viktor looped an arm around his neck from behind and jerked him back. The man wasn't expecting the attack, and his balance deserted him. He sagged against Viktor, his weight coming down on the arm pressed across his throat like a bar of iron. The breath was squeezed out of him.

Frederick folded his arms across his chest and sneered at the crewman in the grip of the big Cossack. "Teach this barbarian a lesson he'll not soon forget, Dorochenko."

Viktor frowned and asked reluctantly, "Are you certain, Count?"

Before Frederick could answer, Lieutenant O'Neal and Captain Harvey, the master of the *Prairie Flower*, came hurrying up. A thickset, red-faced man with a drooping white mustache, the captain looked at Viktor holding the burly crewmen as if he were little more than a naughty child, and blustered, "Let go o' that man! What in blazes is goin' on here?"

One of the other noblemen said, "That lackey insulted Count Orlov. The Cossack was just about to give him a good thrashing for his impudence."

In his most conciliatory tone a tight-lipped, Lieutenant O'Neal asked Frederick, "What seems to be the trouble, Count?"

"The trouble is that you Americans have allowed your commoners to think that they are the equals of those who are obviously their betters," Frederick snapped. "That man insulted me, just as Anton said. It is a matter of honor now." He looked at Viktor again. "You heard me, Dorochenko!"

Viktor sighed. *"Da."*

He let go of the crewman, who stumbled forward a step, grasping his bruised throat and dragging a great breath of air into his lungs. When the man turned and looked at Viktor, his eyes burned with rage.

"You'd better do something about this, Captain," O'Neal said nervously.

Captain Harvey shook his head. "Nothing I can do now, Lieutenant, even if I wanted to. That count fella has been askin' for trouble ever since he got on board. Now I reckon he's got it."

Viktor studied the crewman, taking in the American's broad shoulders, the long arms, the thick chest. The man's strength was obvious. Now that he had caught his breath, a grin stretched across his face, which was marked by scars that proved this was not to be his first fight. He flexed his long, blunt, knobby-knuckled fingers before curling them into fists.

"I'd rather it was your boss I was about to beat the livin' daylights out of, mister," the man said, "but I reckon you'll do."

He should have learned to fight and not talk. The words warned Viktor the crewman was about to make his move. Viktor moved smoothly to the side as the American lunged at him, swinging a wild, overhand blow.

The women had begun hurrying back on board the riverboat as soon as it became obvious there was going to be trouble. As they came up the gangplank to the deck, Alena clutched her aunt's arm and asked anxiously, "Is there any way to stop this?"

Zora laughed curtly. "Stop a man from making a fool of himself over his so-called honor? You might as well try to stop the snow from falling on Moscow in the winter."

As she reached the deck, Alena saw Sasha standing nearby. The young man appeared to be as worried as

Alena. She went over to him and said, "Sasha, you must prevail on Frederick to call a halt to this madness."

He shook his head. "There is nothing I can do. Frederick would be furious if I interfered." There was a look of shame on his face.

Alena swallowed her irritation and looked around to see if there was anyone else who might be able to restore some sanity to the situation. The American army officer and the captain of the riverboat seemed to have washed their hands of the matter, and the two guides were watching intently, obviously as eager for the battle to begin as all the other spectators.

Which was exactly what happened the next instant, as the burly American crewman launched a punch at Viktor's head.

Sasha saw Viktor dart aside so that the crewman's blow passed harmlessly by his right ear. Viktor whipped a punch to the man's midsection, then stepped even closer and threw his arms around the crewman in a bear hug. Both of them staggered toward the railing as the American tried to jerk free of Viktor's grip.

A glance at Alena told Sasha how upset she was. She was watching the fight with her features pale and drawn, her lower lip caught between her teeth as she gnawed at it. He knew that Alena and the Cossack, Dorochenko, were friends—at least, as much as it was possible for a noble and a commoner to be friends. Sasha liked and admired Viktor, too. He had no desire to see the big man get hurt, especially when it had been Frederick who had provoked the battle.

Alena and Sasha were evidently the only ones disturbed by the altercation. The deck was crowded with onlookers now. Shouts of "Fight! Fight!" had brought the rest of the crewmen, at least those who were not engaged in vital tasks. The American army troops were there, too, as were the rest of the Cossacks. As Viktor and the crewman grappled and traded blows, shouts of encouragement rang out, each side supporting their countryman. Sasha saw wagers being eagerly arranged amid the tumultuous gathering.

No matter how the others felt, this was wrong. Someone had to do something to bring the battle to a halt before one of the men was seriously injured.

Looking around, Sasha knew that someone would have to be him.

He skirted the combatants as they slammed hard into the railing. The impact jolted Viktor's grip loose, and the American was able to land two hard punches to his opponent's chest, knocking Viktor back toward the companionway where Frederick stood watching with a satisfied expression on his face. Viktor caught himself and with a roar tackled the American again.

Sasha reached his brother's side and caught at the sleeve of his expensive coat. "Can't you stop this, Frederick?"

"Why should I?" the count asked. "I'm rather enjoying it."

"Viktor might be injured!"

Frederick laughed and shook his head. "Not that dumb Cossack. His skull is as hard as iron."

As if to prove Frederick's statement, Viktor took several blows to the head. His fur cap went flying, but that seemed to be the only effect of the American's punches. Viktor shrugged them off and landed a hard combination of punches of his own, driving the crewman toward the railing once more.

Pressing his momentary advantage, Viktor sent a flurry of blows at the man's head and torso, slugging mercilessly as he forced the American to give still more ground. The crewman's hips bumped against the railing. He flung a desperate punch at Viktor's head, and his fist slipped past Viktor's attempt to parry the blow, catching the Cossack on the chin. There was enough power behind the punch to slow Viktor, making him pause for an instant to shake his head. The American set himself, ready to launch another attack.

He never got the chance. Viktor stepped toward him, bringing around a punch with all the power of his massive body behind it. The Cossack's fist crashed into the crewman's face. Arms thrown wide, the man was driven against the railing again, and this time he flipped up and over it. He plunged into the river between the boat and the shore, sending muddy water skyward in a huge splash.

Viktor stepped back, holding his right hand with his left. That final blow had been a painful one for the man who had thrown it, as well as for the man on which it had landed.

"Bravo, Viktor!" Frederick called, applauding lightly. The other nobles followed his lead. Several of the men slapped Viktor on the back as the Cossacks collected on their bets with the American soldiers, all of whom looked disgusted by the fight's outcome. Frederick strolled over to the railing and looked down at the crewman who had been knocked overboard. The man was pulling himself out of the shallow water, sputtering and cursing, covered with thick, sticky mud. Frederick said to him, "Next time perhaps you will show some respect to your betters."

The American wiped mud from his face and glared up at Frederick, but he did not say anything.

Frederick turned to his friends. "That display was quite invigorating. I believe I could use a drink." He started up the steps to the next deck, followed by the other noblemen and several of the ladies.

Sasha came up to Viktor, who had been left behind by his well-wishers. The Cossack was still rubbing sore knuckles on his right hand. "Are you all right, Viktor?" Sasha asked.

"*Da*. It was a good fight."

"Frederick should not have done that. There was no need."

Viktor shrugged his broad shoulders. "The count does what he does." It was obvious from his demeanor that he thought there was nothing else to say about the matter.

He stepped over to the railing and leaned down to offer a hand to the man he had just knocked into the river. The crewman hesitated for a second, then took Viktor's hand and allowed the Cossack to help him climb back aboard.

As he stood there dripping on the planks of the deck, the man's mud-daubed face split in a grin, and he said, "That's a mule kick of a punch you got, mister. If you ever decide to give up bein' a soldier over there in Russia, you could come back here and work on the river anytime."

Viktor returned the grin and shook his head. "I could not leave Mother Russia forever."

The crewman slapped Viktor on the shoulder. "Well, you think about it," he said. He put his fingers on his chin and worked his jaw back and forth. "Don't seem to be broken, but I reckon I'd better go clean up and get a little medicine for it anyway."

Titus laughed and lifted the jug he held in his hand. "I got the medicine you need right here, feller."

"Thanks." The crewman took the jug and raised it to his mouth, swallowing a long drink of whatever was inside it. Sasha assumed it was some sort of liquor. After a moment the American extended the jug toward Viktor, who took it without hesitation and drank.

"I am much obliged, as you would say," Viktor said as he gave the jug back to the crewman, who passed it on to Titus.

The American went belowdecks, and the rest of the crew got back to their work. The soldiers wandered off toward the bow of the riverboat, no doubt to resume the card games that occupied most of their time whenever the *Prairie Flower* was tied up.

Sasha shook his head as he said to Viktor, "I do not understand this. It was as if you and the American are now friends, and only a few minutes ago you were trying to smash each other."

"He understood I had no choice in what I did," Viktor said. "And I respected what he felt he had to do. There was no hatred between us."

Sasha sighed. "I do not think I will ever know what it is to be a man like you, Viktor."

"You are still young. You have much time to grow." Viktor's fellow Cossacks were waiting for him, motioning for him to come with them. With a smile for Sasha, he turned to join them.

As he watched Viktor with the other men and heard his booming laughter as they talked about the fight, Sasha knew the big Cossack had been wrong.

No matter how much time passed, he would never be like Viktor Dorochenko.

4

AFTER WEEKS OF TRAVELING
up the Missouri through the monotonous, sparsely popu-
lated prairie, the riverboat's arrival at Fort Union, Montana
Territory, was a momentous occasion indeed, Viktor
thought as he leaned on the railing. As a Cossack, he was,
of course, accustomed to the loneliness of the wilderness,
but for the others on board the *Prairie Flower,* the settlement was a welcome sight.

Zephaniah and Titus came up to the rail beside Viktor as
the paddleboat approached the landing near the fort. With a
gesture toward the buildings surrounded by a high stockade
fence, Zephaniah said, "I reckon that there is the last outpost of civilization in these parts. Not that you'd call it real
civilized most times. The place is usually full o' fur trappers lookin' for an excuse to go on a rip-snortin' tear."

Viktor shook his head. "I do not understand."

"The boys bring in the pelts they've taken durin' trappin'
season, and they sell 'em to the fella who works for the fur
company. That puts money in their pockets, and then they
just naturally got to spend it."

"Ah," Viktor said. "On women and strong drink, no
doubt."

Titus grinned. "You got it figgered out, all right. Some of

'em go on a howlin', fightin' drunk and don't stop until they've spent ever' last cent they got for their furs." He chuckled. "I was a mite like that myself, in my younger days."

"Last year, if I recollect right," Zephaniah commented dryly.

"Yeah, well, this year I've hired on as a guide for these Rooshans, and I'm behavin' myself, ain't I?"

"You have been an excellent guide, friend Titus," Viktor assured him.

Up in the wheelhouse, Captain Harvey had apparently tugged on the whistle cord, because two shrill blasts sounded, announcing their impending arrival at the settlement—as if such a warning was really necessary. Viktor saw quite a few people already gathering at the landing to welcome the new arrivals. In such an isolated spot as this, he thought, a visit from a riverboat might be the most exciting thing to happen for quite some time.

The *Prairie Flower*'s passengers had already begun to emerge from their cabins as well. They hastened to the railing and watched eagerly as the settlement drew steadily closer. There was a great deal of talking and excitement.

Footsteps and the rustle of skirts next to him made Viktor look to his left. Alena and her aunt had come to the railing beside him. Alena had the balalaika slung over her shoulder on its strap. Viktor had spent many pleasurable hours during this journey listening to her play, although Alena was probably not aware of that. Though she struggled with the instrument and obviously did not enjoy the practice, the songs she played took Victor back to his homeland, even if it was only for a few minutes.

The redheaded young woman leaned forward anxiously and pointed. "Look, Aunt Zora!" Her tone was a mixture of fear and anticipation.

Viktor saw that she was pointing at a cluster of odd-looking structures near the fort. They were shaped like cones and seemed to be made of animal hides stitched together and decorated with garish paintings. Tendrils of smoke from some of them rose into the pale blue arch of sky.

Zephaniah had heard Alena's words as well. He looked past Viktor and said to her, "Them's Injun lodges, missy. They call 'em tepees. Leastways, that's close to the Injun word."

Several figures emerged from the odd dwellings, drawn by the boat's whistle. The children were clad in buckskins, and the women wore buckskin dresses. The men sported buckskin leggings, but they also had blankets wrapped around their torsos. Several of them held long, spearlike weapons, and Viktor's keen eyes saw that each man also had either a knife or a small ax tucked into the leggings. Their long dark hair was braided, and some of the men had eagle feathers in their hair.

Alena stared at the figures of the Indians, wide-eyed. Beside her, Zora put a hand to her mouth and uttered a prayer in Russian under her breath. The older woman turned to Viktor and asked, "Are they dangerous?"

He was about to tell her that he did not know, when Zephaniah answered the question for him. "Them redskins won't bother you none, ma'am, leastways not here around the fort. Now, if they was to catch you by yourself out on the prairie, that might be a different story."

"What sort of Indians are they?" Viktor asked.

"Blackfeet," Titus said. "Come from the Piegan band, from the looks of 'em."

"Of course they are pagans!" Zora said. "What else could they be, here in this godforsaken wilderness?"

"Titus said Piegan, ma'am, not pagan," Zephaniah explained. "They sound pretty much alike. But I reckon you got a point. There's been a heap o' missionaries come out here to try to convert the savages, goin' all the way back to them French Jesuits who come down from Canada 'fore us Americans ever got out to this part o' the country. Ain't none of 'em accomplished a whole lot, though. Most of the redskins still believe pretty much like they always have."

"Then they are not . . ." Alena searched for the right word. "Domesticated?"

"Tame Injuns? No, missy, they ain't. They come in here

to the tradin' post to swap furs to Mr. McKenzie, him that runs the place for the American Fur Company. They get back beads and blankets, white man's clothes, knives, and such like. They behave theirselves pretty good as long as they don't get likkered up whilst they're here."

"But they'd kill you and lift that purty red hair if you was to give 'em half a chance," Titus put in.

Alena shuddered as both Viktor and Zephaniah frowned at Titus for speaking so bluntly.

"That's why you don't never want to wander off without havin' us or some o' Viktor's Cossacks around," Titus went on.

"Do not worry. I will not wander off."

Viktor was fairly certain of that. Alena was so frightened of the Indians now that she probably would not set foot outside the fort without an armed escort. And she might not want to leave even *then*.

Sensing more movement, Viktor turned his head and saw Frederick coming up behind Alena. He took her arm, and she jumped and let out a small cry. Frederick frowned and said, "Do I frighten you that much, my dear? I hope not. When we are to be married, I would not want you crying out in fear every time I touch you."

"I . . . I'm sorry, Frederick. You just startled me, that's all. We were looking at those Indians, and I didn't know you were behind me."

Frederick sniffed, somewhat mollified. "Come along, darling. As soon as the boat has docked, we shall see what there is to see in this primitive outpost, though I daresay it will not be much."

He led her toward the spot where the gangway would be placed. Viktor watched them go, and he thought about what Frederick had said. The idea of the count touching Alena produced unpleasant images in his head. Resolutely, he thrust those images away and turned his attention back to the people on the bank of the river.

The Indians—Blackfeet, Titus had called them—had come down to the landing to watch the riverboat being tied up, but they kept their distance from the whites of Fort

Union. Nor did they call out greetings to the newcomers, as did the settlers, nearly all of whom were male. Viktor saw only two women and a bare handful of children. He supposed they were the families of a couple of the American officers assigned to this frontier outpost.

Crewmen from the riverboat tossed thick ropes ashore, where they were grabbed by eager hands and quickly snubbed around the thick posts that supported the short pier extending into the Missouri. The gangway was put in place, and a man in the blue swallowtail coat, white breeches, black boots, and peaked black cap of an American army officer strode briskly up the planks to the deck. Lieutenant O'Neal met him there, and the two men exchanged crisp salutes. "Lieutenant John O'Neal reporting, sir," the young officer said.

"Glad to see you and your party made it safely up the Big Muddy, Lieutenant. I'm Captain Davis. Welcome to Fort Union."

Davis was a thin, fair-haired man with a rather haunted look in his eyes, Viktor noted. He wondered if the expression came from being assigned to this post so deep in the wilderness, or if there was something else in his past.

Viktor stood close by as O'Neal introduced Count Frederick Orlov, Alena, and the other aristocrats to the fort's commanding officer. Davis did not act surprised to see the Russians, and when all the introductions had been concluded, he said, "I received the dispatch from St. Louis informing me of your plans to visit, Count Orlov. Welcome to Fort Union, and I hope your stay here is a pleasant one. If there's anything I can do to make it so, please inform me."

Frederick inclined his head in gracious acknowledgment of the commanding officer's greeting. "I shall certainly do so, Captain," he said. "The first thing we would like is a tour of your fort."

Davis smiled and indicated the gangway with a wave of his hand. "Certainly. After you and your lady, Count."

It took several minutes for all the visitors to disembark from the riverboat. Viktor managed to stay close to Alena, knowing that she was nervous about the Indians. He saw her casting occasional glances at the savages, who still stood nearby, watching the proceedings impassively. The Blackfeet made no move to interfere with the group as they started toward the fort.

Viktor looked over his shoulder and saw that his men were ranged along the line of nobles, just as they should have been. With the Cossacks close at hand, their charges would remain safe, even if the Indians were to attack. That seemed highly unlikely to Viktor, especially since the American soldiers, who dealt with the Blackfeet all the time, did not seem particularly worried by their presence.

Lieutenant O'Neal's troop brought up the rear, along with Zephaniah and Titus. The two mountain men had their long-barreled flintlocks canted over their shoulders and appeared to be completely at ease. Not far in front of them, trailing the rest of the Russian party, was Frederick's brother Sasha, whose head swiveled almost constantly from side to side as his wide eyes took in everything. These surroundings had to be quite exotic and exciting for a young man whose entire world until this expedition had been Moscow and his family's *dacha* on the Caspian Sea.

The pair of gates in the stockade fence had been swung wide open. As he passed through the entrance, Viktor got a better look at the fort and saw that there were quite a few buildings inside the fence. Some were made of logs and seemed quite sturdy, while others had been constructed from blocks of sod cut from the ground and stacked up to make walls. Viktor wondered where the logs had come from, since the prairie was virtually treeless.

As if to answer the Cossack's unspoken question, Captain Davis said to Frederick, "We floated the logs to build all of this down from the mountains. Took a while, but I think it was worth it."

"Quite impressive, Captain," Frederick agreed, and Davis looked pleased. Despite the count's faults, he could be a smooth diplomat—when he wanted to be, Viktor thought. On board the riverboat, he had referred to Fort Union as a primitive outpost, and in truth, it was. But Frederick was not going to point out that fact to its commanding officer.

"That's the headquarters building," Davis said, gesturing toward one of the log structures. "Next to it is the sutler's store, then the officers' quarters. Enlisted men's barracks over there, along with our smokehouse and armory." He pointed to a small sod building tucked away in a distant corner of the fort. "Powder magazine," he explained. "And this is the trading post."

The captain paused in front of the largest building inside the fort, larger even than the barracks that housed the enlisted men. A broad roofed porch extended the length of the building's front, and there were several doors leading into its cavernous depths. Through those openings, Viktor saw piles of blankets and bolts of colorful cloth, as well as stacks of what appeared to be dried animal hides.

A barrel-chested man with an impressive upward-curling mustache stepped onto the porch from inside the trading post. Captain Davis steered the visitors in his direction and said, "Count Orlov, I want you to meet Mr. Kenneth McKenzie, the agent for the American Fur Company. Mr. McKenzie, this is Count Frederick Orlov, Czar Nicholas's personal representative from Moscow."

McKenzie came down the steps from the porch. He wore a wool shirt and whipcord pants. As he extended a hand to Frederick, he said, "Pleased to meet you, Count. I got a letter from my employers informing me that the State Department had requested our cooperation during your visit to our country. We have wagons and horses ready to take you out on your hunting expedition. We're glad to have you with us."

Frederick shook McKenzie's hand. "And I am honored to be here. You are the one known as the Emperor of the West, Mr. McKenzie?"

McKenzie threw back his head and laughed. "Some folks have called me that."

"Rather like our czar, eh?"

"Not hardly. No offense, Count. I'm just a fella who works for a fur-trading company. I don't boss a whole country."

Frederick turned and waved a hand at his companions, motioning Sasha forward. "Allow me to introduce my brother Sasha. And this is my betrothed, Alena Galovnin, and her aunt Zora."

"Mighty pleased to make your acquaintance, ladies," McKenzie said, bowing to Alena and Zora. He shook Sasha's hand. "And you, too, Sasha."

The young man looked flattered at the attention, although Viktor saw his eyes widen slightly as he felt the strength of McKenzie's handshake.

Frederick introduced Anton and the other noblemen in the party, and McKenzie welcomed them to Montana Territory. "I hope your visit is exciting enough to suit you, gentlemen," he said.

"Where are the Indians?" one of the men asked impatiently. "We saw Indians in St. Louis, but they were hardly the painted savages we were led to expect. What about the ones outside the fort? Are *they* savages?"

Viktor saw McKenzie and Captain Davis exchange a quick glance, and he had a pretty good idea what the Americans were thinking. The question was a stupid one, asked by a man who had no idea what life on this frontier was really like.

Viktor remembered border clashes with the Tartars back in his homeland, and he was certain those hordes were every bit as savage as the Blackfeet or any other Indians. A wise man did not seek out trouble simply on the hope that it might be exciting.

But no one had ever said that these aristocrats, with their pampered city ways, were wise.

McKenzie was polite in his response. "If it's Indians you want, folks, wait just a minute." He turned toward the trading post and called, "George, can you come out here? There's some folks I want you to meet."

A moment later a man wearing buckskins and carrying what looked like an easel appeared in one of the doorways.

He came onto the porch and was followed by a tall, solemn Indian carrying a lance and wearing a headdress of eagle feathers.

Zora took one look at the Indian and let out a scream.

5

THE MAN IN BUCKSKINS
looked startled, as did his companion. Alena caught hold of
Zora's arm and asked urgently, "Aunt Zora, what is it?
What's wrong?"

Zora leveled a shaking finger at the Indian. "He is going
to scalp us! He is going to carry us off and make us
slaves!"

"I don't think that's very likely to happen, ma'am," said
the man in buckskins.

"Of course not," Kenneth McKenzie added. "He couldn't
do both. Besides, Stu-mick-o-sucks here is friendly."

Alena was not sure why Zora had chosen this moment to
lose her composure, but she could tell that her aunt was
genuinely frightened. Caught in the unfamiliar position of
having to comfort Zora, instead of the other way around,
she said, "It's all right, Aunt Zora. Nothing is going to happen. Viktor and his men are here, and you told me yourself
that they would never allow any harm to come to us."

Zora took a deep breath and calmed herself with a visible
effort. "You are right, of course," she said. She managed a
weak smile as she turned to Frederick. "My apologies,
Count. My outburst was inexcusable."

"Nonsense," Frederick said. "A lady such as yourself,

thrust into this wilderness, has every right to cry out at the sight of a bloodthirsty savage."

Alena frowned. The Indian on the porch of the trading post did not look particularly bloodthirsty, and she hoped Frederick had not offended the man by saying so. An Indian woman and a child came from the building, and the little boy, who looked to be about five years old, ran over to the man. As the man put a gentle hand on the boy's shoulder, the love between them was visible to anyone who bothered to look.

"This is George Catlin," McKenzie said, nodding to the man in buckskins. "He's an artist, and he's come up the Missouri to paint what he finds out here on the frontier."

Catlin, who had dark hair and a slender, sensitive face, set the easel aside and came down the steps to the ground. "Hello, folks," he said to the visitors.

"George, I want you to meet Count Frederick Orlov, from Russia. He and his party have come here to do some hunting and sightseeing."

Catlin grinned. "Well, there's plenty of sights to see out here in the West." He held out a hand that seemed permanently stained with various colors of paint. "Pleased to meet you, Count."

Frederick hesitated only slightly, then took Catlin's hand. "The pleasure is mine, Mr. Catlin," he said. "Allow me to present my brother Sasha and my fiancée Alena."

Catlin shook hands with Sasha, who once again seemed rather embarrassed, nodded politely to Alena and murmured a greeting, then looked past them at Viktor, who stood nearby but made no move to call attention to himself. Catlin's eyes lit up with speculation. "Who's this big strapping fellow?"

Frederick glanced over his shoulder. "Oh, that's Dorochenko, one of our Cossack guards."

Catlin strode over to Viktor and held out his hand. "Wouldn't mind painting you sometime, son," he said.

Viktor looked distinctly uncomfortable, Alena thought. He had never cared for attention, and from the slight frown creasing Frederick's forehead, the count did not care for

Catlin ignoring him to greet a commoner, and a Cossack at that.

Reluctantly, Viktor shook the artist's hand. "What about it?" Catlin prodded. "Would you like me to paint a portrait of you?"

"Perhaps," Viktor said. "I do not know."

"Well, you give it some thought."

As much to distract Catlin from Viktor as to satisfy her curiosity, Alena pointed to the three Indians still standing on the porch, watching impassively, and asked, "Who are they?"

Catlin turned back toward the trading post. "The chief is called Stu-mick-o-sucks. That means Buffalo's Back Fat in the white man's tongue. His wife is Eeh-nis-kin . . . Crystal Stone. Come along, and I'll introduce you."

The artist led the foreign visitors over to the porch. Frederick went without hesitation, and his fellow noblemen followed, unwilling to look like cowards in front of him. Alena, Zora, and the other women hung back slightly. Alena was curious about the Indians, but she wanted to stay close by Zora's side. Her aunt still looked pale and shaken, although she was doing her best to control the reaction. Viktor and the other Cossacks stayed close by, as was their custom.

"Chief," Catlin said, "these are guests of the Grandfather who have come here from a far land to see the country where you and your people live."

Stu-mick-o-sucks nodded gravely. "This is a good thing," he said in reasonably unaccented English. He probably spoke the language better than several of the visitors from Russia, Alena thought. The Blackfoot chief went on, "Our land is beautiful and should be seen by the friends of the Grandfather."

Quietly, Alena asked Catlin, "Who is this grandfather of whom he speaks?"

"That's what the Indians call the president," Catlin explained. "To them, he is a revered figure who rules from far away."

Frederick stepped closer to the porch, putting a short gap

between himself and the others. Addressing Stu-mick-o-sucks directly, he asked, "Do you have good hunting in this land, Chief?"

"Many buffalo," Stu-mick-o-sucks said. "Antelope, moose, elk . . . all good. Good hunting."

For some reason, Alena hoped no one would mention Frederick and his friends' recent slaughter of four antelope.

"I'd better get started on my painting," Catlin said. "I'm doing a portrait of the lad there, and I'm not sure how long he'll be willing to pose for me. Of course, after all he's been through, standing on a porch probably doesn't seem like much of an ordeal to him."

Alena looked at the little boy, who wore an expression every bit as solemn as that of the chief. She indulged her curiosity and asked Catlin, "What do you mean?"

"The Crows keep stealing him. They've grabbed him twice and carried him off from his grandfather Stu-mick-o-suck's village."

For the first time since the brief spell of terror, Zora seemed to recover some of her usual aplomb. She said, "I think that's awful! Why would anyone do such a thing?"

"Well, ma'am, he's going to be the chief one of these days," McKenzie said. "His father is dead, so he'll inherit leadership of the Piegan band from Buffalo's Back Fat. The Crows and the Blackfeet have been feuding for a long time, so the Crows would like nothing better than to deprive their enemies of a future chief. The Blackfeet always steal him back, though."

"What a terrible thing to do to a child!" Alena exclaimed.

"The burdens of leadership are always heavy," Frederick said smugly, "even in an uncivilized country such as this, I suppose."

Alena saw George Caitlin and Kenneth McKenzie exchange a glance at Frederick's casual insult, but they let it pass. The faces of Captain Davis and Lieutenant O'Neal tightened as well, although O'Neal seemed somewhat accustomed to Frederick's heavy-handed manner by now.

As she looked at the solemn-faced little boy, Alena was

struck by an idea. "I think he is very brave," she said, walking toward the porch and unslinging the balalaika as she approached the Indians. She held the instrument out toward the boy. "Here. I want you to have this."

"Alena!" Zora said, startled by the young woman's action. "What are you doing?"

Alena tossed a smile over her shoulder. "I think he deserves a reward of some kind for being so brave."

"But not your balalaika!"

"I have already made the offer," Alena said. "I cannot take it back now."

Zora sighed in exasperation, her fear of the Indians seemingly replaced by irritation at Alena.

The boy did not take the balalaika immediately. Instead, he looked up at his grandfather. Stu-mick-o-sucks spoke to him for a moment in their native tongue. The boy answered quietly, and Stu-mick-o-sucks nodded. As the youngster turned back toward Alena, a shy smile touched his face. He reached out to take the balalaika.

Alena let him turn the instrument over in his hands for a moment, then carefully showed him where to place his fingers. He flinched at first at her touch, then relaxed at a word from his grandfather. Alena was quickly forgetting that the boy was a Blackfoot Indian, a wild savage from an even wilder land. For now, at least, he was just a little boy, not much different from her nephews and cousins back in Russia. If not for his red skin and buckskin clothing, she might have forgotten entirely about his heritage.

"Here, let me show you," she said, knowing that he probably could not understand the words. At the moment that did not seem to matter.

She took hold of his hand and brushed his fingers across the strings of the balalaika. He jumped a little at the sound that action produced. Then he strummed the strings again, this time without Alena's help. The notes were rather discordant, but neither of them cared. The boy looked up at her, and this time his solemn expression disappeared for good. He grinned in joy and began plucking loudly at the balalaika. A laugh bubbled out of him, and Alena joined in.

Zora rolled her eyes.

That evening, as dusk settled down over the fort and the surrounding prairie, Viktor strolled around the inside of the stockade fence and studied its construction. To his experienced eye, the fence seemed strong enough, the thick logs planted solidly in the ground and lashed together with strips of rawhide that had dried to the hardness of iron in the high-country sun. This fort would have turned back a Tartar attack, he decided. Surely it would suffice to hold off any marauding Indians.

The sound of a balalaika being played loudly and badly came to his ears, and he turned toward the trading post. The young Indian boy had been reluctant to set aside his new toy so that the painter, Catlin, could work on his portrait. Finally, his grandfather the chief ordered him to do so, and the boy had obeyed. But now, after the canvas and the paints had been put away and everyone had eaten supper, the boy had taken the balalaika in search of Alena. Judging by the sounds coming from the porch of the trading post, he had found her.

Viktor strolled in that direction, and as he did so, Zephaniah and Titus came up beside him. They were both smiling. Nodding toward the porch, Zephaniah said quietly, "I'd say the little lady has made herself a friend."

Viktor frowned slightly in concern. "These Indians . . . you say they are dangerous?"

"They can be, if you cross 'em. They owe a debt to Miss Alena now, though, since she gave the little'un a present."

"They seem to me a . . . a noble people."

Zephaniah nodded. "I reckon they can be *that,* too."

"The chief, the one called Buffalo's Back Fat, he reminds me of the *hetman* of our village, old Gregori. Though he had many years, no one dared oppose him when his mind was made up. He could drink more vodka than any man in the village, and his sword arm was still strong."

Viktor shook his head. "I would not have wanted to do battle with Gregori."

"I reckon you got a pretty good idea what these Blackfeet are like, then," Zephaniah said. "Sounds like you Cossacks got even more in common with them than you do with mountain men like me an' Titus here."

"All those who live on the frontier, whether they be red or white, American or Cossack, they know many of the same things. The voice of the wind, the touch of the sun, the smell of the earth . . . these things never change."

"We can hope not," Zephaniah said quietly. "But I ain't completely convinced. . . ."

Titus spat onto the fort's parade ground. "You two got more'n that in common. You can be a pair o' long-winded, gloomy cusses when you want to. Why don't you shut up so's we can listen to the music?"

"That is a good idea," Viktor agreed.

"I reckon," Zephaniah said.

They took out their pipes, filled and lit them, and stood there in the gathering shadows, listening to the strains of the balalaika as the stars began to gleam in the night sky.

6

FOR THE NEXT FEW DAYS THE Russians remained at Fort Union, preparing for the journey deeper into Montana Territory. Now that the members of the expedition had arrived at the fort, Kenneth McKenzie could make a better estimate of just how many provisions would be needed. He supervised the loading of the wagons with supplies, including plenty of powder and shot. "Wouldn't want you running dry, Count," he said to Frederick as they watched McKenzie's helpers wrestle several barrels of gunpowder into the back of a wagon. "You ought to be able to do plenty of hunting."

"That is why we are here," Frederick said. "That, and to see for ourselves the noble savages we have heard so much about."

There was plenty of opportunity for that; the Blackfeet were in and out of the fort quite a bit. After a few days even Zora Galovnin became more accustomed to their presence, although she still watched them warily whenever any were near her or Alena.

The grandson of Buffalo's Back Fat spent as much time as possible with Alena. The boy practiced the balalaika with an enthusiasm that Alena herself had never been able to muster. But she was glad to show him what she knew about playing the instrument, and he took to it quite well. In time, she thought, he would be a better musician than she could ever hope to be.

George Catlin was somewhat frustrated, Alena knew, because the chief's grandson was more interested in playing the balalaika than he was in posing for his portrait. The artist was a gentleman, however, and did not complain. Alena supposed he knew that the visitors would be moving on soon, and then he would once again have the Indians to himself.

As for Viktor, his heart leaped the first time he saw the horses McKenzie had selected as the party's mounts. For months, during the sea voyage and the trek across the United States, he and the other Cossacks had been forced to travel by means other than horseback—to such men, a serious sacrifice. In Viktor's opinion, there were no better horsemen in the world than Cossacks. He was anxious to get back in a saddle again.

The horses were rangy and still a little shaggy from the winter. They milled around in the corral outside the fort, snorting and throwing their heads up so that their manes shook back and forth.

Viktor thought they were beautiful.

He leaned on the corral railing next to Zephaniah and Titus and said, "They look like good mounts."

"That they are," Zephaniah agreed. "They got some Injun pony in 'em, from the looks of 'em. That means they're stronger than you might think, and they'll run all day if you ask 'em to. Plenty of sand in those hosses, yes, sir."

"Once we rode for three days straight, pursuing Poles who raided our village," Viktor said. "They thought they could escape us, and they slowed once they believed they were safe. But still we came on, and our mounts never faltered. The Poles were foolish enough to make camp." He sighed at the memory. "Our swords were red with the blood of our enemies that day."

"Wish I could've been there," Titus said with a laugh. "Sounds like a mighty good fracas."

"Yes," Viktor said. "It was . . . a mighty good fracas."

"Well, we won't run into any trouble like that over here, the Good Lord willin'," Zephaniah said. "As long as the count and the rest o' them noblemen do like we tell 'em, there won't be any problems."

"Count Orlov is accustomed to doing as he pleases. But you already know that."

Zephaniah nodded. "Yep, I figgered as much. But 'tween you an' me an' Titus, maybe we can keep him reined in."

"I will do my best," Viktor said solemnly.

Titus pointed at one of the horses, a big, mouse-colored stallion with a darker stripe down his back. "That lineback dun looks like a good hoss for you, Viktor. He's big enough to carry your weight without any trouble, and he's got spirit. You can tell that just by lookin' at him."

"Yes"—Viktor nodded—"there is fire in his eye, as they say. Should I try to ride him?"

"Sure. I'll go get a saddle." Titus hurried off, but not before Zephaniah frowned at him.

Zephaniah ran his fingers through his beard, tugging on the tangles, and said, "Are you sure you want to try out that dun right now, Viktor? We ain't leavin' for a day or two yet. There'll be time later."

"Why not now?" Viktor asked. "If I begin to ride the horse now, he will have more time to become accustomed to me."

"Well, I reckon that's right." Zephaniah took off his broad-brimmed felt hat and scratched his balding scalp. "Go ahead, if that's what you want."

Titus came back to the corral carrying a saddle and trailed by a pair of soldiers from the fort. "These hostlers'll cut out that dun from the herd and we'll get him saddled up for you, Viktor. Won't take but a few minutes."

Viktor waited, pleased that his friends were going to so much trouble for him. The soldiers climbed into the corral and worked their way among the horses to the lineback dun. One of them slid a halter over the dun's nose.

The horse's nostrils flared as it blew out its breath, but it didn't struggle as the soldiers led it to the fence. Titus opened the gate, and the hostlers brought the horse out of the corral.

The dun stood with its feet planted wide, trembling a bit, as a saddle blanket was thrown over its back. Then Titus lifted the saddle in place and poked the dun hard in the belly to make it let its breath out as he drew tight the single cinch of the military saddle. Viktor smiled and nodded. "We use the same method in my homeland to make certain the horse does not loosen the saddle," he said.

"They'll sure do it if you give 'em half a chance," one of the hostlers commented. "You about got that saddle ready, Titus?"

"Just about," Titus replied as he lowered the stirrups. "Step up here and take a ride, Viktor."

Viktor took off his long red coat. Here in the sun, his *rubashka* provided more than enough warmth. He handed the coat to Zephaniah, who folded it over his arm. Viktor pulled his fur cap down a little tighter, then stepped over to the horse and placed his left foot in the stirrup. He grasped the saddle and swung up with the grace of a born horseman, letting his weight come down smoothly and easily.

The lineback dun seemed to explode under him like one of those barrels of gunpowder that had been loaded on the wagons.

Viktor felt himself rising and clamped down hurriedly with his knees. When the horse came down again, Viktor's rump slammed against the saddle with a tooth-rattling jolt. He tightened his grip on the reins and hauled up on them, trying to get the dun's cooperation by jerking on the halter. That just sent the horse spinning wildly in tight circles. The motion made a lump of sickness rise in Viktor's throat.

He didn't have time to get sick, however, because the dun immediately broke off the spinning and went into a series of high-kicking bucks. Viktor was thrown one way and then the other, and it was all he could do to hang on and stay in the saddle. He was barely aware of the raucous laughter and shouts of encouragement that came from Titus and the two soldiers. Were they cheering for him, Viktor wondered, or for the horse?

No matter. The shouts made him more determined than ever not to be thrown.

The horse began to circle again, then bucked some more. For long minutes the struggle between man and animal went on. Viktor's head was spinning, and weariness gripped him. But he hung on, and finally the dun's movements became a bit less spirited. Viktor drove the heels of his high-topped black boots into the horse's flanks, seeming to take it by surprise. The dun lunged forward. Viktor pulled its head up and called out to it, then heeled it again. The horse settled into a steady gallop.

As Viktor raced across the prairie atop the dun, heading away from Fort Union, he heard cries of alarm from behind him. Titus, Zephaniah, and the soldiers probably thought the horse was running away with him. They could not know that Viktor was now steadily exerting more and more control over the dun. He leaned forward over the horse's neck, urging more speed. The wind of his passage whipped at him and threatened to tug the fur cap from his head. Viktor held it on with one hand while he expertly guided the horse with the other and with pressure from his knees. The dun responded instantly, as if sensing that it now carried a man who was truly its master.

Viktor swung the horse in a tight turn and saw that Titus and one of the soldiers had started after him on foot, while the other soldier was hurriedly saddling another horse. Zephaniah stood by and watched, leaning on his long-barreled flintlock. Viktor pointed the dun back toward the fort and once again prodded it into a dead run.

Titus and the soldier saw him coming and stopped abruptly. Viktor reached across his body and slid the curved saber on his hip from its brass sheath. He brandished the steel over his head and let out a battle cry. Titus and the other man turned and began running back toward the fort. Viktor had seen their eyes widen in surprise and apprehension as he charged them.

Titus went to the left and the soldier flung himself to the right as Viktor pounded up behind them. He rode between the two men, and his saber flashed in the sunlight as he struck. The upper two inches of the eagle feather in the brim of Titus's hat flew into the air, cleanly severed by Viktor's blade. The Cossack galloped past the two men and brought the dun to a stop in front of Zephaniah, who was shaking with laughter.

"Lordy, I ain't never seen ol' Titus move so fast!" Zephaniah said between hoots of amusement. "Reckon his little prank backfired on him."

"He expected this horse to throw me off, did he not?" Viktor asked.

"That was pretty much the idea, all right. I figger somebody told him how wild that varmint was, and that's why him and those soldier boys was so eager for you to try him out."

"There is not a horse in the world that cannot be ridden by a Cossack."

"With some folks, I'd say that was braggin'," Zephaniah said. "But you just might be right, Viktor."

Titus came up panting. He jerked his hat off and shook it at Viktor. "Look what you did to my feather!"

"Maybe you'd best be glad he didn't decide to lop somethin' else off," Zephaniah advised dryly.

Viktor patted the dun on the shoulder. "This is such a fine mount you picked out for me, Titus, that I thought you would like to see a demonstration of my horsemanship."

The soldier who had been with Titus came up to them, puffing and bending over to put his hands on his knees. "You like to trampled us!" he accused between breaths.

"I'd say you boys got what you deserved," Zephaniah said. "And Viktor got himself a good hoss."

"*Da,*" Viktor agreed. "I will ride this horse while we are here in Montana Territory." He swung down from the saddle and sheathed his saber.

"Just stay away from me with that pigsticker." Titus glared at the hat he held in his hands and sighed heavily.

The story of how Viktor had turned the tables on Titus had reached the officers' mess by that evening. As the Russian visitors dined with Captain Davis, Lieutenant O'Neal, and the other officers from the fort, the tale was repeated by Anton, who thought it was hilarious. Davis, O'Neal, and the other Americans didn't seem to find the details quite so amusing, but they joined politely in the group's laughter.

Alena wished she had seen the incident. She liked the two mountain men, although their rugged appearance still frightened her a little, but Viktor was her friend and she would have enjoyed witnessing his triumph. She would have to congratulate him later, she decided. The Cossacks ate with the enlisted men, of course, so he was not here at the table with the American officers and the Russian nobles.

"I hope I have as spirited a mount," Sasha commented when Anton had finished recounting the events of the afternoon.

"I think a horse that is more docile would be better for you, Sasha," Frederick said. He sipped a glass of wine drawn from a cask provided by Kenneth McKenzie. "You have never been a very skilled rider."

Sasha flushed, and Alena felt a pang of sympathy. Frederick did not have to be so harsh in his assessment of his brother's riding skills, she thought. But Frederick was usually blunt, and he cared little for others' feelings. She knew that quite well about him. It was one more reason she wished the marriage between them had never been arranged . . . but it was much too late for such thoughts, she told herself.

"We'll see that you have a suitable mount, Mr. Orlov," Lieutenant O'Neal said to Sasha. "Who knows, you might turn into a pretty good horseman before we get back here."

"Thank you, Lieutenant," Sasha said with a nod. "I will certainly try."

Captain Davis turned to Frederick and asked, "How long do you intend to be gone, Count?"

"We will spend at least two weeks hunting and exploring this territory," Frederick replied, "perhaps longer if the expedition is going well. Mr. McKenzie has provided supplies for a month's time. It is unlikely we will ever return to your land, so I want to see all of it that we possibly can."

O'Neal said, "I'd like to get over there to Russia one of these days. I've heard a lot about the place."

Frederick smiled thinly. "Perhaps you will be able to visit someday."

"Right now we've got our hands full just trying to get the frontier pacified," Davis said. "It's going to take a lot of time to spread the country from the Atlantic to the Pacific. Manifest Destiny, you know."

"I believe our settlers in the area known as California may have something to say about that," Frederick pointed out.

"Well, that's for the folks in Washington and Moscow to work out," O'Neal said quickly, obviously wanting to avoid an argument over the politics of expansion.

Frederick nodded. "Certainly. We are here as visitors only, not diplomatic envoys. Although I may be called upon in that capacity sometime in the future. One never knows what form one's service to the czar and the Russian empire may take."

Alena had not thought about that. Someday, as Frederick's wife, she might be required to return to this country. While she loved her homeland without question, the thought of visiting the United States again had a certain appeal. She had especially enjoyed Washington, with its parties and glittering ballrooms.

Perhaps someday she would even come back here to Montana and see its prairie and mountains again. She tried to picture herself doing that with Frederick at her side. . . .

But try as she might, the image would not form in her brain. For that matter, she realized suddenly with a small shock, she could not picture herself *anywhere* with Count Frederick Orlov.

That thought chilled her, and she reached for her glass of wine, hoping it would bring her some warmth.

7

A BLUSTERY WIND WAS blowing on the day of the visitors' departure from Fort Union. Banks of thick gray clouds scudded across the sky. There were occasional breaks in the clouds that allowed rays of morning sun to slant through, but none of them lasted very long.

Zephaniah and Titus were standing just outside the open gates in the stockade fence peering up at the sky as Viktor joined them. "You are concerned about the weather?" the Cossack asked.

"Oh, just a mite," Zephaniah replied. "Sometimes we get a spring snowstorm in these parts."

Titus shook his head. "Ain't no snow in those clouds. I'd be able to smell it if'n there was."

"In Russia, I have seen much snow, my friend," Viktor said, "but never once have I been able to smell it."

"Maybe not, but I can. I'd bet my soogans it ain't goin' to snow."

"No bet," Zephaniah said. "I wouldn't take a man's soogans from him."

Viktor was unsure what "soogans" were, but instead of asking for an explanation, as he normally would have, he merely said, "I hope it does not storm. The count would not be pleased if our departure was delayed."

Zephaniah shook his head. "I wouldn't worry. The wagons are all loaded and ready to roll. The weather won't keep us from pullin' out."

Viktor nodded and turned back to the parade ground, where the expedition was assembled. Three covered wagons were lined up behind an open carriage. The American troops that had accompanied the visitors up the Missouri on the *Prairie Flower* were mounted and flanked the wagons on one side. On the other side, also mounted, were the Cossacks. The lineback dun stood at the head of the group, its empty saddle waiting for Viktor.

Lieutenant O'Neal led Frederick, Alena, Zora, and Sasha from the officers' quarters. The women wore fur wraps again to protect them from the wind, which caught at Frederick and Sasha's capes and made them flutter and pop like the Stars and Stripes on the flagpole at the far end of the parade ground. The rest of the Russian party followed. The men mounted horses held for them by their servants, while the women were assisted into one of the wagons. Alena and Zora went to the carriage. One of the Cossacks waited there, and he helped the two women into the vehicle before stepping up to the driver's seat and grasping the reins. Frederick, Sasha, and Lieutenant O'Neal's mounts waited at the head of the party of soldiers. They swung up into their saddles and settled themselves. Viktor was the last one to mount up, and then only after his keen eyes had darted here and there, checking every detail.

The wagons would be driven by some of Kenneth McKenzie's men, employees of the American Fur Company. McKenzie himself came onto the porch of the trading post to watch the departure. He was followed by George Catlin, who had a sketch pad and pencil in his hands. Viktor was not surprised to see that; Catlin had made several sketches of the group during the past few days, although Viktor had been successful in avoiding having to pose for a portrait by the artist.

None of the Blackfeet were on hand this morning, which

came as something of a surprise to Viktor. He had thought that the grandson of Buffalo's Back Fat would want to say good-bye to Alena, after all the time he had spent in her company the past few days. Perhaps the Indians did not like elaborate farewells.

The same could not be said of these Americans. Captain Davis came out of his quarters with his wife and their two children. The tall, angular officer marched across the parade ground, and the company musicians fell in behind him. Davis came to a stop and exchanged salutes with Lieutenant O'Neal, then walked over and extended his hand to Frederick, who reached down from horseback to take it.

"Godspeed on your journey, Count, and good hunting," Davis said. "I'm certain Lieutenant O'Neal and his men will take good care of you."

"I doubt that your country harbors any dangers my Cossacks cannot deal with," Frederick said. "But you have my thanks for all of your assistance, Captain. Will you convey my gratitude to Mr. McKenzie as well?"

"Certainly, sir." Davis stepped back and threw Frederick a brisk salute, which the count returned desultorily.

The musicians began to play. Zephaniah and Titus, riding a pair of ponies that were a little smaller than the soldiers' mounts, moved up to the head of the procession. Viktor joined them. Frederick and Sasha took their positions on either side of the carriage. The strains of a martial melody followed the group as they passed through the gates and out of the fort.

The final stage of the journey that had brought Viktor and the other Russians thousands of miles from the other side of the world was under way.

Viktor straightened in the saddle as a thrill of anticipation shot through him. The feel of the wind in his face, the play of a good horse's muscles under him, the grassy hills rolling gently into the distance in front of him . . . these were things that took him back to the life he had spent in Mother Russia, living wild and free. More of the shackles of civilization dropped away with each step the dun took. Fort Union and all it represented fell far behind them.

Of course, he could not completely escape from civilization, even here. The American soldiers and the aristocrats from Moscow were constant reminders of that other life. But no matter. For the moment Viktor was happier than he had been in weeks.

He heeled the dun into a trot that carried him alongside Zephaniah and Titus. The older of the two frontiersmen looked over at him and asked, "Remind you of home, Viktor?"

"*Da.* This land is much like the valley of the River Don. You would like it there, Zephaniah."

"Maybe so, but I don't reckon I'll ever see it. I'm gettin' too old to go traipsin' halfway round the world."

"You could make the journey," Viktor said. "You could return to Russia with me when we go back. My people would welcome you. The *hetman* would declare a holiday in the village, and there would be a great celebration to honor you. Much dancing and singing and drinking."

"Sounds like my kind of party," Titus said with a grin. "That invite extend to me, Viktor?"

"Of course. Both of you should come."

Zephaniah sighed. "It's a nice thought, boy, but it ain't goin' to happen. I figgered out a long time ago that St. Louis was the farthest I was ever goin' to get from those mountains again."

Viktor didn't waste his breath arguing. He was too busy inhaling great lungfuls of the crisp, clean air that was tinged with the smell of distant rain. Darker clouds gathered over the far-off mountains, and tiny fingers of lightning darted among them. Viktor pointed to the storm. "There may not be snow, but that may cause trouble anyway."

Titus shook his head. "That storm'll hang there over the mountains for a couple of days, then break up. It shouldn't bother us out here on the prairie." Zephaniah nodded his agreement with the assessment.

Viktor hoped they were right. Still, he kept an eye on the distant clouds.

During the day the storm did not come any closer. Alena was watching it, too, and the dark clouds with their fangs of lightning worried her. Zora seemed to be glad to be away from the fort and the Indians camped outside the stockade walls. The older woman feared the forces of nature less than she did those of man. Alena was not certain she agreed with her aunt on that point.

The wind in their faces was cool, but the fur wraps kept them warm. Alena pulled hers up over her mouth and nose and pulled her fur cap down so that only her eyes were showing. The rocking motion of the carriage as their Cossack driver sent it rolling over the prairie was enough to make her drowsy. So it took her a bit by surprise when Zora said, "I hope we do not see any more Indians."

Alena looked over at her aunt, "But that is one of the main reasons we came to this land," she said. "Frederick wants to see Indians."

"Frederick does not know how to leave well enough alone," Zora said in a low voice, glancing at the back of the Cossack driver's head as she did so. It was unlikely the man would repeat anything he overheard in the carriage, Alena thought; while the Cossacks were fiercely loyal in the face of an enemy, none of them had any great love for Frederick.

Nor did she, she added to herself. . . .

"These Indians remind me of the Tartars," Zora went on. "They are savages who live only to kill. Once, many years ago, before you were born, Tartars came to the village where I grew up. Most of our men were away hunting and chopping wood for the winter. I remember standing at the window of our cottage and watching as the Tartars rode into the village. I was too young to know them for what they were, but I saw them take their swords to an old man they caught on the road." Her voice had taken on a hushed quality. "They cut him to pieces, Alena, then chopped off his head and put it on a pike so that they could parade it through the village. They killed everyone who tried to oppose them, and they put the village to the torch. My mother hid my younger brother and me . . . that was your father. We huddled in a cellar that my father had spent an entire summer digging, when the ground finally thawed from the winter. I was afraid the cottage would burn over our heads and come crashing down on us, but our men returned and drove the Tartars away before they could set our dwelling aflame. But I still have dreams about that day." A shudder went through her, but it had nothing to do with the cold.

Alena felt an extra chill as well. She understood a bit better now why Zora was so frightened of the Indians. In the mind of the older woman, the American savages were little different from the Russian ones.

"Frederick can deal with any Indians we encounter," Alena said. "We don't have to have anything to do with them."

"I certainly hope not. And I will be ever so glad when we finally return to Moscow."

Zora could afford to say that, Alena mused. She was not betrothed to Frederick. An arranged marriage did not await her back in Moscow, as it did Alena.

Nothing more was said about Tartars or Indians. The party stopped for their midday meal, which was simple fare—beans that had been cooked back at the fort, fried bacon, and biscuits. This was what American frontiersmen preferred, to judge by the reactions of Zephaniah and Titus, who ate heartily. The Cossacks did, too. Alena, Zora, Frederick, Sasha, and the other aristocrats were accustomed to a different diet, but Alena had to admit that the food was filling. Still, she decided, beans were an awfully . . . indelicate . . . food for ladies. She would just have to hope for the best during the afternoon.

After all, she thought, if such was the only hardship she would have to endure during the expedition, she would be very lucky indeed.

The group pushed on until late afternoon, and as Zephaniah and Titus had predicted, the distant storm hung over the mountains and caused no problems for the travelers. As they made camp, the sky overhead even began to clear slightly.

Viktor was satisfied with the campsite, in a grove of small trees along the banks of a narrow creek. There was a good view of the terrain around them in all directions, making it difficult for anyone to sneak up on them. Viktor intended to post a night watch anyway. He made sure that the horses and the mules from the wagon teams were properly cared for, then circled the camp on foot as the sun shone briefly through a rent in the clouds and then disappeared behind the distant mountains. Shadows of night gathered quickly.

As he returned to the campfire, Viktor saw that some of the noblemen and their ladies were already retiring to bedrolls underneath the wagons. The day's travel had been wearying to these pampered souls whose idea of hardship was having to eat slightly stale crackers with their caviar. Viktor smiled at the thought. As for himself, he felt more alive than he had in days, even months.

He settled down cross-legged next to the fire with a plate of beans and a cup of coffee. Several of his fellow Cossacks were sitting nearby, and he enjoyed listening to their talk as he ate. Not until they suddenly fell silent did he look up from his plate.

Alena stood there, her wrap around her shoulders. "Could I talk to you for a moment, Viktor?" she asked.

He rose to his feet and cast a look at the other Cossacks that made them stand as well and move off to give him and Alena a bit of privacy. "Of course, miss," Viktor said. "What can I do for you?"

"Please, sit," Alena said. "I will join you."

Viktor could not allow her to sit on the ground as he had been doing, so he gestured toward a fallen log a few feet away. "We will sit there."

"All right." Alena settled down on the log first, drawing the wrap a little tighter around her shoulders. Viktor sat down, making sure there was a respectable distance between them. In a low voice, and without looking directly at him, Alena asked, "Viktor, what do you think of Frederick?"

The question took him by surprise, and he did not answer it immediately. Cossacks were not by nature cautious men, but he knew he had to frame this answer carefully.

"The count is a brave man," he finally said. "He fought with valor against the French."

"That was many years ago, when Frederick was young."

"We were all much younger then," Viktor pointed out. "Some were not even born."

It may have just been the firelight, but he thought Alena blushed a bit at those words. "I know that you think me a mere babe, Viktor, but I am a grown woman. I am to be married."

"I know," Viktor said, unable to keep every trace of disapproval out of his voice.

Alena seemed to seize on that reaction. "Would you think me terrible if I was to tell you that I am not sure I—"

"I would never think you terrible for any reason," Viktor cut in, loath to interrupt her but unwilling to be drawn any deeper into a discussion that was clearly none of his business. "I am here to protect you from wild animals or savages or any other danger this land may hold, miss, but there is nothing else I can do for you."

"You have been my friend."

"And I will continue to be. But I have nothing to do with the arrangements your family has made."

This flat refusal cost Viktor quite an effort. He had known Alena for several years, ever since she *was* a child, though she rightly pointed out that she was no longer one. If she was having second thoughts about marrying Frederick Orlov, Viktor could not blame her. But he could not help her, no matter how much he might want to.

Alena sighed and looked as if she was about to say something else, but then the voice of her aunt said loudly. "*There* you are. I have been looking for you, Alena. Do not wander off like that."

Viktor jumped to his feet as Zora stalked up to the log where he and Alena had been sitting. Alena said sharply, "I was in plain sight right here, Aunt Zora. And I was with Viktor, so you know I was in no danger."

Zora's eyes touched Viktor briefly. "Good evening, Dorochenko."

"Madame Galovnin," Viktor replied.

Zora turned back to her niece. "Come with me, Alena. It is time to retire for the evening."

"It is still early," Alena protested.

"We will be making an early start in the morning. Is that not so, Dorochenko?"

Viktor nodded. "Your aunt is correct," he said to Alena. "It is best that I bid you good night."

"Very well," Alena said, though her tone made it clear she was not pleased. She nodded curtly to Viktor. "Good night."

Viktor watched as Zora led Alena away toward the wagons. A space for sleeping had been cleared inside one of the vehicles—the only ones in the party so privileged. Slowly, Viktor shook his head.

The challenges of this wilderness, this raw young land called America, he would gladly meet. They could be defeated with steel and lead and muscle.

But the challenges of the heart . . . those were entirely different, and Viktor had no idea how to grapple with them.

8

GOOD FORTUNE SEEMED TO follow the expedition. The threatening weather cleared, leaving behind an arching vault of deep blue sky dotted with white clouds, and the wind turned around to the south, bringing warmth. A high-country spring was settling in, according to Zephaniah and Titus, and the group could probably expect good weather and traveling conditions for the foreseeable future.

The mountains in the distance drew gradually closer. Frederick did not plan to go as far as the Rockies themselves, Viktor knew. The rugged ranges formed a spectacular backdrop for their journey, however. Several times as he looked at the peaks, Viktor almost wished he had the talent to paint a picture, like the American artist Catlin back at Fort Union. He would have liked to preserve these scenes in something other than mere memory.

The hunting was good, too. Buffalo, moose, antelope, and elk fell before the flintlocks of the Russian noblemen. The prairie echoed with the roar of black powder exploding; a haze of blue-gray smoke drifted over the rolling, grassy hills. The party always had fresh meat. There would have been enough, in fact, to feed a small army; at least, that was what Zephaniah claimed. He and Titus skinned and dressed some of the kills, but most of the carcasses were left to rot or feed the scavengers.

"I tell you, Viktor," Zephaniah said one day when the two mountain men were standing atop a knoll with the Cossack while down below the servants of the Russian nobles set up the shooting stands, "I've always figgered that the Good Lord gave us this land and all its bounty to use, and killin' an animal for food or for its skin ain't never bothered me none. But this—" He waved a gnarled hand at the hunting party, including the ladies in their finery. "This is just plumb wasteful."

Viktor nodded. "I think you are right, friend Zephaniah. But there is nothing we can do anything about it."

"Reckon not. Them Rooshan aristocrats are payin' a handsome price for hirin' us. Guess that makes us just as bad as them."

"Aw, don't say that," Titus complained.

Zephaniah sighed. "That count feller is bound to get his fill o' shootin' game pretty soon, and then we can start back to the fort. Ain't goin' to happen too soon to suit me."

"The count and his friends are disappointed that we have not seen any Indians," Viktor said. "In fact, we have not seen anyone since leaving the fort."

"Oh, the Injuns've been out there," Zephaniah said. "you just ain't seen 'em, is all. They're keepin' an eye on us, nonetheless."

Viktor glanced around, and his hand moved involuntarily toward the hilt of his sword. He didn't like the idea that the expedition was being surreptitiously observed. "You are sure the Indians are watching us?" he asked.

"Look toward the southwest," Zephaniah said quietly. " 'Bout three hills over. See him?"

Viktor peered in the direction Zephaniah had indicated, but the only thing he saw was the endless prairie. "I see nothing."

"Well, you stand right here for another three or four hours, and if you watch real close, you might see that brave twitch a mite. Maybe."

With a chuckle, Viktor shook his head. "I do not think I

will waste my time in such a manner. Does the Indian pose any threat?"

"Doubtful. More'n likely he's just curious. Long as we leave him alone, he'll leave us alone."

Viktor nodded. He would take Zephaniah's word on the matter, just as he would expect the mountain man to bow to his expertise if they had been on the steppes of Russia.

"Chances are," Zephaniah went on, "the longer we're out here, the closer them Injuns'll come to watch us. They'll figger we don't mean 'em any harm, so they'll get a mite more daring. But as long as nobody panics, there won't be no trouble."

"I will speak to my men and warn them."

"You do that. I've already talked to them American soldier boys and told 'em not to get trigger-happy, happen they should spy an Injun or two."

The days turned into a week, then two. Viktor would have gladly stayed and enjoyed the freedom of the plains for a month or more. Alena, thankfully, had not brought up the subject of her engagement to Frederick again. Viktor was aware, however, that some of the others were becoming anxious to return to civilization. Alena had no interest in the hunting, and Zora Galovnin sorely missed her creature comforts, Viktor knew.

But Sasha Orlov was different. The count's younger brother seemed much more comfortable on horseback now, and the sun had darkened his pale skin. He pitched in eagerly, even when the task was disagreeable, such as helping Zephaniah and Titus skin the animals the other men had shot. Sasha hunted little; he seemed more interested in ranging around the hills, never straying too far from Viktor or one of the other Cossacks.

If Sasha spent enough time out here, Viktor thought, the land would transform him. He would no longer be a pampered aristocrat.

That was not going to happen, however, because that night at the campfire, Lieutenant O'Neal announced, "I reckon we'll be starting back toward the fort tomorrow, folks."

Frederick was seated in a folding chair next to Alena and Zora, who also sat in chairs that the servants had set up. The count looked up sharply at O'Neal's words and frowned. "Is that your decision to make, Lieutenant?" he asked. "I was under the impression that I was in command of this expedition."

"That's right, Count, but we only brought supplies for a month, and we've been out for two weeks now. If we don't start back pretty soon, we might run short of provisions."

"Bah!" Frederick made a curt gesture of dismissal. "Game is abundant, more than abundant, and there are small streams every few miles to provide water. What more do we need?"

"Well, sir, you and your friends *have* been burning a lot of powder," O'Neal pointed out carefully. "We wouldn't want to run low on that, just in case of any trouble."

"What trouble?" demanded the nobleman called Anton. "We have not even *seen* any of the American savages since leaving the fort! I have been severely disappointed, Lieutenant."

"I'm sorry about that, sir, but I still think we ought to go back."

Viktor was following the discussion with great interest. The trip had been so enjoyable that he hated to see it end, but he thought O'Neal was correct. It was time to begin the return journey. And while Anton and the other nobles might not have seen any Indians, Zephaniah and Titus had been right about the behavior of the natives: they had become steadily bolder, approaching the party almost close enough to send an arrow into their midst, had they chosen to attack. Viktor had seen them every day for the past several days. The Indians were so skilled at blending in with the terrain, however, that he sometimes suspected they were allowing him to see them on purpose. He wondered at times if there were scores of the savages out there in plain sight, if only his eyes knew where to look.

Frederick said coldly, "We came to America to hunt and to see Indians, Lieutenant. I do not intend to leave until we have fulfilled both of those goals."

O'Neal grimaced but hid the reaction quickly. "There were Indians at Fort Union. You got to meet the chief of the Piegan Blackfoot band, old Buffalo's Back Fat. Isn't that enough, Count?"

"*I* will decide what is sufficient and what is not," Frederick told him.

"I'm sorry, sir"—O'Neal sighed—"but I've got my orders, and I have to carry them out. We weren't supposed to be away from the fort for more than a month. If we are, Captain Davis will have to send out a search party." The young officer's tone hardened a bit, and Viktor admired him for it. "We'll be starting back in the morning."

Frederick lifted himself up out of his chair. "And if I refuse?"

"You and your friends are our guests here, Count. This isn't Russia."

Frederick breathed in deeply, his nostrils flaring in anger. "I will speak to your superior officers about this matter when we return, and I shall lodge a protest with your State Department as well."

"That's your right, sir," O'Neal said. "I was given this job and charged with getting you safely to and from Montana Territory. I intend to follow those orders."

"Very well. The responsibility is on your head, Lieutenant."

O'Neal summoned up a smile and tried to ease the tension a little by saying, "Who knows, maybe we'll run into some more Indians on the way back."

Frederick's mood was foul as the party turned east the next morning. Zephaniah and Titus planned to take a different route back to Fort Union so that the Russian travelers would not simply be retracing their steps. They would still be seeing country that was new to them. But that wasn't enough to mollify Frederick, who said little and glared coldly at Lieutenant O'Neal as the group got under way. The rest of the noblemen, with the exception of Sasha, were doing quite a bit of grumbling, too.

Knowing the count as he did, Viktor would not have

wanted to be in the young lieutenant's boots when they returned to Fort Union. He admired O'Neal for following orders and standing up to Frederick, though.

By midday, the atmosphere was still tense. The group stopped to eat, but Zephaniah and Titus scouted on ahead. The two mountain men rode back into the temporary camp just as the meal was ending.

Zephaniah didn't dismount. He rested his hands on his saddle horn and leaned forward. "There's a herd of buffalo 'bout two miles farther on down the trail," he said. "You want to have a shot at 'em, Count?"

Frederick shrugged. "We have already killed many buffalo. I am no longer as interested in them as I once was."

"It's up to you. Just thought we ought to let you know."

One of the other noblemen said, "Why don't we try to down at least a few of the beasts, Frederick? Who knows how many more such opportunities we may have?"

Frederick cast a hostile glance toward Lieutenant O'Neal, then nodded. "You are right, my friend," he said. "Since we are being forced to return to the fort, we should seize this chance."

O'Neal hesitated, then said, "That's fine, Count. I have no objection."

"I do not recall asking for your permission, Lieutenant." Frederick's voice was as cold as a Moscow February.

O'Neal flushed but made no reply. He turned to his men and said, "Mount up. We'll be moving out shortly."

A few minutes later the wagons and the carriage were rolling eastward again, flanked by the Cossacks and the cavalry. Within an hour they reached the crest of a rise overlooking a broad, shallow depression in the earth. This huge bowl was blanketed with the shaggy bodies of grazing buffalo.

Despite his lingering resentment at Lieutenant O'Neal's decision to turn back, Frederick was gripped once more by the excitement of the moment as the shooting stands were set up. "Next winter when my wife and I ride through the streets of Moscow in our carriage, we will have a lap robe made of buffalo hide," he said with a laugh.

Alena stood nearby, since Frederick enjoyed having her near when he was shooting. She looked down at the ground so that he would not see the grimace that passed swiftly across her face. The thought of sitting in a carriage, snuggled under a buffalo robe with Frederick Orlov . . . it was almost too much for her to endure. Silently, she cursed her family.

When the shooting stands were ready, Frederick and several of his friends rested the barrels of their flintlock rifles on them. As always, the honor of the first shot would go to Frederick. He lined his sights carefully on a good-sized bull, then squeezed the trigger. The stock of the rifle bucked against his shoulder as the powder exploded with a roar. The shot was immediately followed by a volley from the other men. Down below, the buffalo began to mill about, then several of them suddenly broke into the lurching, awkward-looking run that allowed them to cover ground with surprising speed.

None of the animals fell as the whole herd followed, stampeding madly toward the edge of the bowl where they had been grazing.

Frederick shouted, "Why do they not fall?"

"Not every shot can hit its target, Count," one of the other noblemen said.

Frederick lifted his rifle, shook it, and glared at it as if it was human. "These weapons must be faulty. I must speak to Dorochenko about the loads in them."

He thrust the weapon into the hands of his servant, who asked hesitantly, "Should I reload, sir?"

"Of course!" Frederick snapped. "Perhaps I can get another shot at those creatures before they are all out of range."

Anton spoke up excitedly. "Look over there! Perhaps you just need a different sort of game at which to shoot, Frederick."

Frederick turned and looked in the direction the aristocrat was pointing. On the far side of the vast bowl, two figures had appeared on horseback. The riders sat motionless, watching the stampede below them.

"Indians!" Frederick said, a smile breaking out on his face. He turned quickly to his servant. "Where is my gun?"

The man thrust the reloaded flintlock into Frederick's outstretched hands. "H-here you are, Count."

"Watch this," Frederick said as he adjusted his shooting stand and placed the long barrel of the rifle on it. "I shall prove that my shooting eye has not deserted me."

Alena's eyes widened in horror as she realized what he was doing. "Frederick, no! You can't—"

Frederick ignored her as he settled his cheek against the smooth wood of the rifle's stock and lined the sights on one of the distant figures on horseback.

A score of yards away on the rise, Viktor stood with Zephaniah and Titus. They had seen the Russian nobles miss their shots, had watched as the buffalo began to stampede. Viktor could not find it within himself to be sorry that none of the shots had found the mark. These beasts, at least, would escape being slaughtered for no other reason than the gratification of the count and his friends.

But then the Indians appeared on the far side of the great depression in the earth, and a moment later Alena cried out, and Titus muttered worriedly, "What's that jasper up to?"

Viktor turned his head, saw Frederick aiming his rifle. Around him, his friends called out to him, cheering him on. Viktor's eyes widened as his gaze tracked from Frederick to the pair of Indians. He realized what was about to happen, and his mouth opened to frame a shout.

"Noooo!"

It was too late. Frederick squeezed the trigger, and smoke and flame spurted from the muzzle of the flintlock as it fired.

9

FOR A MOMENT THAT SEEMED much longer than it really was, nothing happened.

Then, with a suddenness that shocked the intent watchers, one of the Indians toppled off his horse.

Cheers rang out from several of the count's friends. "Magnificent shot, Frederick!" Anton shouted as he clapped his hands.

Viktor, Zephaniah, and Titus broke into a run toward the nobles. "You fool!" Titus yelled.

"Now he's gone and done it!" Zephaniah said, and Viktor thought the old mountain man sounded more than angry.

Zephaniah sounded afraid.

Viktor glanced toward the distant rise. The unharmed Indian had hurriedly dismounted and rushed over to his wounded companion. He tried to lift the Indian Frederick had shot, but the man slumped back to the ground. The man was obviously badly wounded. The other Indian straightened and shook something at the whites, probably a bow or a lance, Viktor thought. The man was undoubtedly shouting out his rage at them, but it was impossible to hear anything over the rumble of the buffalo stampede.

As Viktor, Zephaniah, and Titus reached the hunting

party, Frederick turned to the other noblemen with a wide, satisfied grin on his face. "Who will take care of the other savage?" he asked.

The hunters quickly began turning their shooting stands and positioning their reloaded rifles. Like the beat of a deadly drum, shots began to pound out.

"Stop it, you idiots!" Zephaniah bellowed. "Stop that shootin'!"

The Russians ignored him and continued firing. Viktor jerked his head toward the far side of the bowl, and his keen eyes saw clods of dirt and grass leap into the air as the rifle balls struck the ground around the second Indian. None of the Russians had sufficient range, but chances were still good that one of the shots would find its target.

The Indian did the only thing he could. Leaving his injured companion on the ground, he ran back to his horse, caught hold of its mane, and swung himself lithely onto its back. He kicked it into a gallop and disappeared over the ridge.

Maddened with anger and fear, Titus lunged toward Frederick, grabbing him by the shoulders and jerking him away from the shooting stand, knocking his rifle to the ground. "You crazy Rooshan son of a she-wolf! You've got us all killed!"

"Stop it!" Frederick shouted, as outraged as Titus but for completely different reasons. "Someone get this lunatic away from me! Dorochenko!"

Drawn by all the yelling and commotion, the other Cossacks were running toward the hunting party. So were the American soldiers, led by Lieutenant O'Neal. Through Viktor's mind flashed the realization that this situation, as bad as it was, could easily become even worse. He could foresee one of his Cossacks drawing a sword and striking down Titus in defense of Frederick. If that happened, the soldiers might decide to fire on the Cossacks for killing an American, and in a matter of instants this could turn into a bloody melee—with Alena, Zora, and the other women right in the middle of it. Viktor knew he had to prevent that.

He reached out and grabbed the collar of Titus's buckskin shirt. The thick bands of muscle along Viktor's arms and shoulders bunched and corded as he pulled Titus away from Frederick. Titus twisted around, too angry to be aware of who had grabbed him, and threw a punch at Viktor's head. Viktor raised his other hand and caught Titus's fist, stopping the blow short. "Please, friend Titus," he said, "do not force me to hurt you."

Titus's eyes dulled, and he went limp in Viktor's grasp. "Too late," he said in a hollow voice. "Too late for ever'thing now."

Puffing and panting, Lieutenant O'Neal ran up and demanded, "What . . . what's going on here?"

Grimly, Zephaniah answered, "The count here just shot an Injun who was watchin' us from that ridge over yonder on the other side."

"And a magnificent shot it was, too," Anton said with a silly grin on his face. "the rest of us missed that other Indian."

Pallor swept over O'Neal's face. "Oh, no." He turned to the troopers who had followed him. "Get ready to pull out—*now!*"

"I do not understand why you are all so upset," Frederick said, annoyance and impatience edging into his voice. "All I did was shoot a savage. You americans do it all the time, do you not? I assumed they were considered little more than animals."

"This is Blackfoot country, Count," Zephaniah grated. "And after what you just done, they're goin' to want ever' last one of us dead!"

Alena, Zora, and the other women brought their hands to their mouths in horror at the old mountain man's words. Frederick just snorted in contempt, shook his head, and said, "Nonsense." He waved toward the far side of the bowl, where the wounded Indian still lay. From the look of the man's sprawled, motionless body, he was probably dead. "Dorochenko, go make sure that savage is finished. And bring me something of his as a trophy, some of his accoutrements . . . or perhaps his ears. I want to have *something* to show for this day's hunting."

Viktor still had hold of Titus's shirt. He released it, dropped his hand to his side, and stood there for a long moment as still as a statue. Finally, he shook his head.

"No."

Frederick turned sharply toward him. The count had paid little attention after issuing the order, assuming that Viktor would obey it without question. "What did you say?" he asked, his face reddening once more with anger.

"I am sorry, Count, but I will have no part of this."

"How dare you! I've given you an order."

"And I have refused it," Viktor said.

Viktor's gaze was fastened on Frederick. He did not even glance toward the others to see their response to this unexpected defiance. Frederick lifted a hand, which was shaking with the depth of his rage, and pointed a finger at Viktor.

"You will regret this, Dorochenko. I ought to shoot you down right now." The rifle he had dropped when Titus accosted him was empty, but there was a loaded pistol in a holster on his hip. His hand moved toward it now.

Zephaniah and Titus looked at each other, then stepped up on either side of Viktor. "I don't reckon that'd be a very good idea, Count," Titus said.

"In fact, it'd be a right poor one," Zephaniah added. There was no mistaking the menace in the voices of both men.

Viktor looked quickly to right and left, meeting the eyes of his new friends for a fleeting second. He hoped they understood how much he appreciated what they were doing. A glance at the other Cossacks told him that they, too, had their rifles ready.

But if gunfire broke out, on which side would his countrymen be? Viktor wondered. In trying to avoid a battle, had he only precipitated one?

It wasn't going to come to that. Frederick swallowed hard, then looked toward O'Neal. "Lieutenant . . . ?"

The young officer was barely keeping his fear and anger in check. "My orders are to keep you and your friends alive, Count. Right now I figure the best way to do that is to tell you to back off."

Frederick cursed bitterly in Russian. "Very well, then! I shall tend to the matter myself." He turned on his heel and stalked off across the bowl. The buffalo were out of sight now, vanished over the rolling hills. The only sign of their recent presence was the dust floating in the air and the earth that had been churned up by their hooves.

The remaining noblemen looked at each other, clearly at a loss as to how to proceed. Finally, Anton said, "I don't know about the rest of you, but I wouldn't mind taking a closer look at a dead Indian. I'm going with Frederick." he started after the count. Most of the others followed.

But not Sasha. Frederick's brother stood there, an expression of infinite sadness on his face.

Zephaniah lowered his flintlock, rested the butt of the rifle on the ground. "Reckon you made yourself a pretty bad enemy there, Viktor."

"*Da.* But I no longer care. I have endured the count ordering everyone around and—how do you say it?—running roughshod over anyone who crossed him for years now. I will not do it anymore."

What Viktor did not say was that his actions had surprised him as much as anyone else. He had not known he was going to defy Frederick until the crucial moment arrived. To refuse an order from his superior went against his grain, but he knew the time had come. He watched, stonefaced, as Frederick ascended the slope on the other side of the bowl and bent over the body of the Indian.

Alena moved up beside Viktor and put a hand on the sleeve of his *rubashka.* "You should not have made Frederick angry, Viktor," she said. "You know what he is like when he is angry."

Zora came up behind them, and her voice lashed out like a whip. "Alena! You should not speak that way! The count is your betrothed."

Alena looked back over her shoulder at her aunt. "Perhaps *that* is a mistake, too."

"And you, Dorochenko!" Zora went on, as if she had not heard Alena's comment. "You have failed in your duty! You are a disgrace! When the czar hears of this—"

"I do not care," Viktor told her, scandalizing her even more. "I have done what I know is right."

"Right!" Zora repeated. "Since when does right have anything to do with—"

She fell silent as Frederick approached, trailed by the rest of the hunting party. He was carrying a pouch made of some sort of animal hide, decorated with beads and shiny stones.

"I will deal with you when we get back to Moscow, Dorochenko," he said to Viktor. "You will be guarding the Siberian frontier next winter—if you are fortunate. For now, you are no longer in command of these Cossacks." The count turned his icy glare on Zephaniah and Titus. "As for you two barbarians, we have no more need for your services."

"Wait just a minute," Lieutenant O'Neal protested. "These men are under my command—"

"Not anymore we ain't," Titus cut in. "We're gettin' out o' here 'fore the Blackfeet come to call. I'm not goin' to get my hair lifted on account of what this ignorant Rooshan did." He looked at his partner. "You comin', Zeph?"

Slowly, Zephaniah shook his head. "No, I don't reckon I am."

Titus leaned back in surprise. "Why not?" he asked.

"I signed on to guide these folks. Job won't be done till I get 'em back to Fort Union, at least."

"Zeph, don't be crazy! You know what's goin' to happen!"

Zephaniah hefted his rifle, rested it in the crook of his left arm. "Maybe not, if we get movin' fast enough," he said, " 'stead of standin' around and wastin' time jawin'." He turned to O'Neal. "Lieutenant, we'd better get busy."

"Yes," O'Neal said, clearly still quite shaken. "Yes, we should get ready to travel as soon as possible."

Titus stared at Zephaniah for a few seconds, struggling to come to grips with the older man's decision. Finally, he shook his head and walked off. Over his shoulder, he said, "If you want to get yourself killed, old hoss, I reckon that's up to you."

Zephaniah sighed, watched the retreating back of his former partner for a moment, then turned to Viktor. "Come on, son. Let's get these pilgrims movin'."

Alena had not known it was possible to be this frightened. She had been in an anxious state ever since the party had arrived on the American frontier, but this was different. The prospect of actually having to marry Frederick Orlov had come to terrify her the more time she spent around him, as well, but again it was not the same.

This was death staring her in the face, and she knew it.

Frantic preparations were under way to get the wagons and the carriage rolling again. The mule teams had been unhitched when it had seemed that the party would be staying here for most of the afternoon. Now the American soldiers hurried to get the balky animals back in their harnesses. Horses were being saddled, and other men were checking the rifles, making certain that all of the weapons were loaded. The Cossacks handled similar tasks, but they did not seem to be as worried as the American troops. In fact, there was a grim anticipation on the faces of some as they ran their thumbs along the edges of their blades and nodded in satisfaction.

Zora was already in the carriage. Alena could not contain her nervousness; she paced back and forth next to the vehicle. When she saw Sasha striding by, an intent expression on his face, she grasped the sleeve of his jacket.

"Have you heard anything more, Sasha?" she asked. "Are the Indians really going to attack us?"

Sasha shook his head. "I do not know. The Americans are very worried, even frightened. But if the Indians come, Alena, I . . . I will protect—" He broke off his pledge and looked down at the ground, too embarrassed to go on.

Even in the midst of this danger, she flustered him to the point where he could barely talk, she thought with a faint smile. It would have been a sweet moment . . . had their lives not been in such peril.

Acting on an impulse, she stepped closer to Sasha, put her arms around his waist, and rested her head on his chest.

She felt him flinch, heard him gasp in surprise. But his arms went around her as well, and she found that his embrace somehow made her feel better. She closed her eyes and murmured, "Hold me, Sasha."

The moment was short-lived. In a horrified voice, Zora commanded, "Alena! Stop that!"

Alena was prepared to ignore her aunt, but then Frederick spoke from somewhere nearby, his tones hard and cold. "Sasha! Go on about your business. Make sure everything is packed in the wagon."

Sasha let go of Alena, practically jerking away. "Yes, Frederick," he said with a hurried nod. He started to turn away, then stopped abruptly. His eyes met Alena's, and he stood there for a second, obviously reluctant to leave. Frederick's continuing glare forced him to move on.

When Sasha was gone, Frederick turned to Alena. "I hope my brother did not offend you with his rash actions." His eyes searched her face.

She shook her head. "No, of course not. Sasha knew how frightened I am, and he was merely trying to comfort me. I am grateful to him."

Frederick smiled thinly, insincerely. "You have nothing to worry about, my dear. The American lieutenant and those backwoodsmen are acting like whipped puppies. Those savages are no real threat to us." He struck his chest with a clenched fist. "We are Russians! We have nothing to fear."

"Of course, Frederick," Alena agreed, looking down at the ground.

He reached out and cupped his hand under her chin, lifting it so that she was forced to look at him. "I would never allow any harm to befall the woman I intend to marry." He leaned toward her, and his mouth came down in hers in a hard, hungry kiss.

Alena accepted the kiss stiffly, not even making any pretense of returning his passion. If Frederick noticed her lack of response, he gave no sign of it. There was no tenderness in the touch of his lips, and Alena almost gasped in relief when he finally broke the kiss.

"We will be leaving soon," he said as he stepped back away from her.

"Aunt Zora and I will be ready."

"Be brave. Everything will be fine."

He turned and walked away. Alena stood there for a moment, trembling inside from a combination of fear, repulsion, and regret. She wished she had never come to this horrible, barbaric land.

Behind her in the carriage, her aunt sniffed. "You should be careful," Zora advised. "If Frederick suspects that you prefer his brother to him—"

"Really, Aunt Zora!" Alena exclaimed, turning sharply toward the carriage. "Don't you think we have more important things to worry about now? Things like surviving when those Indians attack us!"

A heavy footstep made her glance over her shoulder in trepidation. She was afraid that Frederick had returned. Instead, she saw to her relief that it was Viktor. As always, just the sight of the big Cossack made her feel a little better.

"I will allow no harm to come to you, Princess," he said gruffly.

Alena managed to smile at him. "I am not a princess, Viktor, you know that."

"To me, you will always be a princess, little one. Your father and I fought the mad Frenchman together, many years ago. I promised him I would look out for you."

"Really?" She was pleased by that thought. "Father never said anything . . ."

"It is true," Viktor said. "And I intend to honor my vow." He glanced off, and when Alena followed his gaze, she saw that he was looking at Frederick, who was berating Sasha about something over by the wagons.

Viktor's next words were so soft that she barely heard them.

"As much as I am permitted to do so . . ."

The sounds of mourning filled the Blackfoot village. The mother of Cloud Caller wailed and moaned a death song in her lodge. She had cut off her hair as soon as she had been told of the death of her son, and she had gashed the calves of her legs and cut off the first joint of one finger as well. The pain of that mutilation was as nothing compared with the pain of losing a loved one.

Buffalo's Back Fat was grim-faced as he listened to the sounds of loss. The death of young Cloud Caller had to be avenged, and everyone in the band knew it. Already the warriors had begun to gather so that they could ride after the white men and punish them for their crime. Buffalo's Back Fat strode toward the men as they mounted their ponies.

"May the spirits guide and protect you," the chief said as he held up his hands to bless the warriors. He looked at Lis-sis-tsi, the hawk-faced man known as Wolverine. "You will lead our warriors today."

Wolverine nodded, and Buffalo's Back Fat could tell that he was pleased to have been given this honor, though he said nothing.

"Punish the white men for what they have done," Buffalo's Back Fat said.

"We will kill them all," Wolverine promised.

Buffalo's Back Fat shrugged. He did not care if all of the white men died for the crime of one man.

The warriors rode out a short time later with Wolverine at their head. Buffalo's Back Fat watched them go, then returned to his lodge to pray and meditate. As he entered his lodge, he looked at Crystal Stone, his wife, and their grandson, who had not yet been given a name because of his position as the chief's heir. His naming would come later, when he was older and more ready to assume the duties he would inherit. He was a good boy, Buffalo's Back Fat thought, watching the youngster pluck at the strings of the musical instrument the young white woman with hair like fire had given him at the white man's fort.

Buffalo's Back Fat would pray to the spirits that no more evil would visit his people today.

From a distant hillside, Climbs High sat on his horse at the head of the group of Crow warriors and watched the Blackfeet ride out of their village. Climbs High was known for his keen eyesight, and with it he could see that more than half of the Blackfoot warriors were leaving. The village would be only lightly defended.

A grim smile plucked at his mouth. He had no idea why the Blackfeet were leaving or where they were going, but it did not matter.

The spirits were smiling on him and his people, Climbs High thought. Soon, very soon, the prize he sought would be his.

There would be wailing and lamentations in the lodge of the old chief tonight, because by then the grandson of Buffalo's Back Fat would be in the hands of the Crows.

10

A FEW MINUTES LATER, AFTER leaving Alena at the carriage, Viktor stood beside the lineback dun and patted the horse's shoulder. The dun had been a good, no, a fine mount, full of spirit and fire. As Viktor stroked the mouse-gray hide, the horse turned its head and nipped at his hand, making him draw it back quickly. Viktor grinned. "Ah, there is plenty of fight in you, is there not?" he said quietly. "I should have given you a name before now, my friend." He lowered his hand to the hilt of the wickedly curved blade sheathed on his hip. "I will call you Saber."

The dun looked at him, and for a second Viktor thought the horse had rolled its eyes at the idea of being named Saber. He laughed, then reached down for the saddle at his feet. He lifted the saddle and set it in place on the blanket that had already been thrown over the dun's back.

Not even a half hour had passed since Frederick had murdered the Indian, but it seemed longer than that, Viktor reflected. During that time, Titus had gathered his gear and ridden away, heading south. He and Zephaniah had stubbornly refused to say good-bye to each other, and Zephaniah had been looking pointedly elsewhere as Titus left. Titus rode stiffly, without a backward glance. That partnership destroyed was yet another example of Frederick's handiwork, Viktor thought.

It was possible that the second Indian had not yet even reached his village, wherever that might be. Viktor hated and despised the count for what he had done, but right now survival—for himself and his friends and especially Alena—was uppermost in his mind.

Footsteps made him look around, and he saw Sasha hurrying up to him. The young man's face was pale but composed. Sasha nodded to him and said, "Viktor . . . may I ask you a question?"

"Of course."

"Are you . . . afraid of the Indians?"

Viktor tightened the cinch on the saddle after poking the dun in the side. Without looking at Sasha, he said, "I respect them. I am not afraid. I am a Cossack—despite what your brother says."

"I'm afraid," Sasha said. The admission clearly cost him an effort.

Viktor looked over at him solemnly. "In this situation, any sane man *would* be afraid." A savage grin suddenly tugged at his bearded face. "But as I said—I am a Cossack."

On the other side of the wagons, Lieutenant O'Neal called in a loud voice, "Move out!"

Viktor clapped Sasha on the shoulder. "You must mount up now. If trouble does come, watch me."

Sasha nodded, frightened but clearly eager at the same time. "I will, Viktor. I promise." He hurried away.

Viktor grasped his saddle and swung up onto the dun. He lifted the reins and heeled the horse into a trot that carried him quickly to the front of the procession.

Lieutenant O'Neal and Zephaniah were waiting there. Frederick had removed Viktor from command of the Cossacks, but none of the Russians had stepped forward to take charge. Likewise, none of them challenged him when he took his place at the head of the column with the two Americans. Viktor cast a glance over his shoulder and saw the hate-filled glare on Frederick's face as the count watched him. Frederick had noticed where Viktor was riding, that was certain—and though he did not like it, he could do little about it under the circumstances.

O'Neal called, "Move out!" again, and the drivers of the wagons cracked their whips and called out to the mule teams. The Cossack at the reins of the carriage team slapped the reins against the backs of the two horses pulling the smaller vehicle. One by one, the carriage and the wagons lurched into motion.

"Keep your eyes peeled," Zephaniah advised as he and Viktor and the lieutenant nudged their horses into a brisk walk. "No tellin' which direction them Blackfeet'll come from."

"You sound pretty certain that they *will* come," O'Neal said.

"That buck the count shot off his hoss looked like a youngster to me. Blackfeet won't let that go by without at least tryin' to catch up to us. Thing is, we're goin' to do all we can not to let that happen." Zephaniah leaned forward and reached into one of the saddlebags slung on his horse. "I been thinkin', Viktor. Since that count fella fired you, I reckon you don't have to wear that Cossack hat no more. Here."

He took a cap made from a raccoon's skin, complete with the dangling tail, and held it out toward Viktor.

The big Cossack hesitated for a second, then broke into a grin and reached out to take the cap. "I am honored." He took off his usual fur hat and stuffed it into his saddlebags. Then he carefully placed Zephaniah's gift on his head so that the raccoon's tail hung onto his right shoulder. "How do I look?"

"Like a reg'lar mountain man," Zephaniah said, returning the grin.

O'Neal said impatiently, "You two can trade hats when we get back to the fort. Right now we need to keep our eyes open for those Blackfeet."

"I'm watchin', Lieutenant," Zephaniah said. "I'm watchin'."

The three men rode in silence for several minutes.

Their gazes roved constantly over the surrounding land-scape, which seemed quiet and peaceful, even deserted. That impression could be very deceptive, however, and Viktor knew it. Once again he thought about the Indian Zephaniah had spotted on the expedition's first day out. Viktor had not seen that watcher at all; who knew how many more might be out there at this very moment?

He finally broke the silence. "I did not think Titus would leave us as he did."

Zephaniah sighed. "Yep, that was a mite hard to take. Titus and me been ridin' together for quite a spell." The old mountain man leaned over slightly in his saddle and spat. "But I can't blame him for ridin' off like that. Not with a bunch of Blackfeet probably comin' after us as mad as a stirred-up nest of hornets."

"These Indians are really so dangerous?"

"Of course they are!" Zephaniah replied with a snort. "Blackfeet ain't really cared for white men since Cap'n Meriwether Lewis shot one of 'em, back in ought-eight or so. He was one of the fellas who first explored this part of the country after we up and bought it from France. Lewis, I mean, not the Blackfoot buck he ventilated."

"Bonaparte," Viktor said, with a grimace as if the word tasted sour. "He needed money to supply his army so that he could invade my country. That is why he sold this land to your President Jefferson."

"Well, I don't reckon ol' Tom knew what that little Frenchman was up to when he bought the whole blamed Louisiana Territory from the gent. Fought in that war, did you, Viktor?"

With a solemn nod, Viktor said, "Yes, I did, and it was a cold, cold winter, I can tell you that, my friend. A bloody winter, too . . ."

Those grim memories made Viktor fall silent once more, but his mood was no more bleak than Zephaniah and O'Neal's. Viktor hipped around in his saddle and looked back along the line of the little caravan. Every face he saw was set in tight, worried lines, save for those of the Cossacks.

Viktor summoned up what he hoped was a reassuring smile for Alena and her aunt. Frederick and Sasha rode close beside the carriage. Sasha was making an obvious effort to be brave and not completely succeeding. Frederick, despite the hard-set, angry lines of his face, was frightened, too, Viktor realized, although the nobleman probably would have died before admitting it.

Frederick might get the chance to do just that before the day was over, Viktor thought.

Lieutenant O'Neal kept the party moving at a brisk, even brutal pace. An hour passed, then two, and O'Neal, acting on advice from Zephaniah, called a halt to allow the horses and mules to rest. While the procession was stopped, people stretched their legs and grabbed a bite to eat, although no one was really very hungry. Then they were on the move again, heading a little south of east, bound for Fort Union on the fastest possible route. Seeing the sights of this western country was no longer a concern.

By midafternoon, when nothing had happened, Viktor asked Zephaniah, "At this pace, how long will it take us to reach Fort Union?"

The procession was rolling along the base of a short but rugged ridge dotted with outcrops of rock. "We're makin' a lot better time than we did comin' out here," Zephaniah said after considering the question for a moment. "Not stoppin' to hunt really speeds things up. But we still got a heap o' ground to cover, Viktor. It'll take us four or five days, maybe a week, to get to the fort."

"But surely we will not be in danger that entire time."

Zephaniah nodded. "I'm afraid so. No matter how big a lead we got on them Injuns, a war party on fast ponies'll be able to catch up to us. And with this many horses an' wagons, there ain't no way they can't track us. We're leavin' a trail a deaf, dumb, and blind man could foller."

O'Neal spoke up. "I hope that the Blackfeet will have the sense not to attack such a large, well-armed party. I wouldn't want that insufferable Russian to hear me agreeing with him, but our muskets should be more than a match for their arrows and lances."

"Could be you're right about that, Lieutenant," Zephaniah said. "But what if them Blackfeet don't know—or don't care—just how outgunned they really are? They could jump us anyway."

The young officer shook his head. "I'm going to hope you're wrong. I know I haven't been out here on the frontier nearly as long as you, but—"

His words were cut off by a fluttering whisper followed immediately by a thump and a gasp. Viktor looked over, his eyes meeting O'Neal's. The lieutenant's eyes were opened wide and bulging with pain and horror.

The feathered shaft of an arrow was lodged in his throat, and the bloody tip protruded from the back of his neck.

A ghastly, strangled moan came from O'Neal as he slowly toppled out of his saddle. Before the lieutenant even hit the ground, Zephaniah was jerking his mount around and bellowing, "Here they come, boys!"

Viktor yanked the dun's head to the left, toward the ridge. He was facing the slope squarely as more than a dozen Indians mounted on small, fast ponies charged over the crest. They shouted and whooped as they waved their lances in the air.

"Comin' in on the other side, too!" Zephaniah called out as he pulled his horse around in circles.

Viktor twisted to look to the right and saw even more Blackfeet seemingly rising out of the earth itself. There had to be a some sort of gully over there, he realized, and the Indians had used it for concealment until they were in position to strike. For a moment he looked back and forth at the howling, charging Blackfeet. Then he reached to his belt and slid the long, curved saber from its sheath.

Zephaniah steadied his horse and brought his long-barreled flintlock to his shoulder. Without seeming to take the time to aim, he fired, and one of the Indians went spinning off the back of a horse. Sporadic firing came from the American soldiers, too, although with their leader dead, none of them quite seemed to know what to do.

Viktor wheeled the dun and drove his boot heels into the animal's flanks. The horse lunged forward, carrying him toward the carriage where Alena and her aunt Zora were cowering. Zora had her hands over her face and was shrieking at the top of her lungs. Alena held tightly to her aunt's arm and watched the onrushing Indians with wide, terrified eyes, but she made no sound.

"Princess!" Viktor shouted.

Alena's gaze flicked toward him, and for an instant he thought her pale face was slightly less frightened.

Viktor waved his saber at his fellow Cossacks and called out to them in Russian. The order was not really necessary; the riders from the steppes were already charging to meet the attack of the Blackfeet. Some of the Cossacks fired pistols, while others brandished their sabers in the air and gave weird, ululating battle cries.

The carriage and the wagons had come to an abrupt stop when the Indians attacked. Frederick brought his horse next to the carriage and left the saddle in a dive that sent him sprawling into the front seat opposite Alena and Zora. He pushed himself up and shouted at the Cossack driver, "Go! Get us out of here!"

The Cossack whipped the horses into motion again, sending the carriage jolting forward. That took it past Viktor, who was racing to meet it. The big Russian hauled back on the reins and wheeled the dun once more. He pounded after the carriage, along with Sasha, who bounced wildly in the saddle of his galloping mount, almost coming unhorsed several times.

Viktor saw Frederick stand up in the carriage and fire his pistol at the Indians, who were quite close by this time, sweeping in from both right and left. Several arrows slashed through the air near Viktor's head, but none of them touched him or the dun. He glanced at the corpse of Lieutenant O'Neal as the horse thundered past. The young officer had done the best he could in an almost impossible situation.

The blame for this bloody debacle rested squarely on the shoulders of Count Frederick Orlov.

Placing blame would not save any of them, however, Viktor knew. He caught up to the carriage as Frederick finished reloading the pistol. The count lifted the weapon and fired again, his actions cool and steady. One of the Blackfeet slumped over the neck of his horse but did not fall. Frederick had his faults, but cowardice—and bad aim—were not among them.

One of the Indians lunged at Viktor, thrusting a lance. Viktor twisted in the saddle to evade the wicked point. His saber swept up and then down, shattering the lance. In a continuation of the same movement, he veered the dun closer to the Blackfoot pony and slashed at the rider with a backhanded stroke. The keen edge of the blade sliced across the chest of the man's buckskin tunic, then found the soft flesh of his throat. Blood fountained into the air as Viktor's saber grated on the Indian's spine. The Blackfoot fell limply from his mount, his almost decapitated head flopping grotesquely.

But for every one of the Indians killed, another three or four were waiting to take his place. Their savage, bloodthirsty cries filled the air as they surrounded the American soldiers. Outnumbered and leaderless as they were, the troopers were cut down without mercy.

For a moment it appeared that the Cossacks would break through the closing ring of Blackfeet. Then they began to fall as well, darker stains of blood appearing on their already red coats. They sold their lives dearly, their blades drinking deeply of Indian blood.

Viktor looked around for Zephaniah, saw the old mountain man surrounded by mounted warriors. With no time to reload his rifle, Zephaniah dropped it and jerked a pistol from his belt, firing the weapon at close range into the contorted face of one of his attackers. The Blackfoot toppled off his horse, his head practically blown off his shoulders.

That left Zephaniah unarmed except for the heavy hunting knife and the tomahawk tucked behind his belt.

He grabbed both weapons and began flailing around with them, dealing death to any of the Indians foolish enough to come within arm's length of him.

The carriage was bouncing and careening along crazily. This terrain might look flat, but there were plenty of bumps large enough to send the carriage jolting into the air every few seconds. The horses, wall-eyed and terrified by the gunfire and the screaming and the coppery scent of blood, ran full tilt over the plain. Alena and Zora held on to each other and tried to keep from being thrown from the carriage. Viktor brought the dun alongside the vehicle on the right, while Sasha moved closer on the left. They provided an escort of sorts.

But not enough of one to keep arrows out. Zora suddenly rocked back against the seat and stopped screaming. The shaft of an arrow quivered from the center of her chest. She shuddered and then hung limply, pinned to the seat by the arrow that had passed all the way through her body. Alena saw what had happened and screamed, half out of her mind with terror, then pulled away from her aunt's body and tried to stand up.

"Aunt Zora!" she shrieked. "Oh, dear Lord, no!"

Frederick saw what she was doing and reached out to grab her arm. He practically threw her toward the seat next to her aunt. "Get down! Sit down, Alena!"

At that moment the carriage hit an even larger bump and lurched heavily. Alena slammed against the seat, then was thrown hard toward the side of the vehicle. She tried to grab hold of the edge, but her hip struck the door and popped open the latch. With another scream, she tumbled free and flew through the air to crash into the ground.

"Alena!"

The shout came from both Viktor and Frederick. Viktor jerked back brutally on the dun's reins, bringing the horse to a sliding, skidding halt, while the count turned and pounded on the shoulder of the driver. "Turn back!" he ordered. "Turn back, you fool!"

The Cossack at the reins of the carriage suddenly

slumped forward, doubling over as an arrow struck him in the midsection. He surged to his feet, dropping the reins as he fumbled at the arrow that had been driven through his vitals. As his balance deserted him, he pitched forward off the seat, falling under the carriage so that its wheels passed directly over him. That jolted the vehicle again, knocking Frederick off his feet.

Viktor sent his mount in a hard run toward Alena, fearing the worst. As he neared her, however, he saw that she was moving around slightly. She might be badly hurt, stunned by the fall, but at least she was still alive.

Alive, and surrounded by savages bent on exacting a bloody revenge . . .

The booming of a pistol made the knot of Indians break apart for a moment. Viktor saw Sasha on the other side of the spot where Alena had fallen. With no thought for his own safety, the young man launched an attack on the Blackfeet. One of the Indians fell from Sasha's gunshot, then he was among them, his own sword flashing in the sunlight.

Viktor was proud of the youngster. Sasha's actions were foolhardy, but valiant. There was no time to dwell on his bravery, however. Viktor rode into the small group of Blackfeet, chopping down two of them with bone-crunching saber strokes. The others were driven away a few yards by Sasha's mad charge.

Viktor saw Alena lift her head. Her long red hair had escaped the confines of her cap, which she'd lost in her fall from the carriage. It hung loosely around her head and over her face. She must have seen Viktor, because she called his name and held her hand up toward him.

Viktor leaned down from the saddle, and his hand clasped Alena's wrist. He pulled her up, her weight seeming as nothing to his enormous strength. She sprawled across the saddle in front of him. He shifted his grip to her dress and hauled her into a more secure position, then kicked the horse into a run again. He guided the dun with his knees while holding on to Alena with one arm and wielding the saber in the other. There was a small hill not far away, he noted. He headed for it.

Meanwhile, Sasha had broken away from the Indians he had driven off from Alena. Bleeding from several wounds, he jerked his head around and saw the carriage, still bouncing over the prairie as the horses galloped wildly in sheer terror. Frederick clambered upright again and hung over the rear seat, looking back toward Viktor, Alena, and Sasha. "Alena!" he shouted.

Sasha looked around, saw that Viktor had picked up Alena. She would be as safe with the big Cossack as with anyone, he knew. He rode after the carriage, hoping to stop it so that he and Frederick could rejoin Viktor and the three of them could protect Alena.

A couple of hundred yards to the rear, Zephaniah was still on his horse, fighting hand to hand with the Blackfeet who thronged around him. Blood streamed from several wounds, and he was abruptly knocked forward in the saddle by an arrow that struck him from behind in the left shoulder. Forcing himself upright, he lashed out once more with the tomahawk, but he was too weak to do much damage now. With a whoop, one of the Indians thrust a lance at him, and Zephaniah was unable to avoid it. The lance took him in the stomach and drove completely through him before he was knocked from the saddle by the impact.

Impaled by the lance, covered with blood, the old mountain man struggled mightily to rise to his feet once more. "Come on, you savages!" he rasped at the Indians closing in around him. "Come on an' die!"

They dismounted and surrounded him, tomahawks rising and falling, the heads of the war axes soon daubed with red and gray. In a matter of moments, the struggle was over and the Blackfeet threw themselves back on their ponies to race off in search of more prey.

A pair of Indians tried to block Viktor's path as he rode toward the hill. Holding Alena tightly against him, he angled the dun directly toward one of the warriors and slashed at the other with his saber. The Indian tried to

block Viktor's stroke with his tomahawk, but the Cossack's blade bit deeply into his shoulder. The other
Blackfoot jerked his pony out of the way and tried to
draw a bead on Viktor with an arrow. Viktor's saber
flashed again, and the bow fell, still clutched tightly in
the hand that Viktor had just chopped off the man's arm.
The Indian howled in pain as he flailed the blood-spout-
ing stump.

The top of the hill was where he would make his stand,
Viktor had decided. It was the closest thing to high
ground on this boundless prairie. If some of the others
could rally to his side, they might have a chance.

But there would be no help forthcoming, he saw as he
looked back over his shoulder. The American troops were
all either dead or mortally wounded. A few of his fellow
Cossacks were still fighting, but most of them were
sprawled motionless on the ground, easy to spot because
of their bright red coats. As Viktor watched, another man
fell to an Indian arrow, an old friend from his village.

There was no time to mourn. All he could do was fight
off the savages for as long as he could and protect
Alena's life with his own.

He pulled the dun to a halt as the horse reached the top
of the hill. Sliding from the saddle, Viktor took Alena
with him. She cried out, "Viktor! What—"

Viktor had already seen close to a dozen mounted
Blackfeet circling around the hill to cut off their escape.
More were closing in from behind. He urged Alena to the
ground, saying, "Stay down, Princess. I will protect you."

"No, Viktor! Get back on the horse and get away while
you can! Save yourself!"

Viktor sheathed his saber and jerked his rifle from the
boot attached to the dun's saddle, then slapped the horse
across the rump. It lunged away.

"Too late for that, Princess," Viktor said with a grim
smile. "Now all that is left is to die with our feet awash
in the blood of our enemies!"

Seeing that he intended to make a stand, several of the
Blackfeet leaped down from their horses and attacked on

foot. Viktor felt a strange kinship with them, knowing they did that so his end would be a more honorable one, rather than simply riding him down and riddling him with lances and arrows.

Just before the Blackfeet reached him, he glanced past them and saw the carriage disappearing in the distance, still carrying Count Frederick Orlov. Sasha rode right behind the vehicle, a good-sized group of Blackfeet in pursuit.

Frederick and Sasha would have to meet their own destiny, Viktor thought—just as he was about to meet his.

He jerked the pistol from his belt with his left hand as he lifted the rifle in his right. Both weapons roared as he discharged them into the onrushing horde of Indians. Not waiting to see the results of the shots, Viktor dropped the guns and drew his saber again. As he met the attack with cold steel, the words of a Cossack battle song came unbidden to his lips. They rang in his ears as he slashed at the Blackfeet. Alena huddled at his feet.

Drops of blood fell like crimson rain around him as he hacked at the Indians. A thrown knife lodged in his left shoulder, and a tomahawk grazed his head, leaving a bloody gash behind and staggering him. One of the Blackfeet darted in underneath the whirling saber and grabbed Alena, jerking her away from Viktor. She screamed and struggled wildly.

"Alena!" Viktor bellowed as he swung toward her.

Something slammed into the back of his head, a glancing blow but one with enough power to send him to his knees. A red haze covered his eyes, and he did not know if it came from blood dripping from his head or if he was simply passing out. With a roar, he tried to surge back to his feet and locate Alena, who was still screaming, but before he was able to do that, more tomahawks struck him.

He felt something hit him in the face, tasted dirt in his mouth. He had fallen, he realized. It was over. His eyes were open, but awareness dimmed in them as his features went slack. The sounds of Alena's screams slowly faded in his ears.

But the screams continued for a long time before they finally ceased.

11

THE OLD WOMAN'S FACE
was a mass of wrinkles. She appeared to be at least a hundred years old, and she sported a wrinkle for every one of those years. Her skin was the dark reddish brown of aged mahogany, her eyes blacker than the darkest night. Behind her was a wall of some sort, apparently stitched together out of pieces of buffalo hide.

The sight of that face, staring at him from a distance of a few inches, so startled Viktor that it took him several seconds to realize something even more amazing.

He was alive.

The pain that throbbed inside his skull, surging with every beat of his heart, was proof enough of that. He was certain somehow that dead men did not know such pain. Nor did the smell of rancid buffalo grease fill their nostrils. He was less sure about that conclusion, having no real idea what heaven—or hell—should smell like. But he was convinced it would not be what he was smelling now.

"Ni-tap-i wak-sin?" the old woman said.

Her voice echoed strangely, and the words were meaningless to Viktor. He shook his head and immediately regretted it. The pain, which he had thought could not grow any worse, blossomed throughout his head and made him wince. Even *that* small movement made the pounding ache grow worse.

Gradually, he became aware that the old woman was trying to force something into his hands. Steeling himself against a resurgence of the agony, he pushed himself onto an elbow. Only after he had done so did he realize that he was lying on a thick, soft robe. Close beside him was a small fire, and the warmth it gave off made him feel a tiny bit better.

He was holding a crude wooden bowl filled with food of some sort. The old woman was squatting beside him, next to the fire. Moving his head slowly and carefully, lest it topple from his shoulders, Viktor looked around and saw that the two of them were alone. They were in a circular structure made of buffalo hide. An Indian lodge such as the ones they had seen just outside Fort Union, he decided. Tepees, that was what they were called.

He was wearing his loose-fitting black trousers and the heavy linen shirt. The *rubashka* was torn and stained with blood in several places. His boots were gone, as were his long red coat and the cap made of raccoon skin that Zephaniah had given him.

The thought of the cap made his mind jerk back to what had happened out there on the plains. Zephaniah was dead, as were Zora Galovnin, Lieutenant O'Neal, the other American soldiers, and the rest of the Cossacks. Almost beyond a doubt, so, too, were Alena, Frederick, and Sasha.

So, Viktor asked himself as his brain began to work again, why was *he* still alive?

With a long finger as gnarled and knobby as a twig of a tree, the old woman pointed at the bowl in Viktor's hands and said again, *"Ni-tap-i wak-sin?"*

Viktor found his voice. It was hoarse and sounded as odd and strained to him as the old woman's did. "You . . . you want me to eat?"

She pointed brusquely at the bowl, the expression on her wrinkled face becoming more impatient. She looked like she was dealing with a half-witted child.

"Well . . . I did not expect to still be alive," Viktor said. "I suppose I should eat and try to stay that way."

The world seemed to have stopped spinning the wrong way every time he moved his head, so he pushed himself into a more upright position and studied the contents of the bowl, where chunks of meat appeared to be swimming in thick brown gravy. He fished out one of the chunks with trembling fingers and lifted it to his mouth. Biting off a piece and chewing it took a surprising amount of energy and left him exhausted. But he managed to swallow and then nodded approvingly. The meat was tough but did not taste too bad.

"Good," he said. "What is it?"

The old woman returned his nod, fairly beaming at him as she did so. *"Ni-tap-i wak-sin,"* she said.

"If you say so." Now that he had evidently made a friend of this crone, he ventured a little farther. He was still alive, so he could not be completely certain that Alena had not survived the massacre, too. Knowing the old woman probably could not understand him, he asked, "Where is Alena?"

The smile disappeared from the woman's wrinkled visage. She shook her head and stood up, then moved to the other side of the lodge. The long buckskin dress she wore whispered around her ankles as she shuffled her moccasin-clad feet.

Viktor put the bowl aside. "The young woman who was with me," he said. "The woman with long red hair . . ." He made motions with his fingers, pantomiming long strands of hair. "Where is she?"

The old woman shook her head again, even more stubbornly than before.

Viktor put a hand on the ground to balance himself and tried to stand up. He was less than halfway upright when a wave of dizziness struck him. He slumped back onto the buffalo robe with a groan of frustration. Beads of sweat popped out on his forehead.

Panting a little, he said, "If Alena is dead . . . you should have killed me . . . too. I will avenge her."

The old woman watched him stolidly, obviously not

comprehending what he was saying. After a moment Viktor sighed heavily and reached for the bowl of food again. No matter what had happened before, he had to regain some of his strength if he was going to have any chance to survive. As he began to chew another chunk of meat, the old woman nodded.

Viktor ate slowly. His stomach cramped a little, but he forced himself to continue until all the meat was gone and he had wiped all the gravy out of the bowl and licked it from his fingers. If he lived long enough, he thought, the Blackfeet might have cause to regret feeding him.

He was confident that the old woman was a Blackfoot and felt sure as well that he was a prisoner in the village of the band that had attacked the count's hunting party. For some reason he could not fathom, they had spared his life and brought him here, rather than leaving him cold and lifeless on the prairie. The knife wound on his left shoulder had been packed with something and then bound up. His other injuries were minor enough so that nothing had been done about them, at least as far as he could tell. The pain in his head was still excruciating, as well it should have been after all the blows that had fallen on his skull. But he was hardheaded, like all Cossacks, he thought. He would recover, given time and rest.

Which the Blackfeet might not give him. An explanation for their decision to spare his life suddenly occurred to him.

They might have brought him here to their village to torture him, to make his death a lengthy, agonizing ordeal for their own entertainment. That was something the Tartars of his native land would have done, he thought.

The entrance flap of the lodge was abruptly shoved aside. Viktor looked up as a Blackfoot warrior stepped inside. The dancing light of the fire revealed a strong face that was all planes and angles, seemingly sharp enough to hew wood. The man glowered at Viktor and said in English, "American is awake. Good."

Viktor was not sure which surprised him more: the language used by the Blackfoot or the fact that anyone could mistake him for an American. He lifted his head and said,

"I am no American." He thumped himself on the chest with a clenched fist. "I am a Cossack."

The warrior leaned over and spat contemptuously into the fire. "American . . . Coss . . . Cossack . . . no matter. All the same. All white. All evil. Come with me, American."

Viktor's lips pulled back from his teeth in a grimace at the insult. The warrior put his hand on the hilt of the knife sheathed at his waist. Viktor tried once more to stand.

This time he was successful, although he was pretty unsteady on his feet for several seconds. When his balance had strengthened, he squared his shoulders and asked, "What do you want of me?"

The warrior did not answer the question directly. He said, "I am Lis-sis-tsi. In your tongue, Wolverine."

"I speak it, but it is not my tongue."

Wolverine ignored that comment. "You not do as I say, I kill you," he said, rather matter-of-factly. "Chief says you must live, but I do as I see fit."

That was an interesting bit of information. The chief of this band of Indians—could it be old Buffalo's Back Fat? Viktor suddenly wondered—did not desire his death, at least not yet. That was potentially useful information.

Wolverine stepped back and opened the entrance flap again. "Come with me," he ordered.

Viktor hesitated, but only for a second. Refusing to leave would gain him nothing. Whatever his destiny might be, it awaited him outside.

He nodded curtly and stepped out of the lodge. Wolverine followed and let the flap of hide fall shut behind him.

It was night, and just as Viktor had thought, he was in the center of a Blackfoot village. Perhaps forty lodges made of tanned buffalo hide were scattered along the banks of a small creek lined with trees. Viktor could make out that much among the shadows. The village itself was fairly well lit, because quite a few small fires were burning. People moved busily among the lodges. He heard the laughter of children at play and the barking of dogs. He was in the midst of what appeared to be a vibrant, vital community.

But it was no less dangerous for all that. Several warriors

paused from their activities and cast hostile glares at him. A woman walking by stopped and spat at his feet. A group of small children spotted him standing just outside the lodge where he had awoken, and they grabbed up small rocks and came charging toward him, obviously intent on pelting him with the missiles.

Wolverine stopped them with an upraised hand and a sharp word. The children looked disappointed, but they dropped the rocks and moved back, continuing to stare at Viktor as they did so.

"Come," Wolverine said. He jerked his hand in a curt gesture.

Viktor started walking through the village in the direction Wolverine indicated. He was still a bit unsteady on his feet, but he forced himself not to stumble, carefully planting one foot in front of the other. All of the men he passed glared at him, and some of them fingered their weapons. He was walking on the very brink of death, Viktor realized, and it would be very easy to topple over that edge.

Still, his concern for Alena made him willing to risk the displeasure of his captors. He looked around and called softly, "Alena! Are you here, Princess?"

"Quiet!" Wolverine barked. "American not speak."

"I told you, I am not—" Viktor broke off his protest and shook his head. "Ah! Why do I try to explain to a savage?"

Wolverine stopped short and whirled toward Viktor, reaching for his knife as he did so. "Savage?" he repeated. "You kill Cloud Caller! You are the savage!"

"Cloud Caller? Was that the young man the count shot? I am sorry for his death." Viktor's expression of sorrow was genuine. Not only had the young Blackfoot brave not deserved to be shot down coldly and callously by a man who had regarded him as not even human, but the death had led to much more bloodshed. Viktor would have been a fool not to regret Frederick's brutal action.

But none of that would mean anything to Wolverine and the other Blackfeet. One of their own had been murdered, and they wanted vengeance. Wolverine scowled disdainfully at Viktor and motioned for him to continue walking.

They approached what seemed to be the largest lodge in the village, almost twice as big as most of the other dwellings. The panels of buffalo hide that formed its exterior were decorated with many elaborate paintings. The pictures had a crude beauty to them, Viktor thought. He was not in much of a mood to appreciate such things at the moment, however.

Wolverine called out in his language, and a moment later the entrance flap of the lodge was pushed aside. A tall, stern-faced, middle-aged warrior stepped out. His long, black hair was parted in the middle and hung past his shoulders, except for a small band that was pulled down so that it covered the center of his forehead. Eagle feathers were fastened at the back of his head. The man wore buckskins decorated with beadwork and a large circular painting on the breast of the tunic. Viktor recognized him immediately.

"I have brought the American," Wolverine announced, a note of pride in his voice. Viktor wondered if Wolverine had been the one to strike him down in the battle and had claimed him as a personal prisoner.

The older warrior looked at Viktor and said, "You remember me from trading post at fort."

Viktor nodded. "You are the chief who was there with his wife and grandson."

"Stu-mick-o-sucks," the man said, lightly touching his chest. "The whites say Buffalo's Back Fat."

"The artist, the man called Catlin, was painting your grandson."

Buffalo's Back Fat nodded solemnly. "The great medicine painter has captured my image as well. He is good man. Some of my people say he tries to steal our souls when he paints his pictures, but I do not believe this."

There was no point in postponing the inevitable, Viktor thought. He asked, "Why have I been brought here?"

Evidently Buffalo's Back Fat was not ready to answer that question. He turned back to the entrance of the lodge and spoke in his own tongue as he pulled the flap aside. A second later a slender, red-haired figure appeared, and Viktor's heart pounded so hard with relief that it seemed about to tear its way out of his chest.

Alena rushed into his arms. She was disheveled, her dress ripped in places, her long red hair tangled around her face. But she did not seem to be hurt, and Viktor was thankful for that.

"Viktor!" she cried, then buried her face against his chest. She shuddered as he put his arms around her. He embraced her protectively, patted her awkwardly on the back.

"You are . . . all right, little one?"

"They . . . they have not harmed me," she answered, her voice muffled as she continued burrowing against him. "But Viktor, I am so frightened! Are they going to kill us?"

"If that was their wish, they would have done it before now," he told her, convinced of the truth of his words. For some reason, the Blackfeet—at least their chief, Buffalo's Back Fat—wanted them spared. He looked over Alena's shoulder at the chief and asked bluntly, "What do you want of us?"

He was not the only one who was puzzled. Wolverine's tone was edged with anger and impatience as he asked, "Why you keep this man alive?"

Buffalo's Back Fat would not be stampeded, unlike his namesake. He turned abruptly toward the lodge and said in a voice that brooked no argument, "Come. We smoke."

12

VIKTOR SAT CROSS-LEGGED
on the ground, joining the circle of men around the fire in
the center of the lodge. The sheer strangeness of the situation threatened to overwhelm his brain for a moment, but
then his pragmatic nature came to the fore. He was sitting
in the lodge of a Blackfoot chief, surrounded by men who
had been doing their best to kill him earlier in the day, men
whose brothers and friends *he* had undoubtedly killed during the battle, and he was about to smoke a pipe with them.
It was truly odd.

But he was alive, and so was Alena, and at the moment
that was all that really mattered.

Wolverine sat at his right, and another warrior who
seemed to have just as much dislike for Viktor, judging
from his grim expression, settled down on the left. Buffalo's Back Fat was on the other side of the fire so that the
chief could look over the dancing flames and directly into
Viktor's eyes. Half a dozen other Blackfoot warriors who
had filed into the lodge with them filled out the rest of the
circle. The wife of Buffalo's Back Fat sat nearby but was
not part of the actual circle. Viktor remembered that her
name meant Crystal Stone in English. Alena sat on a buffalo robe next to Crystal Stone. She was still pale and

frightened looking, but at least for the moment she seemed composed.

The men were passing around a large pipe decorated with eagle feathers and strips of fur. One of the men, whom Viktor had taken to be some sort of mystic, had begun the ceremony by standing and chanting something in the Blackfoot language, then taking puffs on the pipe and blowing smoke in each of the four cardinal directions. The other men had watched solemnly as this was going on, and Viktor's own demeanor was equally grave. This was serious business. He sensed that his and Alena's lives were both at stake here.

Each of the men followed the example of the first one to smoke the pipe. Without rising, they took the pipe in turn and blew smoke to the four winds. Viktor watched carefully, and when the pipe came to him, he knew what to do.

Wolverine had a look of unmistakable dislike on his face as he handed the pipe to Viktor. Viktor lifted the pipe to his mouth, took a small puff. The smoke was harsh and biting, but he was accustomed to a rugged blend of tobacco. He honored each of the four winds with smoke, then passed the pipe on to the next man. A glance across the fire told Viktor that Buffalo's Back Fat seemed pleased by his action.

The pipe continued around the circle until the ritual was complete. It was a leisurely journey, none of the Blackfoot warriors hurrying. Viktor could see Alena's growing nervousness and impatience and hoped she could keep her emotions under control. He wanted the Blackfeet to think as well of them as possible.

When the smoking was finally finished, Buffalo's Back Fat peered directly across the fire at Viktor and said, "My warriors tell me that you fought bravely today and that you should have an easy death, American."

"I am not American," Viktor said, wondering how many times he was going to have to explain that. "I am a Cossack. My homeland is Russia, far across the oceans. My name is Viktor Dorochenko."

Buffalo's Back Fat listened as Viktor spoke, but he went on as if the big Cossack had not said anything at all. "All but Wolverine agree. Wolverine thinks you should be tortured before being put to the death."

Viktor looked over at the warrior next to him and could not keep a small, savage smile from appearing on his face. "Give me my saber, and let Wolverine try."

Wolverine scowled, his lips pulling back from his teeth in anger. He leaned forward, and his hand moved toward the knife at his hip. Buffalo's Back Fat raised a hand and made a slight, unhurried gesture. With a hiss of breath between clenched teeth, Wolverine sat back and took his hand away from his knife. But his eyes still burned with hatred as they stared at Viktor.

"Tonight you are our guest," Buffalo's Back Fat said. "No one dies. Tomorrow . . . who can say?"

Viktor nodded. "For what it is worth, Chief, I am sorry about the death of the young man known as Cloud Caller. He was killed by Count Orlov. We tried to stop the count but could not."

"Count Orlov," Buffalo's Back Fat said, the name coming awkwardly from his lips. "The friend of the Grandfather I met at the trading post?"

"Yes. He was the leader of our group. That does not mean we all agreed with everything he did."

"He was your chief."

"He was a bad chief," Viktor said.

Buffalo's Back Fat nodded solemnly. "I know how this can be. Not all in the band always agree with everything their chief does. Is this not true, Lis-sis-tsi?"

Wolverine said tautly, "I hear the words of my chief, and I obey."

Viktor thought he saw a glint of amusement in Buffalo's Back Fat's eyes. Wolverine had not answered the question, and everyone in the lodge knew it.

Buffalo's Back Fat looked at his wife and Alena, then back at Viktor. "Eeh-nis-kin says that you and the girl should live. She says that the girl was kind of my grandson. My grandson has made much music with the gift given to him."

"The balalaika," Viktor said, remembering that first day at Fort Union.

"Now my grandson is gone."

Viktor looked up sharply, startled by the simple, yet dramatic declaration. "Gone?" he repeated.

Crystal Stone let out a wail, a sound like that of a trapped animal in pain. Beside her, Alena looked shocked and leaned away.

Not even a trace of humor remained on Buffalo's Back Fat's face now. "He was stolen from us by the Crows while most of our young men were gone from the village to avenge the death of Cloud Caller."

Viktor was stunned by that news. The Crows must have been watching the Blackfoot village, and when most of the warriors had ridden out in pursuit of the Russian hunting party and their American escort, they had struck.

"We fought as best we could, but the Crows came upon us too fast," Buffalo's Back Fat went on. "They killed three of our men as they rode through the village, and one of them leaned down from his pony to pick up my grandson. He put the boy in front of him and rode away, shouting and whooping. I would have killed him if I could." The chief's voice trembled a little from the intensity of the emotion gripping him as he recounted the story of the Crow raid.

This day had been filled with tragedy all the way around, Viktor thought. Not only had innocents died on both sides in the battle between the Blackfeet and the Russians and Americans, but blood had been shed here in the village, too. And all of it could be laid at the feet of Count Frederick Orlov.

Viktor hoped the count had not died an easy death.

Alena looked like she wanted to say something. She was clearly upset by the news of the kidnapping. Viktor caught her eye and gave a tiny shake of his head. It would be best if he handled the talking here. Instinct told him that the Blackfeet would not appreciate a woman speaking up while the men were holding a council.

"What will you do now?" Viktor asked.

"We will steal him back," Buffalo's Back Fat declared,

as if it was the simplest thing in the world. His next words proved he knew that was not the case, however. "If we raid the Crow village, they will be expecting us. There will be a great battle. Many men will die on each side."

"That is the price of war," Viktor said. It was a price he knew all too well, after facing the armies of the Frenchman Bonaparte and the bloodthirsty Tartar raiders of the steppes.

"The members of the council and I have spoken, before you were brought here among us." Buffalo's Back Fat waved his hand at the other warriors seated around the fire. "We have decided to send only a small party to rescue my grandson, in hopes that there will be less killing. We will send two men. Wolverine will be one of them."

Viktor glanced at Wolverine, saw the warrior straighten his shoulders and lift his chin in pride that he had been chosen for this important, dangerous mission. It was clear to Viktor that Wolverine had not known of his selection until this moment.

Buffalo's Back Fat stared straight across the fire at Viktor, the intensity of the gaze drawing the Cossack's attention once more. "You will be the other," he said.

"No!"

The cry of protest and denial came not from Wolverine, where Viktor might have expected it, but from Alena. He motioned for her to be quiet. In truth, he was just as shocked as she was, and it had taken an effort to hold back the exclamation he felt welling up his throat. Beside him, Wolverine was also staring in stunned surprise at the chief.

"This cannot be!" Wolverine finally said after a few seconds of strained silence.

"It is my decision, and the decision of the council," Buffalo's Back Fat said sternly. He looked at Viktor. "What say you, American?"

Viktor didn't bother correcting him this time. This was neither the time nor the place for such concerns. He said solemnly, "I know little of your land and nothing of your ways, Stu-mick-o-sucks. But I understand that this is an honor."

Smiling faintly, Buffalo's Back Fat said, "It is a way you can save your life, and the life of the girl. Return my grandson safely to me, and you shall both live."

Viktor's mind was racing. He had expected to die by torture and that Alena would be given to one of the warriors as a slave—or a wife. Instead, Buffalo's Back Fat was extending him an opportunity to make sure those things did not happen.

All he had to do was penetrate the Crow village accompanied by a man who hated him and wanted to see him dead, steal the chief's grandson back from those who had kidnapped him in the first place, and return safely to the village of the Blackfeet. That was all. He bowed his head sightly in acknowledgment of the decision made by the chief and the council and said quietly, "I accept."

"Viktor!" Alena exclaimed. "Viktor, you cannot leave me here with these . . . these savages!"

"Be silent, little one," he said sharply. She gaped at him, clearly shocked that he would talk to her in such a tone. He went on, "We are no longer in Russia. I must do as I think best for both of us."

Wolverine came to his feet, uncoiling from his cross-legged position like a snake. "I will not go to fight the Crows with this . . . this white man!" he said.

Quietly, Buffalo's Back Fat said, "You would go against the decision of your chief and his council of warriors?"

Wolverine hesitated before answering. He had to know he was treading on dangerous ground, Viktor thought. Even at the best of times, it was likely that Buffalo's Back Fat was a dangerous man to oppose, and right now the chief would not be in the mood to show mercy to anyone, even one of his own warriors. As long as the child was in the hands of the Crows, there was no time for petty personal resentments.

Wolverine's blunt-hewn face suddenly brightened. An idea had occurred to him. "The American must prove he is worthy," he declared. "He must prove that he is a warrior, too."

Viktor would have thought that he had already proven

his prowess by killing several of the Blackfeet in the battle that afternoon. Somehow, this did not seem to be the best time or place to point out *that* fact, either.

"How will he do that?" Buffalo's Back Fat asked, obviously intrigued by Wolverine's suggestion.

Wolverine thumped his chest. "He must fight me!"

The words came as no surprise to Viktor. Wolverine had been aching for an excuse to kill him. There was only one response Viktor could make.

Before he could speak, Alena said urgently, "Viktor, you can't do that! You might be hurt . . . or worse."

There was that chance, of course. Viktor wondered fleetingly if she was worried more about him—or about what might happen to her if Wolverine killed him and she was left alone here among the Blackfeet. Not that it mattered either way, because he had no intention of allowing Wolverine to defeat him.

"I have no choice, Princess," he said. He stood up and looked straight into Wolverine's eyes. "I accept your challenge."

Buffalo's Back Fat leaned back a little, crossed his arms over his chest, and nodded in satisfaction. "So it shall be," he said. "Tomorrow morning, the two of you will meet in combat."

Wolverine was not finished, however. He flung a hand toward Viktor in a contemptuous gesture. "If this white man bests me, he can come with me to raid the Crows and steal back the boy. But if I best him . . . he dies and the girl with hair like flame is mine." He cast a glance that was almost a leer toward Alena.

Viktor felt his hands clench into fists. He ached to smash them into Wolverine's arrogant face, to blunt those sharp angles of bone and flesh by pounding them into a red pulp. He had a pretty good idea what sort of fate Wolverine had in mind for Alena, should Viktor be defeated and killed. He would not—*could not*—allow that to come to pass.

But from the eager looks on the faces of Buffalo's Back Fat and the other warriors, he knew he could not ignore

Wolverine's challenge, either. Without looking at Alena, he nodded grimly to Wolverine and said, "Yes. So shall it be."

"This is mad!" Alena cried. "Viktor, you cannot agree to such a—"

He turned toward her and fairly roared, "I told you to be silent, woman!"

Once again Alena's eyes widened in shock. But she fell silent, and that was all Viktor was interested in at the moment. He could apologize to her later for his insulting behavior. It was all he could do to bring himself to treat her so roughly.

"One more condition," Viktor said to Buffalo's Back Fat. "If *I* defeat Wolverine in battle and then return the boy safely, the girl is mine."

"Yes," the chief agreed. "This is good. She has much spirit, which is sometimes a good thing in a woman. You will have to beat her often."

"Oh!" Alena was more angry than frightened now.

Without deigning to look at her, Viktor sat down, resuming his place among the warriors as if he truly belonged there. Grudgingly, Wolverine sat beside him. Viktor crossed his arms. An outsider might well have thought he was one of this band of Blackfeet.

Except for the faint sheen of sweat on his forehead that had nothing to do with the heat coming from the fire in the center of the lodge.

13

VIKTOR WAS TAKEN BACK TO
the lodge where he had regained consciousness. Wolverine
and the other warrior who had flanked him during the council accompanied him. The ache in Viktor's head had eased,
and this time as he walked through the Blackfoot village,
he noticed even more than he had the first time. He heard
wailing coming from some of the lodges and suspected that
women who had lost husbands or sons or fathers in the battle were mourning. Those wails were actually songs for the
dead.

He had some mourning of his own to do. The old mountain man, Zephaniah, had been a good friend. Viktor could
not forget that these Blackfeet had killed him. The other
Cossacks and the American troopers had merely been following the orders of their commanders, else they would not
have even been in this Montana wilderness. And there had
been innocent women among the party, as well, wives and
daughters of the noblemen who had accompanied Frederick
on the expedition. All dead now, of that Viktor had no
doubt.

Yet he could not bring himself to hate the Blackfeet for
what they had done. One of their young men had been wan-
tonly shot down for no reason. Their revenge had been

swift, bloody, and brutal, true, but it never would have happened if not for Frederick's rash action.

Viktor truly wished he had forsaken his oath of allegiance to the czar long before now and choked the very life out of Frederick Orlov with his bare hands. Such a simple act, but it would have prevented untold suffering. . . .

The old woman who had prodded him into eating still sat in the lodge. Wolverine and the other warrior practically pushed him inside, and Wolverine spoke sharply to the old woman in the Blackfoot tongue. She nodded slowly.

"Do not think we leave you here with only this grandmother to guard you," Wolverine informed Viktor. "There will be warriors outside the lodge all night, and they have orders to kill you if you try to escape."

"I have no interest in escaping," Viktor told him honestly. "When I leave here for the last time, I will have the girl with me."

Wolverine grunted. "Girl with hair like flame will soon be mine."

Viktor stiffened. "You will not touch her."

"Her name will be Flame Hair. She will be my wife and will bear me many fine children." Wolverine laughed. "She will warm my sleeping robes when snow is on the ground."

With an effort, Viktor controlled the anger flooding through him. He knew that Wolverine was only trying to goad him into starting trouble, in the hopes that Buffalo's Back Fat would change his mind about the plan to send Viktor along on the raid to rescue the chief's grandson. Viktor was not going to allow Wolverine to triumph so easily.

"Tonight, the girl sleeps in the lodge of Buffalo's Back Fat as a guest," Viktor said. "No one will dare disturb her."

Wolverine scowled, and Viktor knew the Blackfoot warrior was disappointed that he had not risen to the bait. "The time will come," Wolverine said ominously.

"We will see."

Still glaring, Wolverine turned on his heel and stalked out of the lodge, taking the other warrior with him. Viktor had no doubt that they would station themselves right outside the entrance, and if he so much as stuck his head out through the flap during the night, they would kill him. Buffalo's Back Fat would be displeased, but Wolverine and the other man could always claim that Viktor had been trying to escape.

Besides, regardless of what might happen to Wolverine in such circumstances, Viktor would still be dead, and Alena would be doomed to a life as a Blackfoot squaw. Viktor could not allow that. As long as he was alive, they still had at least the hope of returning to their home.

He turned and saw the old woman regarding him gravely. With a laugh and a slight shake of his head, he said, "Do not worry, Grandmother. I will not cause any trouble."

She did not understand a word of what he said, of course. He might as well have been speaking Russian. There were thick, shaggy buffalo robes spread on the floor of the lodge. Viktor sat down on one of them and rolled himself in it. The robe made a warm and surprisingly comfortable bed. As he relaxed, he took note of the aches and pains that lingered in his body. His left shoulder and arm were stiff from the knife wound, and he knew that would hamper him in the battle against Wolverine. There was no doubt in his mind that the warrior would try to take advantage of his every weakness. Other than the sore shoulder, though, he judged himself to be in pretty good shape. The throbbing pain in his head had subsided, and now he was simply weary.

There was a cure for that. He closed his eyes and slept.

One thing Viktor had already noticed about the Blackfoot village was that it was full of noise. His exhaustion the night before had enabled him to ignore the racket and fall asleep easily. When he awoke the next morning, the noise continued as if it had never ceased.

As he sat up on the buffalo robe, he heard men and children shouting, women wailing, dogs barking, and the clatter of rattles. Surely it was easy for enemies of these people to find their camps on the trackless plains simply by standing still, listening, and then following the noise. A faint smile plucked at Viktor's face as that thought crossed his mind. When the time came for silence, he was willing to wager that the Blackfeet could be quiet indeed.

He glanced around the lodge. The old woman was nowhere to be seen. She had been there when he went to sleep the night before; he wondered when she had left. There would still be guards outside the entrance, he was certain of that.

He pushed himself to his feet and stretched, wincing at the pull of stiff, sore muscles. He could barely raise his left arm above his shoulder. For a moment he debated what to do next, but he was saved from having to make that decision. The flap of hide over the entrance was thrust aside, and Wolverine stepped into the lodge.

Viktor turned to face the warrior. Wolverine was holding a pair of buckskin leggings and a buckskin shirt. A pair of high-topped moccasins that laced up the front hung from his other hand. He tossed the clothing on the buffalo robe and said, "Wear these. No more white man's clothes."

"All right," Viktor said with a nod. He didn't mind changing into the Indian garb. His clothes were filthy, torn and ragged, bloodstained.

"When you finish, we will fight. I will prove you are no warrior."

"No breakfast?" Viktor's tone was grimly humorous.

Wolverine did not look amused. "When our fight is over, you will not be hungry. Why waste food?"

Viktor ignored the gibe. He pulled his *rubashka*, which was crusted with dried blood, over his head and dropped it on the ground. As he reached for the buckskin shirt, he could feel Wolverine watching him, studying the broad shoulders and the thick layers of corded muscle. Was that a hint of worry in the Blackfoot warrior's eyes? Viktor wanted to think so. He wanted Wolverine to begin to wonder if issuing that challenge had not been such a good idea.

Abruptly, Wolverine turned and slapped the entrance flap aside, stepping out to leave Viktor alone in the lodge. That was all right with Viktor. He finished changing into the buckskins in privacy, then sat down to draw the moccasins onto his feet. The supple leather made for a good fit, and he nodded in satisfaction as he stood up again.

The buckskins were a little stiff with grease, which seemed to be the common way these people wore them. The leggings and the sleeves of the shirt were also a bit short, and the shirt was tight across his broad chest, but he thought he would be able to move fairly easily nonetheless. He bent over so that his great height would clear the opening and stepped out of the lodge.

If anything, the Blackfoot village was busier and louder than ever this morning. An air of excitement gripped the place and competed with the mourning wails of the women who had lost loved ones in battle. Children clustered eagerly around Viktor as he stepped away from the lodge. Today they did not threaten him with sticks and rocks; their curiosity had gotten the better of them, and they just wanted a good look at this massive white man. Viktor felt sure the entire village knew by now that he was going to fight Wolverine for the right to accompany the warrior on the rescue mission. That was why so many openly inquisitive, appraising stares were being directed toward him. Wolverine probably had quite a reputation as a fighter. The Blackfeet had to be wondering what chance Viktor would have against him.

Wolverine and several other warriors were standing a few feet away. Wolverine spoke curtly to the children gathering around Viktor and motioned them away from the big Cossack. They went reluctantly, still chattering and laughing. Viktor smiled at the youngsters and said, "Good morning." A couple of them yelped in surprise and darted away even farther.

"You come now," Wolverine said.

Viktor nodded. "I am ready. Are you?"

Wolverine just glared at him for a second and then turned away. The other warriors fell in around Viktor, virtually surrounding him as Wolverine led them through the village. Women and children trailed along behind them, forming a procession just as they had the night before.

Their destination, Viktor guessed a moment later, was a large open area on the far side of the village. As they passed the lodge of Buffalo's Back Fat, Alena emerged from the hide dwelling, followed by two elderly women. Viktor thought one of them was the woman who had brought food to him, but he could not be certain. One old, incredibly wrinkled woman looked pretty much like another to him.

Alena saw Viktor and darted toward him, so fast that the gnarled, clutching hands of the crones could not grab her. Like Viktor, she had been given fresh clothes and was now wearing a buckskin dress decorated with fancy beadwork. The dress fit her better than Viktor's buckskins did him. The soft material, tanned and faded until it was almost white, hugged her breasts and hips, as if to remind Viktor that she was no longer a child.

Viktor did not need that reminder, nor did he need to see the way Wolverine's eyes lingered on Alena's body as she ran up to him and threw her arms around him. "Oh, Viktor, those old women are awful!" she exclaimed. "They keep poking and mauling me—"

Viktor put his hands on her shoulders and moved her back slightly so that he could look down into her face. "Try to be brave, Princess. If they see that you are afraid of them, they will probably treat you even worse."

"It's hard to be brave." Her voice held a quaver as she spoke.

"I know, but you must try."

"Viktor . . ." A different sort of uncertainty came into her voice. "What you said last night . . . about me being your woman . . ."

He dropped his voice, not wanting the Indians to overhear too much of their conversation. "I meant no offense, Princess. I just thought—"

Wolverine turned and glared, and one of the other warriors prodded Viktor hard in the shoulder. It was fortunate, Viktor thought as he caught his balance, that the Indian had shoved his right shoulder, not the injured left one. That would come soon enough.

He glanced back at Alena as he was forced on toward the open area where he would do battle with Wolverine. The two old women had come up to her and grasped her arms, one on each side. Alena grimaced in pain as their grips tightened.

"Remember, be brave, little one!" Viktor called to her.

A ring of spectators had already formed around the open space, and they were talking excitedly. They parted for Viktor, Wolverine, and the guards. Buffalo's Back Fat was already in the center of the circle, waiting for them. Viktor strode directly up to the chief, ignoring Wolverine's angry look.

"I am ready," Viktor declared. "Are there rules to this fight?"

Buffalo's Back Fat smiled thinly. "The only rule is to survive. Will you fight with tomahawks, knives, or bare hands?"

Viktor glanced at Wolverine and did not bother to hide his contempt, although that was mostly bravado. He knew that Wolverine was a warrior to be feared. "If you give me a tomahawk or a knife, I will kill my opponent. Bare hands will be better."

"I agree," Wolverine said with a sneer. "*I* can kill with bare hands just as well as with a tomahawk or knife."

"As can I," Viktor said quietly.

"Enough," Buffalo's Back Fat said, an edgy tone of impatience in his voice revealing the strain he was under. His grandson was in the hands of his most hated enemies, after all, and every minute Viktor and Wolverine spent standing around and posturing was another minute the boy was forced to spend away from his people. Viktor understood that, and he nodded his readiness to the chief, as did Wolverine.

Buffalo's Back Fat raised his hands and stepped back, nodding as a signal for them to begin. Viktor glanced one last time at the ring of spectators and saw that Alena had somehow made her way to the front, dragging the two old women along with her. She was watching anxiously, her lower lip caught between her teeth.

Wolverine charged suddenly, almost taking Viktor by surprise. Viktor saw the move from the corner of his eye and twisted around, narrowly avoiding the charge and Wolverine's grasping arms. He reached out and grabbed Wolverine's shoulders as the warrior lunged past him. His fingers tightened on the warrior's buckskin shirt and flung him to the ground.

Wolverine rolled over smoothly, down for less than a second before he regained his feet. Viktor's triumph was so fleeting that he had no chance to take advantage of it. Wolverine lunged toward him again.

Viktor tried to knock his hands aside, only to realize too late that the Blackfoot's charge was merely a feint this time. Wolverine grabbed Viktor's arm and twisted savagely. Viktor had to twist with the arm or see it broken. While he was off balance, a blow from Wolverine's knee exploded in his midsection. Viktor stumbled, almost went down.

He righted himself and used his left arm to swing a backhanded blow at Wolverine's head. The Blackfoot was not expecting such a move, obviously, and Viktor's hand cracked across his jaw, staggering him. The blow hurt Viktor as well, pain blossoming in his injured shoulder. He grimaced, unable once again to seize an opportunity. Both men stumbled back a step, putting a little distance between them.

Viktor was vaguely aware that the Blackfoot spectators were making a lot of noise, shouting out their support for Wolverine, no doubt. No one wanted to see him win this fight except Alena, and perhaps Buffalo's Back Fat and Crystal Stone. Having those two on his side was the only thing that had kept him alive this long. Without their intervention, Wolverine or some of the other warriors would have probably tortured him to death.

After a moment's hesitation Viktor and Wolverine both leaped forward at the same time. They crashed together, their arms going around each other as they grappled, each searching for a hold that would give him the upper hand. Viktor was taller, heavier, probably stronger, but Wolverine was quicker and more experienced at this kind of fight. He was making a possibly fatal mistake by wrestling with Wolverine, Viktor realized. His reach was longer than Wolverine's, and he was not taking advantage of that. He managed to get a hand on his opponent's chest and shoved him away, once again opening some distance between them. This time, however, Viktor closed that gap by throwing a long, looping punch.

His fist caught a surprised Wolverine on the mouth. Viktor felt blood spurt across his knuckles. Wolverine was rocked back by the blow, blood welling from his smashed lips. He grunted, but that was the only sound that came from him.

Viktor pressed forward, ignoring the pain in his shoulder and the feeling of wetness where the knife wound had reopened. He threw a hard left to Wolverine's solar plexus, landed another punch to the warrior's face. Wolverine looked groggy now, and the cheers and shouts of encouragement from the spectators took on a desperate quality. They were about to see their champion defeated. Viktor wound up for a punch that would finish the Blackfoot warrior off.

He missed.

Just as Viktor launched the blow, Wolverine threw himself forward in a dive that carried him at the Russian's legs. Already off balance, Viktor tumbled over Wolverine and fell hard, retaining the presence of mind to twist his body in midair so that he would not land on his hurt shoulder. The damage was already done. As he tried to raise himself up off the ground, Wolverine landed on his back, and the Blackfoot warrior's arm looped around his neck. Wolverine held on for dear life, choking the breath out of Viktor.

Somehow, the big Russian managed to get to his feet, but still Wolverine clung fiercely to him. Viktor's greater height lifted Wolverine's feet from the ground. The extra weight just put more pressure on Viktor's throat. His lungs were already desperate for the air that had been cut off from them.

Viktor reached behind his head, searching for the Blackfoot's face. He would gouge the Indian's eyes out if he had to. He found one of Wolverine's braids instead, and he hauled forward with all his strength as he bent sharply at the waist. With an involuntary yell of pain, Wolverine tumbled off Viktor's back. Viktor shoved him away and gasped for breath, gulping down lungfuls of precious air.

"Viktor, look out!"

The scream came from Alena and cut through the tumult. Viktor jerked his head around and saw that Wolverine had clubbed his hands together and was swinging them at the back of Viktor's head. The only way to avoid the blow was to duck. Viktor did so, then lunged forward to slam his shoulder into Wolverine's midsection. The Indian's feet came off the ground again.

Viktor straightened, channeling all his strength, all his anger, all his outrage at the circumstances that had brought him here, into one final effort. A bellow of defiance thundered from his chest as he got both hands on Wolverine and lifted the struggling warrior into the air. A stunned silence fell on the watchers as Viktor lifted the brave above his head and then threw him down.

Wolverine landed hard several feet away, the impact knocking him senseless for a moment. He rolled limply onto his back, and Viktor landed with his knees on his chest. His hands closed around the warrior's throat. Now it was his turn to deny the breath of life to his enemy. It was Wolverine who would gasp and choke and ultimately die.

The killing rage that gripped Viktor lasted only a few seconds, but that was long enough for Wolverine's eyes to bulge out and his tongue to protrude grotesquely from his mouth as he struggled for air that did not come. Then Viktor's senses returned to him, and he realized that Wolverine's death would serve no real purpose. He held the warrior's life in his hands, and everyone in the village knew it. That was enough.

With a snarl, he let go of Wolverine's neck. He pushed himself unsteadily to his feet and moved back a step. The Blackfoot warrior stayed where he was, gasping for breath, unable to get up.

Buffalo's Back Fat stepped over to Viktor and put a hand on his shoulder. "You have won," the chief said. "The flame-haired woman is yours . . . if you bring my grandson back safely to me."

Viktor was still breathing heavily himself, although not as much as Wolverine. He could not speak, but he managed to nod.

Alena pulled away from her aged guardians and ran up to him. Her arms encircled his waist, and she cried happily, "I knew you could do it, Viktor!"

Tiredly, Viktor patted her on the back. "Not . . . finished yet . . . only started."

He slipped out of her embrace and turned toward Wolverine. His right arm came up, and he extended his hand toward the fallen warrior. Wolverine's eyes focused on him, and for an instant the old familiar hate was there. But then it faded somewhat, and he lifted a trembling hand to take Viktor's. The Cossack pulled him to his feet.

When Wolverine spoke, his voice was hoarse and rasping. "Together . . . we steal boy . . . from Crows. But what is between us . . . not over. White man is right . . . only started."

14

WOLVERINE WAS LED AWAY
by several of the other warriors as the crowd around the
open area dispersed. Even though he had lost the fight, the
other men were congratulating him because he had fought
well. Viktor watched them go. No one came up to him to
congratulate him. Buffalo's Back Fat was the only one who
had done so. But Viktor saw the expressions of awe with
which the Blackfeet regarded him.

Alena clung to his arm until the old women tugged her
away. She looked imploringly at Viktor, but he said, "Go
with them, Princess. They will not harm you." He glanced
at the chief for confirmation of that promise, and Buffalo's
Back Fat nodded solemnly. Reluctantly, Alena went with
the women.

Buffalo's Back Fat looked at the shoulder of Viktor's
buckskin shirt and said, "You are bleeding. Our healer will
attend your injury."

The knife wound was hurting like fire again, and Viktor
nodded gratefully.

Buffalo's Back Fat led him back to the big lodge in the
center of the village. Everyone stood aside respectfully to
let them pass. Alena had spent the night in the chief's
lodge, Viktor knew, but was not there now. The old

women must have taken her to one of the other lodges, he thought.

"I will summon Stands with a Stick, of the Bear Cult," Buffalo's Back Fat said. "He is the healer who cared for your wound before."

"Thank you," Viktor said.

Crystal Stone had followed them into the lodge. As Buffalo's Back Fat left, his wife motioned for Viktor to sit down. The big Cossack settled himself on one of the buffalo robes, moving awkwardly now because of the pain in his left arm and shoulder. In the heat of battle, he had been able to ignore it, but no longer.

Crystal Stone brought him a waterskin, and he drank greedily. Until this moment, he had not realized how thirsty he was. He was hungry, too, and when he rubbed his stomach, she brought him what seemed to be strips of buffalo meat that had been smoked and dried. They were not as easy to eat as the stew of the night before, and his teeth soon began to ache a little from chewing, but as the juices of the meat flowed into him, they brought renewed strength.

Buffalo's Back Fat reentered the lodge a few minutes later, accompanied by another man. This man wore a fur headdress with buffalo horns attached to it, curving up and away from his head. Feathers were tied to the horns, and a cape made of feathers hung down his back. He carried a spear in one hand, but the weapon appeared to be more ceremonial than functional. Spiraling around the shaft were bright-painted, elaborate patterns; feathers and strips of fur were tied to it. In the man's other hand was an object that Viktor did not at first realize was a bear's paw, still attached to part of the animal's leg. The thing was dried and twisted, and the fur was coming off of it in places. The claws, which were still intact, were yellow and brittle with age. The man handled it with great reverence.

"This is Stands with a Stick," Buffalo's Back Fat said to Viktor. "He is a healer, a great shaman of the Bear Cult."

Viktor nodded to the man, feeling his way along by instinct now. "I am grateful," he said. "I am sure he is a very good healer."

Stands with a Stick said nothing. He came closer to Viktor and waved the bear's paw over the big Cossack's head, once, twice, three times. He shook the spear and began to chant as he danced in a circle around Viktor. Each time he passed the wounded shoulder, he reached out and tapped it with the bear's paw.

Finally, when he was finished, he had Viktor take off the bloodstained shirt. Opening a pouch made of hide that hung from his shoulder, he took out some strips of sinew and a handful of moss of some sort. Crystal Stone moved to help him, unwrapping the piece of hide that was bound around Viktor's wounded shoulder. Viktor's lips pulled back from his teeth in a grimace as Stands with a Stick raked a wadded-up mass of dried blood and moss from the wound. Crystal Stone cleaned the injury with a cloth dipped in an earthen pot containing warm water, then Stands with a Stick packed it with fresh moss, bound that in place with the strips of sinew, then wrapped another piece of hide around it. He spoke a few words in the Blackfoot tongue.

"Stands with a Stick says that this time you should not fight and undo all of his good work," Buffalo's Back Fat translated.

"Tell him I am grateful for his help and for his advice as well," Viktor said, "but I must fight. I must help Wolverine bring your grandson back from the Crows."

"Tomorrow," Buffalo's Back Fat said before passing along Viktor's words to the healer. "Today and tonight, you rest. Tomorrow you and Wolverine will ride to the land of the Crows."

Viktor nodded, accepting the chief's decision. The rest would do him good, he knew.

But then he thought of the boy, so solemn until Alena had showed him how to play the balalaika, and he remembered how his face had lit up in a smile as the notes came from the instrument. Those memories made him eager to ride, eager to face the Crows who had raided this village and stolen the child.

The Crows would live to regret their crime.

Viktor was left alone during the day except for Crystal Stone, who worked mending several sets of buckskins that belonged to Buffalo's Back Fat. He dozed, woke up and ate, dozed again. The pain in his shoulder faded to a persistent ache. At least he was not feverish, he thought. He had seen wounds like this fester with infection and eventually cause death. It appeared he was going to avoid that fate, and more than likely he had the ministrations of Stands with a Stick—and his own iron constitution—to thank for it.

Of course, just because the knife wound did not kill him, that did not mean he was out of danger. He could still die in plenty of other ways. . . .

Buffalo's Back Fat entered the lodge late that afternoon. He looked at Viktor and said, "You will go back to your own lodge now."

Viktor hadn't known that he even *had* a lodge of his own, and assumed the chief was referring to the dwelling where he had awakened after the battle. He stood up and nodded his agreement, moving more easily now. The pain of the wound had receded so that he could basically ignore it.

"How is Wolverine?" Viktor asked as he left the chief's lodge with Buffalo's Back Fat.

"He is well," the Blackfoot leader replied, a tone of dry amusement in his voice. "Bruised and sore, but he will be all right."

"I was surprised that he did not strike at my wounded shoulder as we fought."

Buffalo's Back Fat glanced over at Viktor, and he looked a bit surprised, too. "Wolverine knew you were wounded. It was his knife that struck you during the battle. But to try to take advantage of such an injury during a later fight would not be honorable."

"Wolverine's honor is that important to him?"

"It is the most important thing he has."

The simple answer impressed Viktor. He knew what Buffalo's Back Fat meant. A man's honor was the only thing he truly possessed. These Blackfeet had much in common, Viktor thought, with the Cossacks of his homeland. He had compared them to the Tartars, but he saw now that he was mistaken. He had not given the Indians enough credit.

The lodge where Buffalo's Back Fat took him was indeed the one in which he had awakened, and the same old woman was waiting in it. She held a wooden bowl in her hands, and just as she had the night before, she extended it toward him and said, *"Ni-tap-i wak-sin?"*

"Yes," Viktor said with a smile and a nod, still not knowing if the Blackfoot words referred to the act of eating or the food itself. "It is good." He sat down on a buffalo robe, took the bowl from the old woman, and began consuming the chunks of meat. After seeing the large number of dogs around the Indian village, he had to wonder if that was what he was eating. He put that thought out of his mind and tried to concentrate on other things.

Buffalo's Back Fat had left to return to his own lodge. Viktor ate the bowl of food, drank deeply from the waterskin the old woman offered him. He felt the beginnings of drowsiness stealing over him, despite the naps he had taken during the day. Perhaps he would roll up in the buffalo robe and go to sleep. He needed to be fresh and strong tomorrow, when he and Wolverine departed for the Crow camp.

Before he could act on the thought, the entrance flap was pushed aside, and Alena stepped into the lodge, followed by the two old women who had been with her earlier in the day.

Alena didn't say anything. The three old women chattered like magpies for a moment, then the one assigned to Viktor got up and all three left. Viktor was amazed. He and Alena had been left in the lodge alone.

That did not mean they were unguarded, however. There might be half a dozen heavily armed warriors just outside. After everything that had happened, he was not going to be foolish enough to try to escape. His and Alena's best chance for survival, he was convinced, lay in cooperating with Buffalo's Back Fat's plan to rescue his grandson.

Those thoughts raced through Viktor's brain as he set aside his empty bowl and stood up. He went to Alena, who stood quietly, her hands clasped together in front of her and her eyes downcast. "You are all right, little one?" he asked anxiously.

She looked up at him and nodded. "Yes. The old women treated me better today than they did last night. I think they are afraid of you since you defeated the one called Wolverine in battle."

"I did not fight to impress old women, but to save our lives." He gestured toward the buffalo robes. "Sit down. I can have food brought. . . ."

Alena shook her head. "I have eaten. I'm not exactly sure what it was, but—"

"Probably better not to know," Viktor told her.

"Yes, that is what I thought." Alena sat down on one of the robes, adjusting the buckskin dress around her legs. She lifted a hand and touched the long, smooth strands of her red hair. "The women brushed my hair and gave me this necklace of beads."

"You look very pretty," Viktor told her as he sat down a respectful distance away.

"I do not see how. I am dressed in some sort of animal skin, and I have not been able to bathe, and I'm sure my hair is still tangled—" She stopped and took a deep breath. "I suppose I should just be thankful that I am still alive. And I *am* thankful. But what will happen now?"

"Wolverine and I will rescue the chief's grandson from the Crows," Viktor said confidently, "and Buffalo's Back Fat will be so grateful that he will allow us to leave. Perhaps he will even take us back to Fort Union."

Alena leaned forward worriedly. "But you will have to risk your life against the Crows!"

"All of life is a risk," Viktor said with a shrug.

"Yes . . . Yes, I suppose you are right. I . . . I am glad you saved my life, Viktor."

He smiled. "So am I."

"Aunt Zora was . . . was struck by an arrow. I am certain she is dead, along wlth everyone else."

Alena's face was pale and her voice was full of grief. There was nothing Viktor could do except nod solemnly and say, "I wish I could have saved her, and all the others, too. You should not think about such things, Princess. There is nothing we can do for them. We must think of ourselves now."

"Yes." A pair of tears trickled down Alena's smooth cheeks. She wiped them away with the back of her hand before continuing. "I know you are right." She reached up to the rawhide thong that held the neck of the buckskin dress closed. She began to untie it.

Viktor's back stiffened in surprise at her actions. "What are you doing?" he asked sharply.

"You said that I was to be your woman." The thong was loose now, and Alena started to pull the dress down over her bare shoulders. "The chief came to the lodge and spoke to the old women. I . . . I assumed that I was to be given to you tonight, before you leave with Wolverine in the morning."

Viktor reached and grasped her wrists to prevent her from pulling the dress down any farther. The white swells of her breasts had just started to appear. Flustered, he said, "Princess, I never meant . . . I said that only for the Blackfeet. So that they would know you were spoken for and none of the warriors would try to claim you as his wife."

Alena looked relieved yet disappointed. "So you . . . you do not want me . . . that way?"

Viktor released her wrists. He took hold of the buckskin dress, pulled it up where it was supposed to be, and drew the rawhide thong tight. As his blunt, strong fingers tied it awkwardly, he said, "You are the little princess, the daughter of my friend and commander from the war against Bonaparte. No matter how beautiful you are—and you *are* beautiful—I could not force myself on you."

As she laid a soft hand on his chest, Alena looked into

his eyes and whispered, "You would not have to force me, Viktor Alexandrovitch."

Viktor shook his head. He stood up and stalked as far away from her as the cramped confines of the lodge would allow, emotions warring inside him. He dared not look at her as he muttered, "This cannot be allowed!"

For a long moment Alena was silent, staring at the resolute stiffness of his stance. Then she threw her head back and laughed. "You Cossack!" she said, making the words sound scornful, yet like an endearment at the same time. "You wild and free Cossack! You are as bound by rules and tradition as any of the czar's court that you so despise."

Viktor turned back at last to look at her. "I am bound by honor," he said quietly.

She stood up and approached him, putting her hand on his arm. There was nothing romantic or seductive about her touch this time. "I know. And I suppose I would not have you do something you think is dishonorable. But the Indians expect me to stay here tonight, with you. If I do not . . . they may think that you do not want me for your woman after all."

Reluctantly, Viktor nodded. "There *is* that to consider, I suppose."

Alena tugged on his arm. "Come with me and sit down on the robe. There is nothing wrong with friends holding each other, is there? After tomorrow, I . . . I may never see you again."

Viktor allowed her to lead him over to the buffalo robe, and they sat down side by side. Alena leaned against him, and after a moment Viktor gingerly slid his arm around her shoulders. Gradually, he tightened his embrace, pulling her more closely against him.

"No, there is nothing wrong with this," he said. "But you *will* see me again, little one. If there is nothing else I can promise you, it is this: I will be back for you."

Alena closed her eyes, rested her head against his shoulder, and made a soft noise of contentment deep in her throat. In a sleepy tone of voice, she asked, "And will we see Mother Russia again?"

"*Da.* We will see Mother Russia again." Viktor's answer was barely more than a whisper.

They sat there together like that for a long time. Although the village outside was as noisy as ever, inside the lodge there were no sounds save their breathing and the crackle of the small fire.

15

THIS WAS AN IMPORTANT day, and the entire population of the Blackfoot village turned out to see Viktor and Wolverine depart on their mission to rescue the grandson of Stu-mick-o-sucks.

Viktor was still unarmed when he stepped out of the lodge with Alena at his side. Though it made him uncomfortable knowing that the Blackfeet thought he and Alena had made love the night before, he was more than willing to maintain that pose if it meant she would be safe while he was gone. He put an arm around her shoulder possessively as he walked forward to meet Wolverine, who was waiting for him along with Buffalo's Back Fat.

The Blackfoot warrior held a sheathed knife and a tomahawk. He extended them toward Viktor and grunted, "Here. These will be yours." In his eyes, Viktor still saw dislike, but there was also grudging respect.

The Russian took the weapons. "Thank you. May they drink deeply of the blood of the enemies of the Blackfeet."

Both Wolverine and Buffalo's Back Fat looked pleased at these words. The chief was holding a small, hide-wrapped bundle. He unwrapped it to reveal Viktor's saber, the one he had carried since the days of the war against the mad Frenchman. About six inches of the blade were missing, snapped off during the battle, no doubt.

Buffalo's Back Fat held out the saber. "One of our warriors found this. Now I return it to you."

The broken blade ended in a jagged point, making the saber look even more wicked and dangerous than before. Viktor took it from the chief and said, "Thank you, Stumick-o-sucks. I will use this blade in the service of the Blackfeet and their chief." He tucked the broken saber, the knife, and the tomahawk behind the rawhide belt that encircled his waist and cinched in the long buckskin shirt.

Still looking pleased, Buffalo's Back Fat turned and gestured. One of the other Blackfoot warriors pushed through the crowd leading a horse. The cavalry saddle had been replaced by a colorful blanket, and the leather harness discarded in favor of a rawhide hackamore, but the horse was unmistakably the lineback dun Viktor had ridden from Fort Union. For a second he stared in disbelief at the animal. He had supposed it had either been killed in the fighting or was now running wild and free over the prairie.

As Viktor stepped forward, the dun threw its head up and gave a sharp whinny, then danced sideways in a skittish step. "Don't you remember me, *tovarisch?*" Viktor asked. He stretched out a hand for the dun to sniff.

The horse gave him a haughty look, but if such a thing was possible, Viktor thought he also saw relief in the dun's expression. Recalling what he had named the horse, he reflected that he had been given two sabers this day.

After a moment the dun nuzzled Viktor's hand. Buffalo's Back Fat looked on in approval. "This fine horse was to be one of my own," the chief said, "but gladly will I give him up to help you in bringing my grandson back to me. You can ride well, I am told."

"In the land of my birth, the young boys ride before they can walk. And they learn to use cold steel when they are almost as young."

Buffalo's Back Fat nodded. "It is good."

The crowd around them parted again, and Wolverine rode up on a big chestnut stallion. Viktor had not noticed the warrior leaving, so surprised had he been to have the broken saber and the horse returned to him. With a scowl at Viktor, the Blackfoot said, "I am ready if the white man is."

Viktor nodded, grasped the mane of the dun, and swung easily onto its back. "I am ready," he announced.

Alena hurried forward, catching hold of his leg and clutching it. Viktor felt his knee pressing against the softness of her bosom, and embarrassment flooded through him.

"Wait!" Alena said. "You would leave without saying good-bye to your woman?"

Viktor frowned down at her for a second, knowing full well what she wanted and knowing as well that he had no choice but to continue the charade. He leaned down from the back of the dun, put an arm just underneath Alena's arms, and lifted her effortlessly in front of him. Alena's arms went tightly around his neck. Viktor's mouth was next to her ear as she embraced him, and he whispered, "I already bid you farewell, and you know it."

She returned his whisper, her breath hot against his ear. "Yes, but you want the Blackfeet to think I am truly your woman, do you not?"

Without waiting for him to answer, she moved her head so that her mouth found his and pressed hungrily to it in a long kiss that shook Viktor to the center of his being. When Alena finally took her lips away, he was wide-eyed, almost in shock, and Alena herself was breathless.

"There!" she said after a moment of recovery. "You will not forget me now."

"Little one, I could *never* forget you."

Impatiently, Wolverine reined his horse alongside the dun. "Are we going to kill Crows," he demanded, "or are you going to say farewell to your woman all day?"

With a sigh from both of them, Viktor carefully placed Alena on the ground, next to Buffalo's Back Fat and Crystal Stone. She looked a little frightened, but managed to summon up a brave smile.

"Go with God, and come back soon, Viktor Alexandrovitch," she said as she lifted her slender hand in farewell.

Viktor nodded to her, then looked at Buffalo's Back Fat. He clasped wrists with the chief. "We will bring the boy back to you and Eeh-nis-kin," he said, dredging up Crystal Stone's Blackfoot name from his memory. "This I swear."

Buffalo's Back Fat said something in the Blackfoot tongue that sounded like a blessing and a shout went up from the villagers. Wolverine wheeled his horse and kicked his moccasin-shod heels against its flanks, making it lunge forward. Men, women, and children scrambled to get out of the horse's path. Viktor followed suit, thinking that Wolverine's actions were somewhat reckless. Someone could have been trampled. But the exit was certainly a dramatic one, and Viktor was willing to take part in it, especially since Wolverine had already cleared the way. With the Blackfeet whooping behind them, they rode out of the village, and Viktor was pleased when the dun drew alongside the racing chestnut and easily ran neck and neck with the big stallion.

During that day's long ride, Viktor realized, not for the first time, how truly beautiful this land was. From a distance, it looked flat and almost featureless all the way to the far-off mountains. However, from the back of a moving horse, all kinds of variations appeared: grassland as flat as a table, gullies that seemed to have been carved in the earth by the clawing fingers of a monstrous hand, dry, sandy creekbeds, and rock outcroppings that thrust from the ground like the shoulders of a buried giant. The Great American Desert, these plains were called, but they were no desert. Numerous streams crisscrossed the land, none of them large, but holding enough water to nurture the small trees and bushes that grew along their banks, the vegetation marking the course of the creeks with tendrils of darker green.

There was an abundance of wildlife, too, besides the roaming herds of buffalo and antelope. Viktor saw several flocks of small, fat birds that seemed unable to fly but could scurry along the ground with surprising speed. At times he spotted wolves loping along in the distance, never coming too close to the two men on horseback. He was especially intrigued by the small, rodentlike creatures that burrowed in the ground and stuck their heads up from their holes to bark and chatter angrily at the riders.

Wolverine gestured at a group of the creatures as he and Viktor rode past. "There are many of them, even more than there are buffalo, but their homes are under the ground where we cannot see them. Be careful your horse does not step in one of their holes."

Viktor nodded in understanding. Such a mishap could be quite dangerous, resulting in a broken leg for the horse and potential injuries for the rider, who would doubtless be flung violently off his mount.

Whenever they crossed one of the larger creeks, Viktor saw beaver dams. The beaver were more numerous in the mountains, Wolverine explained, but there were quite a few of them in these prairie streams as well.

"In the mountains, there are bear, elk, moose, and deer," Wolverine said. "It is a good land. White men are ruining it."

"That is not their intention."

The Blackfoot warrior glanced at him, his expression revealing all Viktor needed to know about his opinion of the intentions of the white men. Viktor let the subject drop. He and Wolverine had to work together on this mission; they could not afford to argue over things neither of them could do anything about.

Viktor was unsure where the Crow camp was located and how long it would take them to reach it. As the afternoon wore on and the day began to draw to a close, it became obvious they were not yet at their destination. Wolverine called a halt and began to prepare a camp in a hollow between two hills. "Our fire will not be seen here, if we make it small enough," he said to Viktor as he arranged a little pile of twigs, buffalo chips, and dried grass. A few minutes' work with flint and steel had a blaze going that was cheerful despite its tiny size. As dusk settled down, the arching vault of sky turned purple and then dark blue before fading to black. In all that immensity, the fire was somehow reassuring.

Wolverine left Viktor at the camp to tend to their horses while he vanished into the night carrying a short spear. For a moment the Cossack pondered that apparent trust—clearly, Wolverine was not afraid that he would escape. But where would he go? Viktor asked himself. He could not have hoped to return to the Blackfoot village and steal Alena away. And he was not going to leave this wild country without her. Obviously, the warrior had figured that out. Alena was an anchor keeping Viktor moored to his captors, and her safety was sufficient motive to ensure his cooperation.

By the time Viktor had finished rubbing down the horses and seeing to their needs, Wolverine had returned, carrying the carcass of one of the small, flightless birds. He cleaned the kill, impaled it on a stick that he first sharpened with his knife, then knelt by the fire and began roasting it. Viktor sat down on the other side of the fire to wait.

When the food was done, Wolverine sliced off some of the meat with his knife, then speared it and extended it across the fire to Viktor. Carefully, because the meat was hot, Viktor took it and nodded his thanks.

"White man would starve if he was not given food like an infant," Wolverine said disdainfully.

"In my land, even the infants can catch and kill their own food," Viktor responded.

Wolverine just grunted in disbelief. Viktor gnawed off a morsel of the meat and began to chew.

After he had swallowed, he asked, "How long will it take us to reach the land of the Crows?"

"Two suns, maybe three."

"You can find the village where the boy is being held?"

Wolverine glared across the flames. "I know this land from the big river of the north to the Shining Mountains. I can find the boy. . . . Probably find him faster if white man was not with me."

"Your chief said we were to ride together," Viktor pointed out. He did not want Wolverine getting any ideas about slipping off and leaving him alone, and probably horseless, in the wilderness.

"I could always tell Buffalo's Back Fat that you were killed by the Crows. . . ." Wolverine mused, as if to confirm the Russian's worst speculations.

Viktor leaned forward slightly, looked Wolverine squarely in the eye, and said, "And I could tell him the same story about you."

For a long moment as the two men looked at each other across the fire, there were no sounds save the faint crackling of the flames and the distant hoot of an owl. Then Viktor's mouth curved in a smile he could no longer hold back, and to his surprise, Wolverine did likewise. Both men laughed out loud.

"I will sleep with one eye and both ears open," Wolverine confided.

"As will I," Viktor agreed. "As will I."

16

THEIR ROUTE WAS SOUTH
and slightly west, angling ever toward the distant mountains, but during the next day's hard riding, Wolverine
mentioned that they would not reach the peaks before arriv-
ing in the land of the Crows.

"Like the Blackfoot, they are not really a mountain people, although we all go there from time to time to hunt," the
brave explained. "We go there to kill our brother the bear."

Viktor recalled the bear's paw that Stands with a Stick
had used as a healing tool. "The bear has powerful medicine, as your people say," he commented.

Wolverine nodded. "I have never killed a bear, but someday I will."

Viktor moved his shoulder, which had been stiff and sore
when he awoke that morning. Most of the pain was gone
and he had to admit that *something* Stands with a Stick had
done had worked. Viktor tended to give more credit to the
moss that the Blackfoot healer had packed in the wound
than he did to any sort of magic, but he was unwilling to
discount the possibility of spiritual cooperation completely.
He had seen too many strange things in his life to be a total
skeptic.

The landscape became a bit more rugged during the

day's journey. Actual hills appeared. Wolverine led Viktor on a twisting path so that they were never skylighted on the high ground. "The Crows will have watchers out," the Indian said. "They know the Blackfeet will come after the boy. This has happened before."

It was almost like a game, Viktor thought. A grim, deadly game, to be sure, but a game nonetheless. The Crows kidnapped the boy, and the Blackfeet stole him back. Men died each time, but that seemed to matter little to either player. Viktor hoped, for the boy's sake, that this was the last time he would serve as a pawn in the rivalry between the tribes.

The weather had been warm and pleasant since their departure the previous morning, with the blue sky overhead dotted with fluffy white clouds, but during the second afternoon, a cool breeze sprang up from the north, following behind them. When Viktor looked back, he saw a low line of dark blue near the horizon. Reining in, he gestured in that direction and said, "There is a storm coming."

Wolverine studied the distant clouds. "Yes. We will need shelter tonight. I know a place. We can reach it before the storm catches us."

From that point on, the Blackfoot warrior set a faster pace. Viktor kept up easily, the dun moving underneath him in a ground-eating trot. The dun and the chestnut stallion were evenly matched; under other circumstances, Viktor would have enjoyed racing the horse against Wolverine's, but neither man could afford to tire his mount needlessly now. The animals would need every bit of their speed and strength when the time came to leave the Crow village with the boy.

The cool breeze quickened into a cold, steady wind that brought with it the smell of rain. Despite his hurry, Wolverine was still careful about his choice of path. Their best hope for success lay in taking the Crow by surprise.

The blue clouds swept on and eventually blotted out the sun, casting a pall over the landscape. Wolverine led Viktor toward a long bluff that rose beside a creek. Their horses splashed across the stream, and Wolverine lifted an arm to point at a dark smudge on the face of the bluff.

"Up there," he said. "We will have to lead the horses. Even if the rain makes the creek rise, we will be above it."

Viktor looked dubiously at the spot Wolverine had indicated. "It does not look large enough for us and the horses," he said.

Wolverine's tone was impatient as he replied, "I have been here before. Come!" He stepped down from his horse, grasped its hackamore, and began leading it up the slope.

With no alternative, Viktor dismounted, grasped the dun's rawhide harness, and followed. The ridge was fairly steep, but he had no trouble climbing it and leading the dun. Above them, Wolverine and the chestnut reached the mouth of the cave and disappeared inside, proof that the hole in the ridge was large enough for one horse, anyway. Viktor hoped his companion was right about the size of the place. He cast a glance at the approaching storm as the rumble of thunder reached his ears. He saw jagged fingers of lightning splayed among the clouds.

The dun jerked its head and whickered nervously when they reached the cave. Clearly, the horse did not want to go into that dark hole. Viktor urged it on, tugging on the hackamore. Reluctantly, Saber allowed him to lead it into the cave. The top of the entrance was barely tall enough for Viktor to step through without bending.

Inside, the cave indeed opened up into a larger space than was evident from outside. The light that came in through the entrance was dim because of the overcast, but Viktor could see that Wolverine was building a fire. Someone seemed to have left a pile of twigs and leaves, dried grass, and buffalo chips for that very purpose.

"My people use this cave for shelter when they need to," Wolverine explained when he saw Viktor watching curiously. "During dry weather, they leave fuel for a fire here so that the next one to use the cave will have heat and light. If we can, we will do the same."

Viktor nodded in understanding. These prairie dwellers looked out for one another. That was the only way they could survive in a land that could be harsh and unforgiving despite its beauty and abundant bounty.

The storm hit only moments after Wolverine had gotten the fire lit. Rain sluiced down from the sky in thick gray sheets. It became almost as dark as night, but that darkness was relieved by near-constant flashes of lightning, accompanied by the rumble and roar of thunder. Smoke from the fire rose to the top of the cave and dispersed, vanishing through several small gaps in the rocky ceiling. Those gaps also allowed the rain to drip through, but the trickles of moisture were small and out of the way. Viktor sat cross-legged by the fire, enjoying its warmth. There was something tremendously appealing about sitting by a fire, warm and dry, as a storm raged outside.

Since the Blackfoot village was to the north, this downpour had already passed through there, the Cossack knew. He hoped Alena had been safe and warm and dry throughout it, too.

The horses huddled together on the other side of the cave, occasionally snapping at each other but generally being more tolerant than normal, as if they realized they were going to have to make the best of these cramped conditions. Wolverine rubbed them down and fed them grain from one of the pouches he carried, and they drank from the puddles formed by the drips from the ceiling.

With their mounts taken care of, the Indian brought out some strips of the dried meat and handed one of them to Viktor, who took it with a grateful nod. They had finished what was left of their previous night's supper at noontime, and he was hungry again. Wolverine had other food in his pouch as well, something he called pemmican, which he explained was a mixture of pounded meat, chokecherries, and buffalo fat. Viktor did not care for it as much as the plain jerked meat, but he ate it anyway, knowing he needed to keep his strength up.

After they had eaten, a particularly loud clap of thunder pealed, and as its echoes died, Wolverine gestured toward the mouth of the cave. *"Sis-tse-kom* . . . you call it thunder."

"Sis-tse-kom," Viktor repeated, trying to shape his mouth around the word the way Wolverine had.

With a grunt of amusement, the Blackfoot warrior said, "And the lightning is *puh-pom.*"

"Puh-pom."

"The sun is *Natos.*"

"Natos."

A frown creased Wolverine's face. "Why do you wish to learn our tongue, white man?"

"I do not know how long I will be with your people," Viktor said. "I should be able to talk to them in their own language. I learned the language of the Americans for that reason."

Wolverine snorted. "You will not be with us long. This I can promise you."

"We will see," the Cossack said.

Outside the cave, the rain continued the rest of the day, and long into the night.

By the next morning, sunlight poured into the cave as Viktor stepped to the entrance and looked out. The creek at the base of the slope had indeed risen during the night, to about twice its original size, and it was flowing swiftly. The stream had not been large to start with, however, and Viktor thought he and Wovlerine could cross it with no trouble.

The Blackfoot said as much as he stepped up beside Viktor. "The earth will drink deeply of the gift of rain," he went on. "It will not be long until the ground is dry once more."

Viktor pointed at the muddy slope. "We will have to be careful going down."

Wolverine nodded. "Are you as surefooted as the antelope, white man?" he asked.

"We will see who slips and falls first," the big Cossack confidently.

As it turned out, neither of them fell in the mud. After making a short breakfast on dried meat, they led the horses down the ridge and mounted beside the stream. The horses forded the creek with ease, the muddy water reaching only halfway up their legs. Once across, the two riders turned south again, heading ever deeper into the land of the Crows.

By midday, most of the puddles on the ground had dried up, making the land appear as if a storm had never passed. Viktor was hungry again and was about to suggest looking for some game when Wolverine suddenly halted the chestnut at the top of a rise and pointed into the broad, shallow valley below.

"*Kyai-yo!*" Wolverine said excitedly. "*Ni-tap-i wak-sin!*"

Viktor immediately recognized the words that the old woman in the Blackfoot lodge had spoken as she urged him to eat. He brought the dun to a stop and looked out over the valley. A small herd of buffalo was grazing on the thick clumps of grass.

"*Ni-tap-i wak-sin!*" Wolverine repeated.

"What?"

Wolverine lifted his lance and shook it at the buffalo. "Real food. Buffalo meat."

"So that was what the old woman was saying," Viktor mused. "I thought she was just telling me to eat."

"What?" Wolverine frowned and shook his head. "Never mind. I long for the taste of fresh buffalo. It is the only true food of the Blackfeet." He looked over at Viktor. "Will you hunt?"

Viktor shrugged his broad shoulders. "I have no rifle."

"Bah! Those things you call rifles stink up the air and make the ears hurt from their noise. Watch me!"

With the exuberance of a young warrior, he heeled his horse into a run down the hill. Viktor hesitated only a moment, then rode after him.

Thoughts of Zephaniah explaining how the buffalo had never really learned to fear those who hunted them until it was too late crowded into Viktor's head. It seemed impossible that only a few days had passed since the death of the old mountain man. To Viktor, it had seemed like weeks. The still-healing wound on his shoulder reminded him of just how recent the battle with the Blackfeet had been, though.

Staying back so that he could observe Wolverine's actions, he watched as the warrior galloped among the startled buffalo and used his lance to smack one on the head. Wolverine veered away from that lumbering beast, rode alongside another of the huge, shaggy creatures, and struck again with the lance. Viktor had no idea what this process represented; it was as if Wolverine was searching for a suitable target, rather than simply driving his lance into the first buffalo he came to. Wolverine gave a yipping cry and whirled his mount to lash out at another of the buffalo.

Viktor was on the outskirts of the herd by now, and he had to take his eyes off the Indian for a second to make sure his own horse was under control. When he glanced up again, it was just in time to see one of the buffalo lunge heavily against Wolverine's horse, unseating the warrior. Viktor gave a startled cry as the Blackfoot flew through the air and crashed to the ground among the milling herd. Wolverine rolled over a couple of times and then came to a stop, evidently too stunned by the fall to get to his feet.

"Wolverine!" Viktor shouted. He drove his heels into the flanks of the dun, sending it racing forward. Some of the buffalo obstructed his view, but he thought none of them had trampled the warrior—so far. It was only a matter of time, however, before those sharp hooves found his sprawled body and crushed him into the earth.

Heedless now of his own safety, Viktor rode like a madman through the herd, thankful for the surefooted lineback dun. The horse darted around the slower buffalo, and abruptly a clear path opened between Viktor and Wolverine. The Cossack knew the opening might last only a few seconds, so he drove the dun forward with desperate urgency.

Wolverine lifted his head, and his dazed eyes followed Viktor's progress toward him. More of the lumbering beasts swerved toward the fallen Blackfoot, and they were picking up speed now. But the dun was still faster, and Viktor was able to get in front of the stampeding buffalo.

The warning Wolverine had given him the day before about avoiding the holes dug by the little subterranean rodents flashed through his mind, but there was no time for such caution now. Speed was the only thing that would save the warrior's life.

And if the dun stepped in one of the holes and went down before the thundering herd, then all of them would die. It was as simple as that.

"Forgive me, Princess," Viktor muttered. He had no right to risk his life this way when Alena was still a prisoner in the Blackfoot village. But he could not stand by and watch Wolverine die, either.

The Indian raised his arm, holding out his hand. Viktor slowed the dun just enough to reach down, slap his fingers around the proffered wrist, and heave upward. Wolverine helped as much as he could, grasping tightly, but it was the Cossack's enormous strength that lifted him onto the back of the dun. They rode on, Wolverine clinging to the horse for dear life as Viktor guided it expertly through the herd and gradually worked their way clear of the stampede. There were moments when tons of shaggy flesh were racing along on both sides of them, only inches away, but Viktor skillfully avoided any catastrophes.

Once they were free, he brought the dun to a halt. "Are you all right?" he asked.

Instead of answering, Wolverine slid down from the horse. Still a little unsteady on his feet, he stalked away a short distance before turning around sharply and glaring.

"I do not thank you!" he spat out. "You are a fool! You should have let me die under the hooves of the buffalo!"

Viktor rested his hands on the dark stripe that ran down the dun's back and leaned forward to ease the ache in his shoulder. "Would you have let me die if I had fallen?" he asked quietly.

"Yes! And I would have thanked the spirits for taking you!"

"You know where to find the Crow village," Viktor pointed out. "I do not."

Wolverine just continued glaring and made no reply.

After a moment Viktor indulged his curiosity and asked, "Why did you merely strike the buffalo with your lance, instead of killing them?"

Sullenly, Wolverine said, "We have no way to carry the meat and the hides. To waste so much of the buffalo would anger the spirits, so I could not kill them, no matter how hungry I am. I rode among them only to show you our ways."

Viktor was surprised. "You never meant to kill one of them?"

"I may long for the taste of fresh meat, but I will not waste the life of one who brings life to my people. We have dried meat and pemmican. And there are prairie hens to eat, too." Wolverine held out his hand. "Now give me your horse so that I can catch my pony."

"I will catch him for you." Viktor straightened to his full height and peered around, looking for the chestnut stallion. Spotting it atop the rise on the far side of the valley, he turned the dun and rode off.

Behind him, Wolverine called, "Come back here, white man! I will catch my horse!"

The Cossack ignored him, a smile tugging at his mouth. Wolverine's attack on the herd had been all for show, a prideful demonstration of the warrior's hunting skills. At least, that had been the intent. The reality had been nearly fatal.

But then, reality had a way of being like that, Viktor mused.

He rode on, leaving Wolverine to stare after him and seethe in frustration.

17

WOLVERINE REMAINED sullen all through that day, speaking little until late in the afternoon. Then he slowed his horse and said, "We will be near the village of the Crows soon. We must be careful now."

Viktor thought they had been quite cautious so far, but he understood what the warrior meant. Now that they had almost reached their destination, it was more important than ever that they not be discovered.

They swung wide to the east, then back to the west, and Viktor knew they were approaching the Crow village by a roundabout route. He agreed with Wolverine's thinking on the matter. It was best never to do what an enemy expected.

Wolverine led the way to a hill dotted with small trees. He halted at the base of the slope and swung down from his mount. Viktor followed suit. "We will leave the horses here," the Blackfoot said as he tied the chestnut's reins to a thin sapling. Viktor did likewise, then started up the hill on foot with Wolverine.

The top of the hill was bare of trees, and before they reached it, the Indian went to his hands and knees and motioned for the Russian to do the same. Cautiously, they crawled until they could peer over the crest down to the other side. The glare of the lowering sun was in their eyes, but Viktor could still see the Indian village below them, situated, like the Blackfoot village, beside a small creek. Also like the Blackfoot village, warriors, women, and children bustled among the lodges.

"That is the Crow camp?" Viktor whispered.

"One of them," Wolverine replied, also keeping his voice low. "This is the biggest band. The chief's grandson should be here."

Suddenly Viktor pointed as excitement gripped him. "There!" he hissed. "Is that the boy?"

Down in the village at the bottom of the hill, a child was playing with a scrawny dog in front of one of the Crow lodges. It was difficult to tell much about him except for his size and the fact that he was dressed in buckskins—just like all the other children in the village. But Viktor's instincts told him they had found what they were looking for.

"I cannot tell from here," Wolverine said. "It could be him. . . ."

They watched as the boy edged away from the dog toward some nearby horses. Abruptly, with no warning, he lunged toward the horses, using the stump of a fallen tree as a boost and leaping atop one of the Crow mounts. Faintly, Viktor and Wolverine heard the boy shout as he drove his heels into the flanks of the animal and kicked it into a run. He seemed to be holding tightly to the horse's mane.

Viktor started to rise, but the Blackfoot's hand caught his arm and held him down. "Watch," Wolverine said.

The boy's path took him too close to a group of Crow warriors. One of them darted forward and plucked him off the horse. The boy struggled wildly for a moment, flailing at the warrior. The man laughed, put the boy on the ground, and gave him a shove that sent him sprawling. The youngster seemed unhurt by the fall, and leaped up immediately and began shouting at the Crow warrior.

Atop the hill, Wolverine gave a short bark of laughter. "That is the grandson of Buffalo's Back Fat. Did you see the way he tried to get away from the hated Crow?"

"If he had chosen his moment better, he might have succeeded," Viktor said.

"He is still young and has much to learn," Wolverine pointed out with a shrug. He and Viktor watched as, down below, a pair of Crow warriors herded the boy into one of the lodges. Wolverine went on, "Tonight, when the village is asleep, we will go down there and take him. The Crows will not know he is gone until it is too late. I wish I could kill some of them first, but the boy will be safer this way."

Viktor gave a short laugh. "If they discover us, you will get to kill Crows."

"And it will be a good fight. Many will die."

"Including the boy?" Viktor asked.

Taken by surprise by the question, Wolverine scowled. "The boy must be saved."

"Then we must be careful."

"Do not think to give me orders, white man." The warrior's voice was still pitched low, but it held an unmistakable tone of menace. "Just because you helped me when the buffalo knocked me from my horse—"

"Just because I saved your life, you mean," Viktor cut in.

"You do not know that," Wolverine snapped. "I might have gotten out of the way." He slid down the hill a little so that he could stand up in a crouch. "Come. We will wait where the Crows cannot find us."

Viktor nodded and followed him back down the hill to the spot where they had left the horses. Now would come one of the hardest parts of the entire mission, the Cossack thought as he untied the lineback dun and led it away.

Waiting for night. Waiting for possible battle.

Waiting for death.

A young Crow woman walked through the village holding the Blackfoot boy's hand. The grandson of Buffalo's Back Fat went with her reluctantly, dragging his feet every step of the way. He did not try to pull away from the woman and run, however. The two Crow warriors who trailed several feet behind him probably had something to do with that, Viktor thought as he and Wolverine watched from a small gully near the village.

They had spent the time since they had first spied on the camp working their way ever closer. Wolverine had found this narrow gully, its bottom still slightly muddy from the recent rain. During the storm, the gouge in the earth had probably widened into a small stream, but all the water had run off, leaving the gully as the twisting, brush-choked passage it normally was.

Wolverine and Viktor had crept along its bottom as the shadows of night thickened. When necessary, they had traveled on hands and knees in order not to be seen; in the deeper sections of the gully, they had been able to raise up into a crouch and finally to stand at their full height, even the towering Cossack. In fact, they had been forced to climb a few feet up the side of the gully in order to peer into the Crow village from this particular vantage point. The nearest of the lodges was perhaps twenty yards away, Viktor estimated. Quite a few fires were burning in the camp, so it was easy to distinguish details. They had spotted the grandson of Buffalo's Back Fat almost right away, accompanying the young woman back to the lodge that was evidently his quarters.

His prison was a better description, Viktor thought.

The boy was taken into the lodge by the young woman, both of them disappearing from sight as the flap of hide over the entrance fell shut. The two warriors did not enter the lodge but stood talking nearby for several minutes. Viktor was worrying if they intended to remain there all night when the woman stuck her head out and spoke. One of the men replied, and then both warriors moved off into the village. Viktor heaved a mental sigh of relief.

"That is the same lodge where the boy was taken earlier," Wolverine whispered. "I can reach it from here without being seen."

"You are sure?"

It was difficult to read the Blackfoot's expression in the shadows of the gully, but Viktor thought he cast him a disdainful look. "I can move so quietly it will seem I am one with the night," he announced.

The big Russian let that boast pass. All that mattered was that Wolverine could back up his claim. "Will the Crows post guards? I thought they had done so earlier."

"There are always guards around a village, but no one stands near the lodge where the boy is being held. This is the land of the Crows. They will not be as watchful as if they were on Blackfoot land."

"You said they will be expecting Buffalo's Back Fat to send someone after the boy," Viktor commented.

"They will look for a raiding party—not for two men." Wolverine pointed to the other side of the village. "I will go into the lodge for the boy. You wait on that side of the camp. If there is trouble, you make noise, lead the Crow warriors away."

Viktor shook his head emphatically. "We go together," he protested, "as Buffalo's Back Fat said."

"If we are together and the Crows find us, the boy will die or be captured again. Is that what you want?"

"No," Viktor said slowly, seeing the logic of Wolverine's decision but not liking it very much. "Of course not."

"Then do as I say." Wolverine turned and pointed toward the horses. "I will meet you on the prairie when the moon is a hand's width above the horizon."

Viktor nodded and slipped down to the bottom of the gully again. He began to work his way farther along it, intending to use it for concealment until he was as close to his destination as possible. He could not tell in the darkness, but reason told him the gully probably ran all the way to the creek beside which the village was located. If that was the case, he could follow it until he was where Wolverine wanted him to be.

Viktor paused and glanced over his shoulder. The shadows and the twists and turns of the gully had already taken him out of sight of Wolverine. He mouthed a silent prayer and wondered if the Blackfoot was praying to his own gods right about now. He hoped that was the case, because if

they—and the boy—were going to survive this night, they
would need all the assistance they could get.

Inside the Crow lodge, the grandson of Buffalo's Back Fat
sat sullenly beside the fire. A bowl of food lay in his lap
untouched. The young woman who had brought him here
sat on the other side of the fire, next to another, slightly
older boy who had already been in the lodge when they entered. This boy had a bowl of food, too, but unlike the captive, he was eating hungrily.

These stupid Crows believed he would be happy as their
prisoner as long as they gave him food and had the other
boy try to befriend him, the grandson of Buffalo's Back Fat
thought. The other boy was named Rabbit's Hind Foot, and
he was the son of the young woman, who was called Grass
Waving in the Wind. The Blackfoot boy had picked up that
much from listening to them the past few days; he spoke
enough of the Crow tongue to understand most of what he
heard. But he did not speak to them or even acknowledge
their existence. He would not give them that satisfaction.
More than once before he had been captured by the Crows,
and he knew how to conduct himself with the dignity expected from the grandson and heir of a Blackfoot chief.

Rabbit's Hind Foot finished his food and set the bowl
aside. He pointed at the captive and spoke to Grass Waving
in the Wind, asking if he could have the untouched food.
The Crow woman shook her head. "He will eat later," she
said.

They would see about that, the grandson of Buffalo's
Back Fat thought. They would see just how stubborn he
could be.

Grass stood up and came around the fire to kneel beside the
captive. In a harsh voice, she said, "Take off your clothing."

The chief's grandson could not suppress a look of surprise. He said nothing, but he shook his head.

"Yes," Grass said. "It has been decided."

The boy did not know who had made that strange decision,
or why, but he did not care. He was not going to cooperate

with anything these Crows wanted him to do. He started to
scuttle away as the woman reached for him.

"Rabbit!" she said sharply to her son, and the older boy
came to his feet and hurried around the fire. The grandson
of Buffalo's Back Fat saw that they were closing in on him
from both sides, and he tried to leap to his feet and dart between them.

He was not fast enough. Rabbit's Hind Foot grabbed
him, and Grass Waving in the Wind caught hold of his
buckskin shirt. She began tugging at it, trying to work it up
and over his head.

The boy struggled mightily, but he was outnumbered by
larger adversaries. Within moments, they had stripped him
of his buckskins, which were decorated with beadwork and
painted symbols and were much fancier than the Crow
lad's. Rabbit laughed as he picked up the shirt and looked
at it in admiration. A second later, following his mother's
orders, he took off his own shirt and began pulling on the
one taken from the Blackfoot captive.

Tears of anger and frustration and embarrassment sprang
into the eyes of the boy. He blinked them away rapidly.
The grandson of a chief could not be seen crying, no matter
what. He had to be strong and brave. Grass picked up the
shirt her son had discarded and threw it at him. The gar-
ment struck him in the chest, and he caught it instinctively.
"Put on the clothes of my son," she told him.

This strange behavior just proved what the Blackfeet had
always known, the grandson of Buffalo's Back Fat told
himself. In addition to being thieves, the Crows were also
madmen. Their spirits were evil. The boy wished that
someone would come and take him away from this place
and all those who dwelled here.

Someone *would* come. His grandfather would not leave
him here among the Crows. Buffalo's Back Fat would punish those who had dared to steal him.

The boy clung tightly to that hope as he put on Rabbit's
Hind Foot's plain buckskins.

18

VIKTOR HAD GONE ONLY A
short distance when alarm bells suddenly began ringing in
his brain. He stopped in his tracks and put out a hand,
pressing it against the side of the gully. Every instinct in his
body told him that something was wrong, but to save his
life—and the life of the grandson of Buffalo's Back Fat—
he could not have said what it was.

All he knew was that he had to turn back now.

But if he did, he would be disobeying Wolverine's orders. The Blackfoot warrior was counting on him to be in
position when the time came for him to penetrate the Crow
camp. The boy's safety might depend on Viktor's ability to
provide a distraction and slow down the Crows' pursuit.

Wolverine had said that he would not attempt to reach
the lodge where the boy was held until the village was
asleep. There was plenty of time, Viktor decided, for him to
return to the spot where he had left Wolverine and make
sure everything was all right. Perhaps then his taut nerves
would relax a bit so he could proceed with his part of the
rescue.

Hurriedly, the Cossack retraced his steps. Even in the
thickest darkness, a hand on the wall of the gully as he
moved made it impossible to get lost. His eyes were well

accustomed to the darkness by now, and he had little trouble finding the place where he had last seen Wolverine a few minutes earlier.

The only trouble was that the Blackfoot warrior was now nowhere to be seen.

Viktor clenched his hand into a fist and struck it softly into the side of the gully, cursing. Unless the Crows had discovered, and captured or killed, Wolverine, he could think of only one place the Blackfoot warrior could be. Pulling himself up to the lip of the defile once more, he peered anxiously toward the Crow village.

After only a moment, he spotted the Blackfoot ducking around one of the lodges. And if *he* could see the warrior, surely the Crows would, too, if they chanced to look in the wrong direction at the wrong time.

"The village is not yet asleep, you fool," Viktor hissed, as if Wolverine could hear him. "Or is that what you wanted, Wolverine? Are you so full of the desire to kill Crows that you would risk the life of the boy?"

Viktor knew the answer to that question. He knew, as well, what he had to do. He began to scramble up out of the gully.

Fewer people were moving around in the village, Wolverine judged. That was why he had decided it was safe to try to reach the lodge containing the boy, even though the big white man would not yet be in position to help him if he needed it.

He'd just have to do it alone, Wolverine told himself. Buffalo's Back Fat never should have sent the white man in the first place, he thought . . . although the one who called himself a Cossack, rather than an American, *was* a formidable warrior. And a horseman as well. Not that the brave would have admitted as much to the man, even under the threat of torture.

With such thoughts running through his mind, Wolverine moved from lodge to lodge, using the dwellings as cover for his approach. He would soon be at his destination.

A footstep nearby made him freeze in his tracks as he

crouched next to one of the lodges. He heard a man say something inside the lodge, and a woman replied. They were no threat to him, Wolverine knew, as long as they remained inside and unaware of his presence. But then another footstep sounded, and suddenly a Crow warrior was coming around the buffalo-hide structure. He saw Wolverine.

The sight of a Blackfoot warrior here in the middle of his own village no doubt startled the Crow, but he had little time to react. Before the Crow could let out a sound, Wolverine struck, spinning him around, looping an arm around his throat, and pulling his head back. With his other hand, he drew the keen edge of his knife across the man's throat, slicing deep.

Hot blood spurted over Wolverine's hand, the smell quickly mixing with another odor as the Crow's bowels spasmed and voided and he shuddered and died. Wolverine lowered the corpse to the ground and wiped his gore-splattered knife and hand on the dead man's buckskin shirt. For a moment he was filled with a fierce exultation. One of the enemy was dead.

But the boy was still a captive, and freeing him was the reason he had come here, the Blackfoot reminded himself.

He rolled the body onto its stomach to hide the gaping wound in the neck. If anyone saw the man, they might think he was sleeping, at least until they noticed the pool of blood that was beginning to form around his head. Wolverine glanced around. No one was in sight at the moment. The spirits were still smiling on him.

He headed toward the lodge that held the boy, moving more quickly now. With a dead man behind him, he could no longer afford to choose his moments for action carefully. Discovery was only a matter of time.

Inside the lodge, the grandson of Buffalo's Back Fat glared at Rabbit's Hind Foot as the older boy proudly showed off the stolen garments to his beaming mother. The grandson of Buffalo's Back Fat wanted to snort in contempt. As if that stupid Crow boy could ever be a chief, no matter whose clothes he wore!

The buckskins that he had been forced to wear stank of Crow, the boy thought. When he got back to his own village and the weather was warm enough, he'd have to plunge into the creek and wash the stink off him . . . if it would even wash off. The thought of having to smell like a Crow for the rest of his life was a fate too horrible to even contemplate.

Soon, he told himself, the warriors of his grandfather's band would swoop down on this village and kill all the Crow warriors. He'd return to his home, and the village would celebrate his rescue with a feast. Stu-mick-o-sucks and Eeh-nis-kin, his grandparents, would welcome him with great solemnity, but later in the lodge, out of sight of the rest of the Blackfeet, they would hug him and tell him how glad they were to have him with them again.

The boy prayed to every spirit he knew that this would come to pass, and soon.

When Wolverine was within a few paces of the lodge, he reached for the tomahawk tucked behind his rawhide belt. As far as he knew, the boy was alone with the Crow woman. The Blackfoot hoped he could frighten the woman into submission. He made war on warriors, not females. But to keep her quiet and force her to turn over the boy, he was prepared to kill her.

Just as he reached for the flap of hide that hung over the entrance to the dwelling, he caught sight of another Crow warrior. Surprise worked in Wolverine's favor once again, and he sprang toward the man and struck with the tomahawk. With a dull thud, the weapon buried itself in the Crow warrior's forehead. He staggered backward, a strangled gasp welling up from his throat.

This was bad, very bad, Wolverine thought as he wrenched the tomahawk free and a torrent of blood and brains spilled from the dying Crow's shattered skull. But the damage had been done. The sound that the man had involuntarily uttered was unmistakably anguished and terrified, and it had been loud enough to carry to the nearby lodges. Already, another man was calling curiously, asking what was wrong.

Within a matter of moments someone would come to investigate, Wolverine knew. He whirled around and darted toward the lodge.

An angry shout came from his left, and he glanced in that direction in time to see a Crow warrior running toward him. Suddenly halting, the man flung a lance at him. Wolverine dropped to one knee and let the weapon pass over his head. With the speed and ease born of long practice, he tucked the tomahawk away, unslung the bow from his back, and fitted an arrow to the string. The Crow had drawn a knife and was charging him, but Wolverine's arrow caught him in the chest and stopped him short. The Crow stumbled and fell, dropping his knife to paw futilely at the arrow embedded in his body.

As the dying man wailed in pain, Wolverine saw another Crow emerge from a nearby lodge. He nocked a second arrow in his bow and let fly. The shaft took the man in the belly. Doubling over and grunting in pain, he ran a few steps farther before collapsing in agony, his writhing body curling around the arrow buried in his vitals.

Without pausing, Wolverine rose to his feet and again lunged toward the lodge—only to discover that another man had gotten between him and the dwelling. The shadowy figure slashed at him with a knife, and Wolverine felt the blade rake a fiery line across his midsection. A few inches closer, and the stroke would have disemboweled him. As it was, he was able to lash out with the bow and crack the stout wood across his enemy's face. Wolverine dropped the bow, grabbed the wrist of the man's knife hand, and twisted with all his strength. A bone broke with a sharp snap, and the Crow cried out.

Wolverine batted him aside, but another man immediately took his place. Although the people of the village had been going about their usual business, they were expecting the Blackfeet to retaliate sooner or later, and now that the threat had materialized, they sprang into action quickly.

Even as Wolverine grabbed his tomahawk again to ward off the thrust of a lance, he glimpsed Crows coming at him from all sides.

He had been so certain that his stealth would allow him to reach the lodge without being detected. Now he feared that the grandson of his chief would pay for that mistake with his life.

But there was still time, Wolverine reminded himself as he slammed the head of his tomahawk against a Crow's skull and felt a surge of satisfaction at the sound of splintering bone. No matter what else happened tonight, he had already killed several of the Crows, and come what may, he could take some grim satisfaction in that fact.

Whirling madly, Wolverine held his attackers at bay for a moment with the deadly tomahawk. He could not defend every direction at once, however, and suddenly a wedge of icy fire drove into his side. One of the Crows had just thrust a knife into him. He staggered, spreading his legs wide to keep from falling. The cold fire was racing through his body, and he knew he could not maintain his balance much longer. It was going to take a miracle now to save his life, to say nothing of the life of the grandson of Buffalo's Back Fat.

That thought had barely had time to form in his mind when he gasped at the sight of the head of one of the Crows seemingly springing off the man's shoulders, leaving a corpse that stood upright, jerking and twitching madly as blood spouted from its neck.

Viktor had put all his strength behind the stroke of the broken saber. The Crows had been so busy with Wolverine that they had not seen him coming, so he was able to set himself before striking. Enough of the saber's blade remained to cleave muscle and bone, though it grated on the Crow's spine before shearing through it. The man's head went one way, then Viktor kicked the body in another as he sprang into the melee.

Wolverine was hurt; Viktor was able to tell that much, though he could not tell how seriously. He used the broken saber to drive the Crows back and give him some room, then grabbed Wolverine's arm and half shoved, half dragged the Blackfoot warrior toward the lodge.

Wolverine, as it turned out, had provided the distraction, not Viktor, but instead of trying to enter the lodge and snatch the boy during the fighting, Viktor decided to try to rescue the Blackfoot as well. He hoped this would not mean the death of them all, but just as had happened during the buffalo stampede, he was unable to stand aside and allow Wolverine to die.

Together they burst into the lodge, tangling for an instant in the entrance flap. Viktor's eyes searched desperately for the boy, even as the Crow woman threw herself at them, screeching angrily. To his surprise, Viktor saw not one but *two* boys, both roughly about the same age and size. But one was dressed in the familiar beaded buckskins that marked him as the grandson of Buffalo's Back Fat.

While the woman clawed at his eyes, he let go of Wolverine long enough to backhand her and knock her aside. As he was reaching to support Wolverine once more, the Blackfoot warrior cried out, "I am all right! Get the boy!"

Viktor turned toward the child in beaded buckskin and saw him duck away and draw a small knife. That was reasonable, Viktor thought. The grandson of Buffalo's Back Fat had seen him only a few times at Fort Union, and that had been several weeks earlier. At that time he had been wearing his Cossack clothing, instead of buckskins. Now, dressed like a Blackfoot but with white skin and a beard, he knew he had to appear a pretty bizarre figure in the eyes of a youngster. No wonder the boy seemed afraid.

A long step brought him next to the boy. Viktor looped an arm around him and scooped him off the ground, lifting him roughly enough so that the knife jostled loose from the boy's grip. "Stop struggling!" the Cossack told him. "We have come to help you!"

The words seemed to have no effect. The boy continued writhing and flailing at Viktor. The big man ignored the blows and turned toward the entrance of the lodge.

As he did so he felt the weight of the Crow woman land on his back, almost knocking him down. Wolverine grabbed her and jerked her away. He still held his tomahawk, and he used the flat of it to strike the woman in the head. She moaned and folded up, stunned by the blow. Viktor hoped she was not dead.

Now he held the boy in his left arm and the broken saber in his right hand. He put the saber away and reached toward Wolverine, who was barely able to stay on his feet. Blood welled between the fingers of the Blackfoot as he pressed his hand to the wound in his side. Viktor took hold of his arm and steadied him, then tugged him toward the entrance.

"No!" Wolverine said. "They will be waiting for us that way!"

Viktor knew he was right. As soon as they set foot outside the lodge, they would be riddled with lances and arrows. They had to take the Crows by surprise. . . .

Viktor wheeled around and plunged toward the back side of the lodge, almost trampling the boy he assumed was a Crow lad told to make friends with the captive. He clamped his left arm tighter on the squirming body of Buffalo's Back Fat's grandson and bent down to grasp the bottom of the lodge's wall. As he straightened, he heaved upward, tipping the entire lodge over. It fell into a cluster of Crow warriors.

Viktor and Wolverine stumbled away from the overturned lodge in the cool night air. Behind them, the lodge, which had fallen into the fire in its center, burst into flames. The Cossack looked back at the red glare and saw several Crow warriors aiming arrows.

He called out a warning to Wolverine and veered to the side. The Blackfoot followed his lead, and the arrows whipped harmlessly through the air.

More furious screeching came from the woman, who had by now recovered her wits and her rage and was chasing after them as well. She bounded past Wolverine, who staggered as he ran, and threw herself at Viktor again. This time she was able to throw him off balance, despite the fact that she was half his size. Victor tumbled like a felled tree, taking the struggling boy with him.

But the fall turned out to be a blessing in disguise. While it slowed them down, the boy was stunned when his head hit the ground. He stopped fighting and lay limp in Viktor's grip. The same, unfortunately, could not be said of the woman. She was scratching and clawing at Viktor like a crazed mountain lion. He tried to bat her away, muttering harshly, "Stop it! I don't want to hurt you!"

At that moment Wolverine stumbled up, looming over them with a knife in his hand and announcing, "I will *kill* her."

"No!" Viktor shouted. Closing his hand into a loose fist, he struck quickly. Coming as it did on the heels of Wolverine's tomahawk blow, the punch knocked the woman senseless. Viktor scrambled to his feet, glad that the woman was at last subdued and that she and the boy were quiet for the time being.

"Take her, too!" Wolverine said.

"What?"

"Take the woman! We will use her as a hostage!"

Viktor hesitated only a second, warring briefly with his concept of honor. Then practicality won out, and he bent over to pick up the unconscious woman. Carrying both her and the boy like two rag dolls, he loped toward the prairie where he and Wolverine had left their horses.

19

In the Crow village, an imposing figure in a feathered headdress shouted orders, then turned to the small figure who stood in front of him. The Crow chief reached down, caught hold of the boy underneath the arms, and jerked him up to glare into his face. Despite his upbringing, despite the courage and dignity that had been bred into him, the grandson of Buffalo's Back Fat was more frightened at this moment than he had ever been in his life, more frightened even than when he had first been captured and taken from his home.

The Crow chief shook him and let out a howl of rage. By the light of the burning lodge, the hawk-nosed face of the chief was the most terrifying thing the boy had ever beheld. He expected his life to end at any moment.

If only Wolverine would come back . . . ! The boy had recognized the warrior in the moments of confusion and violence when Wolverine and the other man had come crashing into the lodge. He thought the other man had been one of the strangers he had seen at the fort, where the girl with hair like fire had given him the magical thing of wood and string that made music. But he wasn't sure.

All he knew was that he was scared, and that he wanted to go home, and that even though he was the grandson of

Stu-mick-o-sucks, the mightiest chief of the Blackfoot nation, tears were running down his cheeks and there was not a thing he could do about it.

Wolverine hurried to keep up with Viktor. They would have to cross the gully to reach the horses, but if they could manage that before the Crows caught up to them, they stood a good chance of getting away. The dun and the chestnut were good strong mounts, capable of much speed even when carrying double, and Viktor was a good rider. Besides, Wolverine told himself, he was a Blackfoot, and that meant that even wounded, he could ride better than any Crow ever born.

The thought provided little satisfaction, for just then Wolverine felt something like a fist strike him in the back. The impact knocked him ahead and threatened to make him fall, but he managed to keep from pitching forward onto his face. A fresh wave of pain rolled through him. Reaching behind him, he felt the shaft of an arrow. It was high on his right side, luckily away from his heart or anything else vital enough to kill him right away. He had to keep moving, had to help the Cossack escape from the Crows and get started back toward the village of the Blackfeet.

Once that was done, Wolverine told himself, he could die.

Viktor slid wildly down the bank of the gully, dropping the boy as he did so. Once he reached the bottom of the slope and caught his balance, it took only a second to yank the child up from the ground and loop an arm around him again. He had managed to hang on to the woman at the same time.

Viktor looked back and saw Wolverine appear at the edge of the gully. The sky was faintly lit with red, no doubt from the flames of the burning lodge, and the glow enabled him to see the shaft of an arrow protruding from Wolverine's back as the Blackfoot turned and half slid, half fell down the side of the gully.

"You are hurt!" Viktor exclaimed.

"I was hurt before," Wolverine said. "This is nothing. Go!"

Viktor did as the warrior ordered, running along the gully until he came to a spot where he could climb the opposite bank without much trouble. Carrying the double burden of the woman and the boy meant that he could not use his hands to help him scramble up. A glance behind told him Wolverine was following.

"Hurry!" Viktor urged. "They are coming!"

The gully had slowed down their flight, but it would also slow down the pursuit. At least Viktor hoped so. The biggest danger now was arrows, and as he and Wolverine emerged from the gully and raced across the prairie, more of the deadly missiles came flying out of the night, passing them with ugly whispers. Viktor was grateful that the moonless night made aiming difficult.

"Go! Go!" Wolverine muttered, just loud enough for his companion to hear him. The Blackfoot was staggering from side to side as he ran, and Viktor knew that his wounds had to be taking a toll. Still, there was some small consolation in the fact that Wolverine's erratic path would make him a more elusive target for the Crow arrows.

Viktor called out encouragingly to the Indian, then began searching for the place they had left the horses. If Wolverine had been in the lead, he'd have brought them unerringly to the spot, Viktor suspected, but despite all the similarities between the American frontier and the Russian steppes, they remained two completely different places. Viktor did not know this land. All he could do was hope he was going in the right direction.

Two big shapes loomed up out of the thick shadows, and the sharp whinny from the dun was just about the most welcome sound Viktor had ever heard in his life. He looked back, saw that Wolverine was about ten yards behind him. As Viktor came up to the horses, which were tied to small clumps of brush, the boy began to struggle again. The woman was still senseless, though she let out a groan from time to time. Viktor let her slip to the ground.

He turned to Wolverine as the Blackfoot warrior came panting to a stop. "Can you mount and ride?" Viktor asked.

"I am . . . Blackfoot!" Wolverine replied, his pride intact despite his injuries. "I can ride!"

"Can you hold the boy?"

Wolverine stumbled over to the chestnut, jerked its reins loose, and tried to swing up onto the horse's back. Viktor had to step forward quickly and grab him with his free hand, steadying him until he was settled down on the chestnut.

"Hold on to him tightly," Viktor warned the wounded warrior as he placed the boy in front of him. "He is still so frightened that he does not know who we are."

Wolverine put an arm around the boy and spoke sharply in the Blackfoot tongue. The child's struggles eased. Good, Viktor thought. Perhaps Wolverine was finally getting through to him.

Viktor picked up the woman and flung her over the back of the dun. She would not be very comfortable when she finally woke, but there was nothing he could do about that. He mounted behind her, then reined the dun over next to Wolverine's horse. "Are you ready?" he asked. He heard the howling of the pursuit close behind them now.

Wolverine nodded, the motion strained and jerky. "I am . . . ready."

"Hang on," Viktor muttered. He brought the palm of his hand down in a hard slap on the rump of the chestnut, and the horse leaped into a gallop. Viktor's heels drove into the flanks of the dun, and it surged ahead as well, drawing even with the chestnut.

It looked as if the race between the horses that the Cossack had hoped for earlier was going to come to pass after all. But now, the dun and the chestnut would not be competing against each other, but against the horses of the Crows. And the stakes were much higher. Not pride, but life and death, were riding on the outcome.

Wolverine blinked several times, and finally his eyes stayed open. He peered up at Viktor from the floor of the cave, where he lay on his side, breathing harshly.

Viktor smiled. "You are not dead after all. Good."

More than once during the long night, he had thought that the Blackfoot had died. Wolverine had swayed wildly on the back of the chestnut, more unconscious than not, and several times Viktor had been forced to ride close beside him, holding him upright with one hand while guilding the dun with the other. At the breakneck speed they had traveled over the plains, that was a tricky, dangerous maneuver. But Viktor wanted to keep the Indian alive. His own survival and that of the boy depended on it.

Just then Wolverine's lips moved. Viktor had to lean close to make out the words. "Wh . . . where . . ."

"In the cave," Viktor told him. "The cave where we waited out the storm. It was the only hiding place I could think of. The only one I could find, too, and I almost did not do that."

He had not started a fire this time, even though twigs and grass and leaves remained from their previous sojourn here. He couldn't take the chance of any smoke giving away their hiding place.

The confines of the cave seemed even more cramped this time what with the Crow woman and the boy sitting against the far wall. Their wrists and ankles were tied with rawhide thongs Viktor had taken from the long fringe on his buckskins, and they were glaring daggers at him. He knew he would be dead in an instant if either one of them had anything to say about it.

"The . . . boy . . . ?" Wolverine rasped.

"He is all right," Viktor said. "The woman, too. I tied her so that she cannot escape." He hesitated, then added, "I had to tie the boy, too. He kept trying to run away."

"He must be . . . frightened. Does not know why . . . a white man . . . would try to help him."

"Do not worry. I will get him back to your people."

Somewhere, Wolverine found the strength to lift his hand. Clawlike fingers closed around Viktor's arm as he raised his head. "The Crows . . . ?"

"I have not seen them," Viktor said quietly. "I hid our trail as best I could."

Wolverine's head fell back, and his eyes closed. Viktor thought he had passed out again, but after a moment he murmured, "Good. Stay here until . . . night falls again. Then . . . then you must leave me."

Viktor shook his head. "I would never find the Blackfoot village again," he said. "You must come with us, Wolverine."

Wolverine's tongue rasped over dry lips. "Then . . . if I am to live . . . you have to get this arrow out of me."

Viktor leaned over so that he could look at the shaft of the Crow arrow protruding from Wolverine's back. The buckskin shirt was stiff and dark with dried blood around the torn place that marked the arrow's entry. Blood still flowed from the warrior's side, where he had evidently been stabbed with a knife or a lance. He was weak, very weak. Viktor feared for his life.

"You are sure?" the Russian asked.

"There is . . . no other way. If you do not . . . I will die."

Viktor nodded grimly. It was Wolverine's decision to make. He reached for the arrow and gripped the shaft firmly.

Before he could tug on it, Wolverine lifted a trembling hand to stop him. "No," he gasped. "You must . . . push it through first . . . then break off the shaft."

"I cannot," Viktor said, stunned by the grisly suggestion.

"You must. It is . . . the only way. If you pull the arrow straight out . . . it will kill me."

For a moment Viktor sat silent. Then he took a deep breath and reached for the arrow again. He grasped it as tightly as he could with his right hand, while with his left he gripped Wolverine's shoulder to hold the warrior still. This procedure would have been easier if he had had several men to help him. But Wolverine was depending on him.

Viktor took another breath, held it, and shoved the arrow forward into Wolverine's body as hard as he could.

The Blackfoot warrior's eyes snapped open and practically bulged from their sockets. His lips pulled back in a grimace of agony, and he hissed loudly through clenched teeth as Viktor forced the arrow through layers of muscle until the head finally emerged high on the right side of his chest. It was dripping blood.

Several inches of the other end of the shaft still stuck out from Wolverine's back. Using both hands now, Viktor gripped the arrow as he snapped the shaft just in front of the feathers at its base. With that end gone, he could finish pulling the shaft out the front of Wolverine's body. Thankfully, the warrior had passed out by this point. His eyes were closed and his body was covered with sweat, but his chest was still rising and falling in a rapid, labored rhythm.

Viktor threw the broken arrow aside, making sure he did not toss it in the vicinity of the Crow woman. The last thing he needed was for her to get her hands on it. Then he looked at the unconscious Wolverine and said quietly, "Rest . . . my friend."

They had endured too much together now for him to refer to Wolverine as anything else.

20

ONLY A LITTLE FRESH BLOOD had welled from the wounds when Viktor pulled the arrow out, and he was grateful for that. He gathered some of the dried grass they'd left in the cave for fuel and used it to dress the wounds, pressing a handful over each ragged hole in Wolverine's body and binding them tightly. Viktor wished he had some of the moss that old Stands with a Stick had used on his knife wound. His shoulder was still sore from it, but there was no festering and it had not slowed him down during the battle with the Crows.

Wolverine was too weak to eat, but several times during the long day, Viktor managed to dribble some water into his mouth and convince him to swallow it. The Blackfoot warrior passed in and out of consciousness. When he was awake, he didn't seem to recognize Viktor, for he spoke only in his native tongue. The Cossack could make little sense of the ramblings. Wolverine was clearly out of his head from fever. Viktor bathed his forehead, hoping that would help, but the Indian was still hot to the touch when shadows of dusk began to fall over the land.

They could not stay here, Viktor told himself. They had not put enough ground between themselves and the village of the Crows. He had no doubt that at this moment, pursuers from the camp were searching the prairie, and if they remained here in the cave, it would be only a matter of time before they were discovered.

Of course, leaving this hiding place put them at great risk, too, but it was clearly the lesser of two evils. Viktor just hoped that by travelling at night, they could avoid the Crows.

A pale red glow still lingered in the western sky as he led the horses out of the cave. He took them down the slope and across the little creek at the base of the bluff, then returned for Wolverine, gently cradling the warrior in his arms. Carefully, he emerged from the cave and made his way down to the horses, where he lifted the half-conscious man onto the back of the chestnut.

"Will you be all right here?" Viktor asked.

Wolverine just grunted as he sat slumped forward over the neck of the horse. Viktor prayed that he wouldn't fall off into the creek.

Hurrying now, Viktor returned to the cave. He picked up the boy first and took him down to the horses, setting him on the chestnut in front of Wolverine. The boy's hands were still tied, but he jabbered angrily, using words that Viktor could not understand. The youngster's attitude was clear, though. Wolverine was not coherent enough to hold him on the horse if the boy tried to get away, so Viktor took another length of rawhide and bound the boy's feet, passing the rawhide underneath the belly of the horse. He didn't like doing that—as a horseman virtually since birth, he knew how important it was to be able to dismount in a hurry—but he had little choice in the matter.

That left the woman, and for a moment Viktor considered doing just that—leaving her in the cave with her hands tied loosely enough that she could eventually work herself free. Then he remembered that Wolverine thought she had value as a hostage, and vehemently insisted that Viktor bring her along. The Cossack was willing to give Wolverine the benefit of the doubt in this matter, at least for the time being.

For the final time he climbed up to the dark mouth of the

cave and went inside to fetch the woman. When he emerged, he had her slung over his shoulder again. Not surprisingly she was screeching imprecations at him, and she kept it up until he slapped her sharply on the rump. She seemed more startled by the blow than hurt, but at least it silenced her for a few minutes.

Mentally thanking God for this respite, Viktor put her in front of him on the lineback dun. She squirmed some, but the tight pressure of his arm kept her in line. Thankfully, Wolverine and the boy were still mounted on the chestnut, and the Blackfoot had even managed to raise his head a little. In the gloom, Viktor saw the expression on his weary face. He seemed to be waiting for his Russian companion to tell him what to do.

The Crow woman, now fully recuperated again, looked at Wolverine, too, and without warning she curled her lip and spat at him. "Blackfoot die!" she cried.

"He is feverish, but he will not die," Viktor told her confidently, wishing that he felt as sure as he sounded.

"White man die, too!"

The boy added something at this juncture, sounding just as angry as the woman. His continuing hostility puzzled Viktor, but there was no time to waste brooding about it. He just shook his head and said, "We are taking you home, boy. You should be happy, instead of sounding like you want to kill us."

"I will kill you," the Crow woman threatened. "Kill white man, kill Blackfoot." Her knowledge of English seemed rather elemental, but she had definitely mastered the basics, Viktor thought with a dry chuckle.

"Well . . . at least you are not calling me an American," he said.

Viktor was able to get through to Wolverine enough so that the warrior muttered in Blackfoot and pointed with a shaky finger. They rode in that direction. As the sky darkened and the stars became visible, Viktor studied the little pinpricks of light and decided that they were indeed headed north, toward the territory claimed by the Blackfeet. The constellations were different here, of course, than those with which he was familiar in Russia, but since the expedition's arrival in America, he had tried to familiarize himself with his surroundings, and that included the stars in the sky. It was possible, Viktor thought as he rode alongside Wolverine, that he could have found the Blackfoot village on his own ... but by pleading ignorance, he had given Wolverine a reason to live.

They rode all that night, their pace slow and careful. In a more lucid moment, Wolverine informed him that the Crows would not be searching for the fugitives at night, but Viktor was not willing to risk all of their lives on that opinion. Despite his weariness, he was keenly alert for any sight or sound of pursuit.

When the sky to the east began to turn gray, then pale pink, Viktor started looking for a place to rest themselves and the horses. The dun and the chestnut were holding up well, but he did not want to risk having either animal give out. The party stopped for a time in the thick brush along one of the small, meandering creeks, and when Viktor had satisfied himself that no one was on their back trail, they pushed on again.

Through the morning and the long afternoon, they rode on, sticking to the low ground as much as possible. Viktor had learned this strategy from Wolverine during the first part of the journey. It was very much like making a trip through some of the more dangerous regions back in Russia. No Cossack wanted to be jumped by a group of bloodthirsty Tartars.

By now, the boy and the Crow woman had grown too tired to complain. They rode listlessly, heads drooping. So did Wolverine, but his condition was more serious than exhaustion. After rallying at times during the day, the fever came on him strongly again as night fell. He babbled incessantly in the Blackfoot tongue and sometimes waved his arms around to emphasize his words.

There was nothing Viktor could do for him. Wolverine's only real hope was to survive until they returned to the

Blackfoot village where Stands with a Stick could tend to his wounds.

A short while after dusk, Viktor found another gully, narrow and brush-choked like the one that had allowed them to get close to the Crow camp. He led the others down into it, knowing that they could go no farther. They all needed rest, and more than a few minutes of it. He would let them sleep until around midnight or so, Viktor decided.

He got the woman and the boy off the horses and tied their ankles, regretting that he had to do that to the grandson of Buffalo's Back Fat. Once the boy realized he was going back to his grandfather, Viktor told himself, he would understand and be grateful. Then he helped Wolverine down from the horse and made him as comfortable as possible on the dry, sandy bed of the gully.

Their supplies were beginning to run low, since they were being used to feed four people. Viktor gave dried meat and pemmican to the woman and the boy, both of whom seized the rations and ate greedily, glaring at Viktor the whole time. It was a good thing he was not waiting for a declaration of gratitude, he told himself.

Wolverine was able to eat some of the pemmican, though Viktor had to practically force him. He was more interested in the water, which he gulped thirstily from the waterskin. The fever had dried him out, Viktor decided. After he had eaten and drunk, Wolverine sank back against the side of the gully and fell into a fitful sleep.

Viktor wished his companion was strong enough to stand guard for a while. Exhaustion clawed at him, and his eyes were gritty and aching. He longed to close them, even for a few moments. He could not remember the last time he had slept.

But he had to remain alert, he told himself sternly. Someone had to watch the woman and the boy and remain on the lookout for searchers from the Crow village. Wolverine could not do it, so it was up to him. He ate last, washing the food down with a long swallow of water, then sat down on the opposite side of the gully from the wounded Blackfoot. He wanted to keep an eye on his friend, although now that the sun had set, shadows filled the gully and made it difficult to see anything. Viktor rubbed the heel of his hand hard against his eyes and yawned mightily.

Ten minutes later, good intentions or not, his head was falling forward onto his chest.

Something woke him, but he never knew what it was. Perhaps the faint rattle of dirt clods falling down the side of the gully as the boy scrambled up it toward the light of a new day.

Viktor's instincts took over, and he surged to his feet, lunging across the gully to grab one of the boy's ankles. The boy kicked at him and pulled free for an instant, forcing Viktor to climb up the slope after him. They were almost at the top when the Cossack caught up to him again, wrapping an arm securely around the boy this time.

Both of them could see over the edge of the bank. Viktor's eyes widened at the sight of the riders about fifty yards away. They were being led by a big man in a feathered headdress, and Viktor knew they must be the Crow search party. Without even thinking, he clapped his free hand over the boy's mouth to keep him from crying out.

"Hush, little one!" Viktor hissed, wishing he could make the boy understand. "I do not know why you think I am not your friend, but if you call the Crows over here, we will all die."

The boy continued struggling, but he was no match for Viktor's massive strength. As the Cossack held his breath, he watched the Crows ride on, never veering toward the gully or even glancing in his direction. Viktor stayed where he was, head lifted just enough to discern the enemy, until the Crows had disappeared into the distance.

Though surprised and still groggy from sleep, he had noted that the Crows were heading east. He thought they were not too far from the Blackfoot village now, and a hard run might bring them to safety by midday. With the Crows momentarily out of the way, he and Wolverine could afford to throw caution to the winds and ride as fast as possible.

He slid back down the slope and checked to see how the

boy had gotten loose. From the condition of the boy's ankles, which were raw and bleeding, the youngster had simply pulled and strained on the rawhide bonds, rubbing them
back and forth until he was able to slip out of them. His
hands were still tied in front of him.

They were fortunate, Viktor knew, that the woman had
been unaware of the proximity of the Crows. He could not
have silenced both of them at the same time if they had
tried to cry out to the pursuers.

Viktor tied the boy's legs, this time looping the rawhide
cords around his calves to avoid irritating the already-sore
ankles. Then he turned to Wolverine, who sat silent and motionless, eyes open, against the bank. For a terrifying moment he thought that the warrior had died during the night,
but then he saw the slight motion of his chest. Wolverine
was alive, but the fever still gripped him, and whatever
those wide, staring eyes saw, Viktor would never know.

Deep inside, he was furious with himself for dozing off,
but there was no time to waste in self-recrimination. Nor in
eating. Viktor gave water to the woman and the boy and
awkwardly made Wolverine drink. Then he gulped down a
swallow of water himself and started preparing to leave the
gully. By now he had gotten quite good at loading the others onto the horses. This time, however, Wolverine was too
weak to stay atop the chestnut by himself. Viktor had no
choice but to tie him onto the horse, just as he did the
woman and the boy.

When they were ready to ride, Viktor swung up onto the
dun, then took the reins of the chestnut and led it back up
the caved-in section of bank they had used to enter the
gully the night before. With the sun to his right, he pointed
the horses north and urged them into a run. From horizon to
horizon across the prairie, nothing seemed to be moving,
and Viktor wanted it to stay that way.

A little more luck . . . They had already had perhaps
more than their share, but it was all they needed now.

A person could live in terror for only so long, Alena had
discovered, before even fear began to dull. After a week in

the village of the Blackfeet—a week that seemed much, much longer to her—she no longer expected to he scalped and killed at any moment. True, she was treated a bit roughly at times by the old women in whose charge she had been put, but no one seemed interested in really hurting her.

Still, she knew she was alive only because Viktor had accompanied that warrior to rescue the grandson of the chief. If Viktor never returned . . .

After this much time, she told herself, the Indians probably would not kill her. But they *would* make her a slave; either that, or give her to one of the warriors to be his wife. Neither alternative appealed to her. And her dreams were still haunted by visions of the battle, of her aunt Zora's death at the hands of these savages. She would never be able to forget this nightmare, and she would certainly never forgive the Blackfeet, no matter what the provocation had been for their attack.

She spent her days clumslly mending buckskins under the tutelage of the old women, who corrected her mistakes with impatient slaps. Alena tried hard to master the bone needles the women used to pull string made of buffalo gut through the tough buckskin. Her fingers were red and sore and swollen from the countless times she had jabbed herself with the needles.

She was sitting in front of a lodge with the old women when Crystal Stone came up and sat down beside her. The wife of Buffalo's Back Fat had been the closest thing to a friend that Alena had in the village. Whenever she was around, the old women were less likely to slap and poke her, and Alena was grateful for that. She summoned up a pleasant smile and a nod for the older woman now.

"Your man . . . come back soon," Crystal Stone said in labored English.

"I hope so," Alena said fervently. She prayed every day that Viktor would return and take her away from here.

"No," Crystal Stone said. "Your man come back soon."

"But that's what you just said—" Alena began, but then she looked up from the work in her lap and saw that Crystal Stone was pointing across the prairie.

Far out there in the distance, moving steadily closer to the village, she could make out two small dark dots that soon resolved themselves into riders even as Alena watched wide-eyed, the breath catching in her throat.

It was . . . Could it be? It was!

Viktor had come back!

Alena jumped to her feet, dropping the buckskins she had been working on and ignoring the angry reprimands that came from the old women. She ran toward the edge of the village, shouting, "Viktor! Viktor!" Her route took her past the lodge of Buffalo's Back Fat. Seeing the prisoner racing through the village, several warriors moved to intercept her, but the chief emerged from his lodge at that moment and motioned them back. Buffalo's Back Fat watched Alena for a moment, then looked past her and saw the riders approaching from the south. A smile creased his leathery face.

Alena came to a stop at the edge of the village, her heart pounding wildly. She could tell now that although there were only two horses, more than Viktor and the warrior called Wolverine were mounted on the animals. Of course, she told herself. They had the boy with them, the grandson of the chief. But there was someone else as well, she thought. . . .

Just then, Buffalo's Back Fat stepped up beside her. "Your man had returned with Wolverine. If he has my grandson with him, the two of you will go free. Buffalo's Back Fat promises this to you."

Alena glanced over at him, reluctant to take her eyes off the riders, and saw that practically the entire village had gathered to welcome the returning warriors. Crystal Stone moved close to Buffalo's Back Fat, slipping her hand inside his arm.

"I'm just so glad Viktor is safe," Alena said, then added, "and that your grandson has been rescued, too."

The riders were close enough now so that she could see the boy, perched on the back of the chestnut in front of Wolverine. Viktor also had someone riding with him, and that someone was definitely a woman, Alena realized, feeling a sudden, unexpected surge of jealousy.

The dun and the chestnut reached the outskirts of the village. Viktor was leading the chestnut, Alena saw. Something had to be wrong with Wolverine. Perhaps the warrior was wounded. Viktor seemed to be unhurt, and that was really all Alena cared about at the moment.

Viktor brought the horses to a stop, and as he did so, the women of the Blackfoot village began pointing at the woman riding with him. They called out harsh words that could only be jeers and insults. The woman had to be one of the Crows, Alena decided. For some reason, Viktor and Wolverine had brought along a captive.

She could worry about that later. Right now, she wanted Viktor to take her into his arms and tell her that everything was going to be all right.

But it was not all right, she realized suddenly. The children of the village were shouting at the boy who rode with Wolverine, just like the women were doing with Viktor's prisoner. A couple of the young men even picked up pebbles and threw them at the boy until Viktor roared, "Stop!" From the look on his face, he was as bewildered as Alena.

She glanced again at Buffalo's Back Fat. The smile that had been on the chief's face a few moments earlier had disappeared. It had been replaced by a cold, stony mask. He barked orders to his warriors, and several of them sprang forward to help Wolverine down from the horse. Alena could see now that the man was badly wounded, more dead than alive. He had been tied onto his mount so that he would not fall off.

A grim-faced Viktor lowered the Crow woman to the ground, where several of the Blackfoot women promptly grabbed her and shoved her toward one of the lodges, slapping and kicking and striking her with sticks all the way. Another Blackfoot woman stepped forward and took charge of the boy, speaking sharply to the children who were still trying to pelt him with stones.

Viktor swung a leg over the back of the dun and slid to

the ground. Unable to restrain herself any longer, Alena darted forward. "Oh, Viktor," she cried, "are you all right?"

"Of course, little one," he said, and his deep, rumbling voice was the most welcome sound she had ever heard. "To a Cossack, this harsh land is as nothing. You should know that by now." He gave her a quick, awkward embrace, then turned to Buffalo's Back Fat. "Wolverine is badly hurt. I did what I could for him, but he needs more attention than I could give him."

"He shall be cared for," Buffalo's Back Fat said. "He will be taken to his lodge, and Stands with a Stick will see to him." He gestured curtly at the woman and the boy as they were being led away. "Who are these people, and why have you brought them here?"

Viktor's look of puzzlement grew as Alena glanced up at him. "The woman is a Crow who was looking after your grandson."

"That is *not* my grandson! That is a Crow whelp!"

21

Viktor gaped at the chief in astonishment and shock. When he was finally able to talk again, he said, "A Crow? Are you sure?"

"I know my own grandson," Buffalo's Back Fat gritted. Beside him, Crystal Stone stood with tears glittering in her eyes. "Why have you brought this boy to our village, white man?"

"I . . . I thought he was the right one."

The revelation came crashing down on Viktor like a great weight. To have gone through all the danger, to have risked his life a dozen times over, to have suffered through the hardships of the past few days . . .

All for *nothing*!

He became aware that Buffalo's Back Fat was speaking to him again. "Wolverine did not tell you the boy was a Crow?" the chief asked.

"Wolverine has been out of his head from his wounds and the fever that grips him ever since we fled the Crow village," Viktor explained. A fresh wave of dismay washed over him. It was nothing short of miraculous that the wounded warrior had lived this long. He might still die, and if he did, the sacrifice of his life would be in vain.

Crystal Stone was speaking quickly to her husband in

their language. After a moment Buffalo's Back Fat turned to him again, and in a voice that was not quite as cold and menacing, said, "The boy wears the clothes of my grandson. He is a thieving Crow. He must have stolen them."

"There was another boy in the lodge," Viktor muttered. "I thought *he* was a Crow. But he must have been the one we sought."

For an instant a look of pain flickered across Buffalo's Back Fat's face. Viktor and Wolverine had been so close to his grandson . . . and yet the boy was undoubtedly still a captive of the Crows.

"What about the woman?" Viktor asked.

Buffalo's Back Fat turned and called out to the Blackfeet women who were forcing the captive into one of the lodges. They stopped, and the chief went over to her. His hands moved in what Viktor knew to be the almost universal sign language of the Indians roaming the American plains. The Crow woman responded angrily with curt gestures of her hands. Buffalo's Back Fat sighed heavily and motioned for the women to take the prisoner away. He came back to face Viktor and Alena, who stood trembling slightly in the circle of Viktor's arm.

"The woman is Grass Waving in the Wind, the wife of Climbs High, the Crow chief," Buffalo's Back Fat said. "And the boy is their son, Rabbit's Hind Foot."

"Then I have truly failed." Viktor knew what this might mean to both him and Alena. He looked over at her and said, "I am sorry, little one."

She rested a hand on his chest. "You did the best you could, Viktor. You did more than any other man could have." She was obviously upset and worried, but the admiration in her voice was genuine.

To Viktor's surprise, a faint smile appeared on the face of Buffalo's Back Fat. "Perhaps you have not failed, white man," the chief said. "Perhaps what you have done is a good thing, whether you meant for it to be or not."

"But this Crow chief, Climbs High," Viktor said, not understanding, "surely he will come after his wife and son. He will make war on the Blackfeet to get them back."

"Perhaps . . . perhaps not." Buffalo's Back Fat turned to the warriors who had gathered at the edge of the village. He began calling out in his native tongue, the tone of command unmistakable. The chief was giving orders of some sort. But orders to do what?

Viktor and Alena looked at each other, frowning in confusion. They had no answers to the questions, but Viktor was sure they would find out what Buffalo's Back Fat had in mind.

Perhaps all too soon.

Not long after that, riders galloped out of the Blackfoot village on swift Indian ponies. Viktor was in the chief's lodge by that time, sitting by the fire and hungrily eating the bowl of stew Crystal Stone had cooked. Alena sat beside him, reaching out from time to time to touch his arm or his shoulder, as if to reassure herself that he was really there. As Viktor ate, Buffalo's Back Fat sat cross-legged nearby and explained the plan he had conceived when he discovered the identities of the Crow captives. To Viktor's way of thinking, seasoned as it was by years in the service of the czar, the plan sounded feasible. But it would be dangerous for all involved, there was no denying that.

Not long before nightfall, Stands with a Stick entered the lodge and spoke solemnly and at length to the chief. For a moment Viktor suspected that the healer had brought bad news: that Wolverine had finally succumbed to his injuries. But then Buffalo's Back Fat nodded to the medicine man, turned to Viktor, and said in English, "Wolverine will live. His fever has broken."

Viktor closed his eyes and muttered a prayer of thanks in Russian. Alena seemed less affected by the chief's words, but that was understandable. She had not fought alongside Wolverine, had not risked her life with him as Viktor had.

Stands with a Stick spoke again to Buffalo's Back Fat, who listened intently and then translated for Viktor and Alena. "Wolverine will be very weak for a few days, but his strength will slowly return. Stands with a Stick says that you saved the life of Wolverine by caring for him as you did, white man. You could have easily let him die. You could have abandoned him."

Viktor sensed a question behind these words. He said, "I could not do that. We had faced the enemy together. We are like brothers now."

"Wolverine may not feel this way," Buffalo's Back Fat warned.

Viktor shrugged. "I cannot control the way Wolverine feels. I know only what is in my own head and heart."

Buffalo's Back Fat nodded, a light in his eyes saying he wanted to smile but considered the situation too grave to allow it. "It will take time for the messengers to reach the village of the Crows and return to us with Climbs High's answer. Perhaps by then Wolverine will be able to ride with us when we go forth to meet them."

Viktor hoped so. Considering what Buffalo's Back Fat had in mind, he would feel better knowing that Wolverine would be going with them, even though the warrior would not be strong enough to take part in the chief's plan.

"The council will meet tonight," Buffalo's Back Fat went on, "and I will tell them what I intend to do. We will smoke a pipe and say prayers to the spirits. We will ask them for their help and guidance."

Hearing the reverence in his voice, Viktor nodded. "Yes. That will be good." He left unspoken the thought that they might need more than the assistance of the spirits to be successful this time.

It took five days for the fast riders to reach the Crow camp and return to the Blackfoot village. Viktor admired the bravery of the warriors Buffalo's Back Fat had chosen for this task. They risked death by venturing into the land of the Crows, riding in the open as they did in the hope that the curiosity would temporarily overwhelm the Crow's hostility. Such proved to be the case, and after being spotted and surrounded by a party of Crow warriors, the Blackfoot emissaries had been able to sign that they carried an urgent message for Climbs High, chief of the Crows, from Buffalo's Back Fat, chief of the Piegan Blackfeet. They were taken to the village of the Crows, where they delivered their message and were given one to take back.

Viktor learned all of this only after the warriors' return. In the meantime he and Alena had been given a lodge to share. Viktor tried not to think about the way Alena had offered herself to him before he left on the mission with Wolverine, but that incident was in his mind, and he could tell by the way she blushed when he looked at her for too long that she remembered it, too. But the offer was not repeated, and Viktor was thankful for that. At night, since they were alone, they spread their sleeping robes on opposite sides of the lodge. The Blackfeet could think whatever they wanted.

During the days, Alena continued learning Blackfoot ways under the tutelage of Crystal Stone and the old women. Once she had begun to master the bone needles, they taught her how to take pieces of buckskin and fashion clothing. Her first efforts brought hoots of derisive laughter from the old women. Their reactions made Alena burn with anger and embarrassment. She was determined to show them that she could perform whatever task they set for her. Crystal Stone was a better teacher, and after a couple of days of working with her, Alena was able to piece together a shirt and pair of leggings for Viktor. She would have given the clothing to him then, but Crystal Stone explained in halting English and more fluent gestures that they would decorate the garments first. Alena enjoyed the beadwork much more than she did stitching the clothes. The Blackfeet used what they called pony beads, large beads made of opaque glass, as well as smaller beads of glass and metal, all of which came from the trading posts of the white men, and natural beads of stone and wood, along with berries and seeds. The wide variety of colors and sizes made it easy to fashion elaborate patterns on the clothes. As she worked, Alena hoped that Viktor would be proud of her accomplishment.

For his part, Viktor spent most of his time with the warriors of the band. Wolverine had recovered enough of his strength to talk more easily, and he told stories of how he and Viktor had raided the Crow camp and killed many of the enemy in battle. The fact that they had brought back the wrong boy was never mentioned; such a mistake did not detract from the courage and gallantry with which they had fought. Viktor understood and appreciated that.

But he could not forget that if he had scooped up the right boy in the Crow lodge, he and Alena might well be free by now. They might even have returned to Fort Union. As for himself, Viktor did not mind too much the days spent here with the Blackfeet, but he knew that Alena longed to return to civilization.

There were worse ways to pass the time than telling stories with men who loved to ride and fight, and in that respect, the Blackfeet were little different from the Cossacks. With Wolverine acting as translator, Viktor spun yarn after yarn about his people, the Free People, for that was what the name *Cossacks* meant. He told the Blackfoot warriors about the legendary Cossack hero Yermak, who had conquered all of Siberia at the head of an army of bloody-handed reivers. He told them of Khlit of the Curved Saber, who helped turn back an invasion of the Tartars, and Bogdan Hmelnicky, who liberated Poland from oppressive overlords. He spoke of Mazeppa, the Cossack boatman who helped Peter the Great defeat the Ottoman fleet. And he spoke as well of his own exploits during the bitterly cold winter of 1812, when the Cossacks under the command of the great *hetman* Platov played a major role in thwarting Napoleon's mad schemes of conquest.

The Blackfeet listened and nodded soberly for the most part, although during the most stirring passages they sometimes let out small yipping cries and shook their tomahawks over their heads. Viktor lowered his head at those moments so they would not see the smile that plucked at his mouth. Fighting men were much the same the world over, he reflected later as he listened to the Blackfeet tell stories of how they had battled for centuries against the Crows, the Hidatsas, the Assiniboins, and the Crees, as well as any other bands foolish enough to venture into their territory. Viktor could easily imagine a group of Cossacks listening to the stories of the Blackfeet and rattling their sabers in appreciation.

So the days passed enjoyably for Viktor and tolerably well for Alena, but both of them were still very glad when Buffalo's Back Fat's emissaries to the Crows returned, bearing Climbs High's response to the Blackfoot chief's proposal.

They spoke of this first to Buffalo's Back Fat alone, but then the council was summoned to the lodge of the chief, and Viktor was invited as well. When he stepped into the lodge, he could feel the sense or urgency and anticipation in the air. The way these people reckoned time, nearly a moon had passed since the Crow raid on the village. The kidnapped boy was still with the enemy, and that situation could not be tolerated much longer, even if it meant all-out war.

The weary riders were seated on the ground next to the cooking fire in the center of the lodge. Buffalo's Back Fat sat opposite them. He rose and turned to face the members of the council, as well as Viktor. With an expression that betrayed no emotion, he spoke for several minutes in the Blackfoot tongue. The members of the council nodded, and Viktor could read no more from their faces than he could from that of Buffalo's Back Fat. Then the chief looked directly at him and said in English, "The chief of the Crows, Climbs High, has agreed. He will trade my grandson for his wife, Grass Waving in the Wind, and his son, Rabbit's Hind Foot."

Viktor felt a surge of relief. He might yet have a chance to rectify the mistake he had made in the village of the Crows.

"We will leave tomorrow and ride south," Buffalo's Back Fat went on. "The Crows will meet us between our land and theirs, at the river known as the Little Sleep. There we will trade." The chief came closer to Viktor and laid a hand on his shoulder. "You and I will ride forth with the prisoners to meet the Crows."

Viktor tried to keep the surprise off his face. Buffalo's Back Fat was honoring him, he knew, simply by inviting him to come along with the Blackfeet, and this after Viktor had brought the wrong boy back from the Crow village! The gesture showed the chief still had faith in the Cossack.

"I pledge my life to your cause, Stu-mick-o-sucks," Viktor said, a slight catch in his voice. "I will see your grandson brought back safely to this village, or I will draw breath no longer."

The hand of Buffalo's Back Fat tightened on his shoulder. Viktor glanced at the other warriors, expecting to see disapproval on their faces because he had been selected to accompany their chief, but instead they were all regarding him with expressions of admiration and encouragement. Viktor realized something at that moment that had never occurred to him before.

Somehow, in spite of the differences in their cultures and the bloodshed that had accompanied his journey to this land, he was now one of them.

He was as much a Blackfoot as a white man could ever be.

22

ALENA WAS LESS IMPRESSED by this new development.

"Why do you have to go again?" she asked in a voice that was almost a wail. They were in the lodge they had been sharing. "You already went with Wolverine to rescue the boy."

"And we failed," Viktor pointed out. "*I* failed. The boy was there, but I did not free him. Now I have another chance."

"Another chance to die and leave me here alone with these savages," Alena said bitterly. As soon as the words were out of her mouth, she realized how they had sounded, and she threw herself in Viktor's arms and cried, "I'm sorry! I did not mean that, Viktor. I am only worried about you."

Viktor knew that wasn't true, but he could not blame Alena for being frightened. She was thousands of miles from her home, she had seen her beloved aunt killed before her eyes, and she had spent the past few weeks never knowing what sort of danger the next moment might bring. That was enough to put quite a strain on anyone, let alone a young woman who was really little more than a girl.

He patted her on the back. "It will be fine. Nothing will

happen except that the chief's grandson will come home safely."

Tears glistened in Alena's eyes. She wiped them away with the back of her hand as she stepped away from Viktor. A brave smile appeared on her face, though it cost her a visible effort. "I will not complain anymore," she promised. "I made something for you."

"What would that be, Princess?"

"These." Alena took a bundle from under one of the buffalo robes and extended it toward Viktor. "They are yours, and you would honor me by wearing them."

He smiled as his blunt fingers untied the thin length of rawhide fastened around the bundle. As he shook out the contents, he saw that they were a pair of buckskins. Fringe and a row of beads ran down the sides of the leggings, and the shirt front was decorated with an elaborate, colorful sunburst design, with beaded arrowhead shapes on the back. Viktor looked up at Alena in surprise.

"You made these?"

"Yes," she said. "Crystal Stone showed me how. Do you like them?"

"They are . . . beautiful." The big Cossack swallowed hard, as surprised by the depth of the emotion he felt as he was by this evidence of skills he had not known Alena possessed. Probably she had not known, either.

"Will you wear them," she asked, "when you go with Buffalo's Back Fat to trade for his grandson?"

Viktor nodded, still having trouble speaking. "I will be honored," he finally said.

"And I will go with you."

That comment brought his head up again in surprise. "What?"

"When you and Buffalo's Back Fat and the other warriors go to meet the Crows, I am coming, too."

Without hesitation, Viktor shook his head. "That is impossible, little one," he said. "This is a matter for warriors, not for—"

"Not for women?" Alena gave a defiant toss of her head,

which made the long red hair swirl around her shoulders. "Are none of the Blackfoot women going?"

Viktor knew that Crystal Stone was planning to travel with the Blackfoot party, but that was different: she was the boy's grandmother. Several other women, wives of some of the warriors, were going as well, to help stand guard over the Crow prisoners. Grass Waving in the Wind and Rabbit's Hind Foot had been in their charge.

But that did not mean Alena should travel with them. He said, "What the Blackfeet do does not matter. You are Russian, not Blackfoot."

"That was once true of you as well, Viktor," she said. "Now I am not so sure."

He scowled. Her words were perhaps even more on target than she suspected. She was just trying to win an argument, but in truth, Viktor was beginning to think of himself as a Blackfoot. Their way of life was hard and brutal, filled with violence and death—but so was that of the Cossacks. It was said that Cossacks were born with a horse underneath them and a saber in their hands. If a tomahawk or a lance or a bow was put in place of the saber, the same could be said of the Blackfeet.

"The Blackfeet think I am your woman," Alena went on. "If this was true, I would want to be at your side."

"But it is not true," Viktor said quietly. "You are nobility. My mission is to protect you."

"In Russia I was of noble blood. Here that means nothing, and you know it. Here I am only a woman, as you are only a man. And if I cannot truly be your woman, Viktor Alexandrovitch, I am still your friend. I would be at your side when you ride with the Blackfeet to meet the Crows."

Viktor sensed this was an argument he was not going to win. And he knew that he could count on Buffalo's Back Fat to see to Alena's safety. The final part of the plan would be carried out by Viktor and Buffalo's Back Fat alone; Alena could remain behind with Wolverine, the rest of the warriors, and Crystal Stone and the other women. Whatever the outcome, she would be on hand to witness it.

"If this is what you really want, I will speak to Buffalo's Back Fat," he said. "I cannot promise that he will allow you to accompany us."

"I know that." She put a hand on his arm and smiled warmly. "Thank you, Viktor. I hope we are never separated again."

Once more she embraced him, and he said, "I hope so, too, little one. I hope so, too."

But whether or not he actually meant it, he could not have said.

A good-sized party left the Blackfoot village early the next morning. Buffalo's Back Fat, Stands with a Stick, and several important warriors who were part of the council rode in the lead, followed by a group of other warriors including Wolverine and Viktor. Wolverine's wounds were tightly bound up. He had lost weight during his ordeal, and there was a hint of pallor beneath his coppery skin. But he sat straight on the back of the chestnut stallion and carried a lance like the other men.

Viktor was mounted on the lineback dun he had named Saber. He wore the magnificent buckskins Alena had given him. They fit him better than the ones he had first worn, and he was filled with pride for her every time someone looked at his garments in admiration.

In the next group of riders came Crystal Stone and the other women, Alena in their midst. The two prisoners were there, too, the Crow woman and her son, looking as sullen and hostile as ever. As far as Viktor could determine, they had not been mistreated during their captivity. He hoped the same could be said of the grandson of Buffalo's Back Fat.

Bringing up the rear was another party of warriors. Despite the considerable size of the group, plenty of warriors had been left behind to guard the village in case another tribe decided to attack. This time, anyone foolish enough to try to raid the Blackfoot village would be in for a deadly welcome.

Viktor had no idea which of the streams he and Wolverine had crossed during their earlier trip was known to the Blackfeet as the Little Sleep. He would see it for himself soon enough. Buffalo's Back Fat estimated that they would arrive at their destination late the next day. If the Crows were there, too, the exchange of prisoners would take place on the following day. That was the arrangement the messengers from Buffalo's Back Fat had reached with Climbs High.

The group rode boldly all day, taking no pains to avoid the high ground as Viktor and Wolverine had done. No one would attack a party this large without stopping to think twice. They would be safe enough—until the rendezvous with the Crows. After that, who could say?

They camped that night in a little valley that was bursting with the new life of spring. Wildflowers carpeted the meadow. It was as beautiful a place as Viktor had ever seen, and he could easily imagine staying here the rest of his life. Even Alena seemed taken by the surroundings. Early the next morning, as the camp was awakening and the Blackfeet were preparing to leave, he found her looking out over the flower-covered landscape with a smile on her face.

"It's lovely," she said. "For all its dangers, this land can be very appealing."

Viktor nodded. "I have felt the same thing."

"But it is not like Mother Russia, of course," Alena added quickly. "Nothing can take her place."

"Of course not," Viktor said with a shake of his head, but he was only going along with Alena so that she would not have something else to worry about.

Already, he had begun thinking about staying here when Alena returned to civilization. He would accompany her back to Fort Union, naturally, and perhaps even farther than that if need be, until he felt confident that she would soon be safe in the bosom of her family in Moscow. But then he could come back here, to this wild, beautiful land, to the people among whom he had surprisingly found such kindred spirits. The idea was quite . . . intriguing.

But first, there was the matter of the grandson of Buffalo's Back Fat. The boy had to be brought back safely to *his* family, just as Alena had to be returned to hers. Viktor was willing to risk his life to see both of those goals fulfilled.

The Blackfeet, the Crow prisoners, and the two Russians rode on, heading due south, Viktor judged. Around the middle of the afternoon, Wolverine nudged his horse up next to Viktor's and pointed at the tree-dotted knoll to the east.

"That is the Bear's Mound," the Blackfoot warrior said. "Not far now to the River of the Little Sleep."

"I will be glad when we get there," Viktor said. "I am ready to meet the Crows and be done with this."

"A Blackfoot warrior is always ready to meet the enemy." Wolverine glared as if he could already see the Crows. "I wish I could fight them at your side, white man."

"There will be no fighting, if all goes as Buffalo's Back Fat has planned."

Wolverine's snort of contempt clearly expressed his view of the plan.

Viktor had sensed a change in the warrior during Wolverine's period of recuperation. The hatred the Indian had felt for him, even after Viktor had saved his life during the buffalo stampede, had vanished. Like the other men of the band, he now accepted Viktor as one of them, or at least as close to that as a white man could ever attain. Perhaps that was because Viktor had saved his life a second time, during the flight from the Crow village, or because the big Cossack had proven his bravery in battle. Viktor did not know the exact reason, nor did he care. What mattered to him was that now he and Wolverine could call each other "friend" and mean it.

Alena would never reach that point, Viktor sensed. She could neither forgive nor forget what had happened to the others in the Russian expedition. Nor should she, he decided. She had to be true to herself, just as he did.

Not long after passing the Bear's Mound, they reached the River of the Little Sleep, just as Wolverine had predicted. As Buffalo's Back Fat called a halt atop a hill overlooking the wide, slow-moving stream, Viktor glanced around and recalled passing through here with Wolverine. The river ran from west to east through a narrow valley. Viktor suspected that in rainy seasons, or when the snowmelt from the distant mountains was abundant, the river would run much faster. Now it was lazy but still almost majestic as it twisted through the hills.

"This is the place," Buffalo's Back Fat announced, and with that simple statement, he dismounted, folded his arms across his chest, and stood peering across the river at the hills to the south while the others in the Blackfoot party began making camp.

As a woman, Alena was expected to set up the small, tentlike structure that would serve as their shelter, but Viktor helped her, knowing that setting up a tepee would be difficult for her. The Blackfoot women frowned in disapproval at this, but Viktor ignored them and hoped Alena would, too. Just because *he* had adapted so well to Indian ways did not mean that she should have.

That minor problem soon ceased to matter. A series of yips from the warriors told Viktor that something was happening. He hurried over to the crest of the hill, where Buffalo's Back Fat still stood, solemnly regarding the hills on the other side of the river.

Viktor saw what the other men had seen: riders had appeared on the hill directly opposite. In the lead was a tall man wearing a feathered headdress that made him seem even taller. There was something familiar about the man, and after a moment Viktor recognized him as the warrior who had ridden at the head of the Crow search party that had come so close to discovering him and Wolverine and the captives in the gully where they had camped on the way back to the Blackfoot village.

"That is Climbs High," Buffalo's Back Fat said. "He is the chief of the Crows."

"And the husband and father of our prisoners," Viktor said.

Buffalo's Back Fat nodded. "He has come as he said he would. He has kept this part of the bargain."

"What about the rest of it?"

Without taking his eyes off the distant figure in the feathered headdress, who seemed to be staring right back at him, Buffalo's Back Fat said, "Tomorrow, we will see."

23

As soon as the Crows appeared, a feeling of tension began to grow among the Blackfeet. It was still there the next morning when Viktor awoke. He had not slept well, and Alena had been restless as well. He suspected they were not the only ones in camp whose slumber had been uneasy.

What he felt had disturbed his sleep was not fear so much as it was anticipation. Of course, he was worried that something might go wrong and jeopardize not only his life and Alena's, but the boy's as well. But at the same time he was anxious to proceed with the trade of the hostages. The sooner it began, the sooner it would be over, one way or another.

Buffalo's Back Fat stood stop the hill, as if he had not moved from that spot since dismounting there the day before. As Viktor started up the slope to join him, Alena came hurrying up beside him.

"I am going with you," she said as she caught at his arm.

"You cannot," Viktor told her, wanting to be careful of her feelings but preoccupied now with other concerns. "Buffalo's Back Fat and I must go alone with the prisoners."

"You cannot stop me from going to the top of the hill so I can see."

Viktor frowned. He wished he could do that very thing, but again, he knew he was not going to win the argument with her.

The two of them were not the only ones climbing the hill. Wolverine strode up on Viktor's left side and exchanged a grim nod with the big Cossack. Several other Blackfoot warriors joined them. Crystal Stone came up to her husband and stood beside him with stoic patience that betrayed none of the raging emotions she had to be feeling. As the group gathered around Buffalo's Back Fat, Viktor peered across the river and saw a similar gathering on the opposite hill. Climbs High stood surrounded by perhaps a dozen of his men. For a long moment the Blackfeet and the Crows watched each other warily.

In a quiet voice, Viktor said to Alena, "You should not be here, little one. There may be much danger."

"I do not care," she said. "I want to be with you, Viktor."

"You will stay here when we go down to the river," he said firmly, reinforcing what he had told her earlier. Alena nodded. Viktor turned to Buffalo's Back Fat. "Can Climbs High be trusted to trade your grandson for his wife and child?"

"He is a Crow," Buffalo's Back Fat said. "He can never be trusted. But he agreed to the trade when the warriors I sent as messengers proposed it. We must believe he means what he said—for now."

Wolverine grunted. "I am still surprised he let our warriors live."

"He wants his wife and son returned to him. Even a Crow may sometimes be smart."

"Or cunning," Wolverine pointed out.

Buffalo's Back Fat inclined his head in acknowledgment of the veiled warning. "As I said, I do not trust him." He looked at Viktor. "Come."

Wolverine spoke again quickly, saying to his chief, "I still say I should be the one to go with you. If I had seen that the boy was not the right one—"

"You were hurt," Viktor said. "You almost died."

Buffalo's Back Fat said, "And you are not yet strong

enough to come with us to meet the Crows. You will stay here, Lis-sis-tsi. That is my decision."

Wolverine's jaw tightened, but he said, "And I will abide by it."

Buffalo's Back Fat made a gesture of command, and horses were brought up the hill for him and Viktor. The lineback dun was well rested and well fed; Viktor had seen to that himself. Not that they would need any great amount of speed or stamina from their mounts today, he mused. Whatever happened, it would happen right here, at the River of the Little Sleep.

Both men swung up onto their mounts. Alena raised a hand, as if she wanted to reach out to Viktor, but stopped the motion. Her chin lifted and she stood straight, a picture of courage much like Crystal Stone.

The women and a couple of Blackfoot warriors prodded the Crow prisoners up the hill. Buffalo's Back Fat reached down, took hold of the boy, and lifted him onto the horse in front of him. The boy was not struggling this morning, having perhaps figured out that he was soon to be reunited with his father. The woman mounted behind Viktor and slipped her arms around his waist. He was not worried about her escaping, not when they were this close to completing the arrangement.

On the other side of the river, Climbs High had also mounted his horse, and in front of him was a smaller figure that Viktor assumed was Buffalo's Back Fat's grandson. For a second the Cossack worried that Climbs High might have substituted another Crow boy to trick the Blackfeet, but then he discarded the idea. Buffalo's Back Fat never would have considered such an act of treachery, Viktor knew, and he suspected the chiefs of the Blackfeet and the Crows had more in common than they would ever admit.

Climbs High was not coming to meet them alone. Another Crow strode forward, a massive warrior whose size and strength was evident even from this distance. The man mounted up and moved his horse alongside Climbs High's. Together, they started riding slowly down the hill toward the river.

On this side of the stream, Viktor and Buffalo's Back Fat did the same.

It seemed to take much longer to reach the northern bank of the river than the few minutes that were actually required. Viktor would not have been surprised to discover that an hour had passed since he and Buffalo's Back Fat had started down the hill, though he knew logically that was not the case. He wondered briefly if time was passing equally slowly for Climbs High and the other Crow.

The hooves of the horses finally splashed into the river, sending up droplets of water that sparkled brilliantly in the morning sunlight. On the other side of the stream, which Viktor estimated was about fifty yards wide, Climbs High and his companion were also entering the water on horseback. Now that they were closer, Viktor's keen eyes could clearly see the face of the boy riding in front of Climbs High. He recognized the youngster from the few times he had seen him at Fort Union. If not for the darkness and the confusion of battle in the Crow camp, Viktor would have been able to pick out the right boy, he was sure of that.

But what was past was past, and now all Viktor could do was try to make up for the error he had committed on that fateful night a couple of weeks earlier.

Slowly, the two small parties rode toward each other. In a matter of moments they would meet in the center of the stream which rose several feet on the legs of the horses. Viktor felt the arms of the Crow woman, Grass Waving in the Wind, tighten around his waist. He sensed that she was looking at her husband. A glance over at the boy perched on the horse in front of Buffalo's Back Fat showed the same intensity on his face that Viktor sensed coming from the woman. The Blackfeet and the Crows watched from the hills without making a sound. Even the birds and insects of springtime had fallen silent, as if they, too, sensed the gravity of this situation.

Quietly, Buffalo's Back Fat said to Viktor, "My grandson and this Crow boy will trade places when we reach the middle of the stream. Let the woman go then as well. But be ready for the Crows to try some sort of trick."

"What can they do when we are out here in the middle of the river?" Viktor asked. "We are out of range of the bows on both sides."

"Just be ready."

Viktor grunted in acknowledgment of the command. With all the history of trouble between the Blackfeet and the Crows, he could not blame Buffalo's Back Fat for being suspicious.

Thirty yards separated the two small groups, then twenty, then ten. Viktor saw the hatred on the haughty face of Climbs High. The other Crow was as big as Viktor had thought him to be, making him something of a rarity. Viktor himself towered over most of the Blackfeet, and this warrior seemed equally tall. The man's coarse black hair hung in two thick braids, and his face was set in a permanent scowl. His features were heavily scarred, the result of some disease, though, rather than of battle. But he had battle scars, too, Viktor noted.

Climbs High brought his horse to a stop and lifted his hand in a signal to his companion to do likewise. Buffalo's Back Fat reined in his mount, and Viktor followed suit. The two groups were now ten feet apart.

Buffalo's Back Fat had his arm around the son of Climbs High. Moving slowly so that his actions could not be mistaken, he lowered the boy into the river. The water came up to the youngster's waist. Buffalo's Back Fat kept a hand on the boy's shoulder.

Just as carefully, Climbs High lowered the grandson of Buffalo's Back Fat. The river, which was still receiving melting snow from the mountains, had to be cold, but neither boy's face revealed anything. They wore the same stony masks as their elders.

Buffalo's Back Fat signed to Climbs High, who signed in return. Each man released the boy standing next to him. The two children walked forward slowly, glaring as they passed each other.

Viktor turned his head and said over his shoulder to the woman, "You can go to your husband now." He motioned for her to dismount, knowing she could not understand his words.

Grass Waving in the Wind slid off the dun into the stream. The water billowed her buckskin dress slightly. She took two steps toward Climbs High and the other Crow.

Then she turned and lunged toward Buffalo's Back Fat, and the sun glinted on something she gripped tightly in her upraised hand.

Too late, Viktor realized that she had somehow slipped his knife from its sheath. She could have murdered him at any time, he thought, but instead she had waited until she could strike at the chief of her enemies. Buffalo's Back Fat was turned away from her and could not see her coming.

Those thoughts went through Viktor's mind in a bare fraction of an instant. He rammed his heels into the flanks of the dun and sent the horse plunging forward in the river. He left its back in a dive that sent him toward the Crow woman, even as he shouted a warning to Buffalo's Back Fat. Grass Waving in the Wind jabbed the blade toward the Blackfoot chief, but Viktor grabbed her arm and crashed into her before the desperate thrust could reach Buffalo's Back Fat. Both of them fell into the frigid water with a huge splash.

Meanwhile, the big, ugly Crow warrior yanked a tomahawk from his belt and swung it toward Buffalo's Back Fat with a harsh cry. At the same time Climbs High jerked his horse toward the spot where Viktor and Grass were struggling, his own tomahawk upraised for a slashing blow at Viktor's head.

Viktor sensed the danger and shoved the furious, sputtering woman aside. He twisted her wrist as he did so, forcing her to drop the knife, which fell into the muddy water and vanished. Viktor ducked under the blow from Climbs High and wheeled around to face the Crow chief. As he did so, he saw Buffalo's Back Fat blocking the tomahawk of the other Crow with the short lance he carried.

A few feet away Rabbit's Hind Foot and the grandson of Buffalo's Back Fat were wrestling, engaged in just as serious a struggle as their elders.

The plan might have worked, Viktor thought fleetingly, and the exchange of prisoners might have been successful, had not Grass Waving in the Wind tried to kill Buffalo's Back Fat. But now everything had collapsed.

On the hill overlooking the river from the northern side, Alena saw what was happening, and the tightly wound ball of nervousness inside her belly exploded into pure fear. "Viktor!" she cried as she watched the big Cossack narrowly avoid Climb High's tomahawk. "Look out!"

Close beside her, Wolverine lifted his lance and shook it in fury. "*Kyai-yo!* I knew the Crows could not be trusted!" he shouted in his own tongue to the other Blackfoot warriors.

Howling and yipping in rage and defiance, they surged down the slope toward the river on foot, not bothering to go back for their ponies. Their only thought was to rush to the aid of their chief and the big white man who had allied himself with them.

Across the river, on the other hill, the Crows were doing the same thing. They swept down the slope toward the stream, ready to do battle with the hated Blackfeet.

In a matter of moments those two forces would come together, and the waters of the River of the Little Sleep would run red with blood.

Viktor had no time to think about the imminent battle. It was all he could do to avoid the blows of Climbs High and keep the Crow chief's horse from trampling him. The water around his legs slowed him down, and he knew that sooner or later Climbs High's tomahawk would connect.

It was time to take the fight to the enemy, Viktor decided.

He waited until he had parried another of Climbs High's blows, then surged up out of the water, leaping to wrap his arms around the Crow chief. Climbs High cried out as Viktor's great weight slammed into him and knocked him off the back of the horse. The animal shied away as Viktor and Climbs High landed in the river with another big splash.

Viktor clamped his fingers around Climbs High's wrist, holding the tomahawk away from him. He groped with his other hand for the man's throat, but the water in his eyes half-blinded him and prevented him from accomplishing his goal—which was to choke the life out of the Crow chief. The next moment, something else intervened. Huge hands took hold of Viktor's shoulders and tore him away from Climbs High with incredible strength. Viktor sprawled once more in the river.

He saw the other Crow warrior looming over him. The man must have abandoned his struggle with Buffalo's Back Fat when he saw that Viktor was about to overwhelm his chief. The massive Crow threw himself at Viktor with an incoherent shout.

Viktor rolled aside, thrashing in the water. He knew that if the Crow landed atop him, the man could hold him underneath the surface until he drowned. But the leap missed narrowly, and Viktor reached out to grapple with the Crow.

Not far away, Buffalo's Back Fat lunged toward the two boys and wrapped his arms around one of them, lifting him and pulling him away from the other boy. A quick look told Buffalo's Back Fat that he held his grandson in his arms once more. The Crow lad, Rabbit's Hind Foot, started after them, but Climbs High splashed around the milling horses and caught hold of his son's buckskin shirt, jerking him to a halt. Climbs High spoke sharply in the Crow tongue. He and Buffalo's Back Fat stood facing each other across several feet of water, each man panting slightly from exertion. The two boys trembled with the need to attack each other, but their elders restrained them.

On the banks of the broad river, the Blackfeet and the Crows had arrived, and several warriors nocked arrows to bowstrings. Someone on each side called out before the warriors could fire, warning them that they risked hitting their own chiefs. For agonizing seconds the two forces faced each other across the river, while in the middle of the stream, the desperate struggle between Viktor and the huge Crow warrior continued.

The Crow fought bare-handed at first, but Viktor threw

off every wrestling hold he tried to use. He even spilled
the Crow off his feet with a well-timed punch, catching the
man full in the face as he charged. This time, when the
Crow came up out of the water, he was clutching a knife
with a long, heavy blade.

Up on the hill, Alena and Wolverine stood with Crystal
Stone. Alena saw the sun glinting off the knife in the
Crow's hand and said, "Why doesn't someone help Viktor?
Why are your warriors just standing there on the bank?"

"This is between the two of them now. The Crows sense
that, as well as my people. No one shall interfere." Wolverine looked at Alena. "Your man would want it that way."

She sighed. "I know. . . ."

Near the confrontation between Viktor and the huge
Crow, Buffalo's Back Fat and Climbs High were still staring at each other in hatred, but they were holding their
emotions in check. A soaked, bedraggled Grass Waving in
the Wind came up beside Climbs High and took hold of
their son, pulling the boy into an embrace. Climbs High
motioned them away, and Grass started for the southern
bank of the river, tugging Rabbit's Hind Foot with her.

Buffalo's Back Fat told his grandson to go to the northern bank. The boy argued, saying that he wanted to stay
and kill Crows, but Buffalo's Back Fat repeated the order
sharply. Grudgingly, the boy began to trudge through the
sluggish current toward the bank where his grandfather's
warriors waited.

Slowly, Buffalo's Back Fat and Climbs High backed
away from each other, neither man willing to take his eyes
off the other.

In the water, the Crow giant feinted with the knife, then
swung it at Viktor's chest with surprising speed for a man
so large. But the big Cossack reacted quickly as well, and
the feint did not fool him. He was able to jerk back in time
to avoid the worst of the sweeping blow. The tip of the
blade still raked across his chest, slicing through the buckskin shirt Alena had made for him and leaving what felt
like a line of fire on his skin. Viktor roared, not so much

from the pain of the wound as from anger at the damage the Crow had done to Alena's handiwork.

The Crow charged, and Viktor met him squarely. He got both hands on the Crow's wrist and held the knife away from him. Twisting his body, he thrust his foot between the Crow's legs and unbalanced him. Like two trees toppling, the men fell, disappearing under the rolling surface of the river.

They came up again a moment later, Viktor still holding the wrist of the Crow's knife hand, as Buffalo's Back Fat and his grandson reached the bank where the rest of the Blackfeet waited tensely. Across the river, Climbs High, Grass Waving in the Wind, and Rabbit's Hind Foot had also reached safety. Now it came down to the struggle in the center of the stream. No one on either side wanted to interfere or even take their eyes off the battle.

The Crow balled his free hand into a fist and struck at Viktor's head. Viktor saw the blow coming and was able to move aside so that it merely grazed his skull above his ear. The Crow was off balance again, and Viktor was able to yank the man's arm behind his back, spinning him around. With blinding speed, Viktor let go of the Crow's wrist with his left hand and looped that arm around the man's throat from behind. The muscles in Viktor's shoulders bunched under the wet buckskin as he put his massive strength into pulling up on the Crow's trapped arm. Even over the splashing as they staggered around in the water, Viktor heard the cracking sound of the Crow's arm breaking.

The Crow cried out involuntarily, and the knife slipped from nerveless fingers. Viktor pressed his advantage, driving forward with his feet and legs so that both of them fell. The Cossack landed on top, his head still above the water. He added his other arm to the grip on the Crow's neck and increased the pressure. Viktor's breath hissed between his tightly clenched teeth as he struggled to hold the thrashing warrior under the surface. The man's struggles were growing desperate, but Viktor had a death grip on him, and it would not be budged. The old knife wound in his shoulder, which he had thought completely healed, began to throb and burn.

This fight had gone on long enough. Viktor could not wait for the Crow to drown. He tightened his grip even more and heaved.

He sensed more than heard the snapping of the Crow warrior's neck.

The sudden limpness of death that seized the man was unmistakable. Viktor released the body and let it slip completely under the surface. He stood up, his pulse pounding in his head like all the drums of all the tribes that inhabited this vast wilderness. Turning away from the dead man, he staggered toward the shore where Buffalo's Back Fat and the other Blackfeet were waiting.

On the other bank, the Crows lifted their bows again, ready to send flint-tipped missiles of death across the river at the man who had just killed their champion. Climbs High barked a command and gestured curtly before any of the Crows could fire, and slowly, reluctantly, they lowered their bows.

Buffalo's Back Fat was waiting to greet Viktor. He grasped the Cossack's arm to steady him as Viktor stumbled out of the river.

"Climbs High does you an honor," Buffalo's Back Fat said. "He refuses to let his warriors kill you."

Viktor looked back over his shoulder. He saw Climbs High using sign language while shouting defiantly across the river.

"He says that one day he will kill you himself," Buffalo's Back Fat translated.

Viktor drew several lungfuls of air into his body, trying to catch his breath and calm his racing pulse. He said, "How . . . how do I tell him . . . I will be waiting for that day?"

With a grunt of admiration and a smile, Buffalo's Back Fat demonstrated the sign for Viktor. Viktor turned, stepped away from the chief so that Climbs High could see him clearly, and repeated the sign. He ended with an unmistakable sign of his own, a clenched fist held high in the air over his head.

"Viktor! Viktor!"

The sound of Alena's voice made him turn away from the river, ignoring the Crows on the opposite shore. He saw Alena running down the hill toward him, trailed more slowly by Wolverine. The Blackfoot warriors along the bank parted to allow her through. She ran into his arms when he held them out to her, and her own arms went around him tightly.

Viktor patted her head, his big hand gentle on the thick red hair. "There, little one," he said. "Everything is all right now. You are getting your dress wet."

"I don't care," she said through the tears that rolled down her cheeks. "I thought you were going to be killed!"

Viktor glanced over his shoulder as he held her. On the other side of the river, the Crows were leaving. "No one else will die this day," he said quietly.

Wolverine reached him then and pounded him on the shoulder. "A good fight, my friend! A very good fight!"

"Friend?" Viktor repeated with a grin. "You said you would have let me die and claimed the Crows killed me if you had the chance."

Wolverine drew himself up and said haughtily, "Even a Blackfoot warrior can make a mistake."

Viktor left an arm around Alena's shoulders as he turned to Buffalo's Back Fat. "Will there be a war with the Crow on another day?"

"Of course," Buffalo's Back Fat replied, clearly surprised by the question. "It is the way of our people. But today my grandson is once again with his people, and there is peace. When we return to our village, there will be a feast to celebrate his homecoming."

Flanking the boy with Crystal Stone, Buffalo's Back Fat led the Blackfeet away from the river. Viktor and Alena walked among them, and once again Viktor was struck by the way the Blackfeet had accepted him. He glanced back one last time at the hill on the far side of the river, just in time to see the last of the Crows disappear. That was

Climbs High, Viktor noted from the distant figure's head-dress, and the Crow chief now held a lance, which he thrust above his head and shook in defiance at the Blackfeet—and Viktor. Then he vanished.

Viktor tightened his arm around Alena's shoulders and walked on, tired but triumphant.

24

A HUGE FIRE BURNED brightly in the center of the Blackfoot village. Around it dancers shuffled in ageless ritual while drummers beat out the rhythm on tight-stretched buffalo hide and chanted songs that had been old when the ancestors of these people were young. It was a spectacle that took some getting used to, Viktor thought, but once one did, the dancing and drumming and chanting had a tremendous power.

He sat near the fire, Alena at his right hand, Wolverine to his left. To Alena's right was the grandson of Buffalo's Back Fat, who held the balalaika she had given him. Earlier, he had proudly demonstrated how well he could play the instrument for the young woman the Blackfeet all called Flame Hair.

The proud grandparents of the boy sat on his other side, Crystal Stone beaming with happiness, Buffalo's Back Fat looking more reserved, as befitted a chief. But his eyes shone brightly, and anyone looking at him could tell that this was a good time for him.

The celebration had been going on for hours, and according to Wolverine, it would continue all night and probably into the next day. The group led by Buffalo's Back Fat had ridden into the village late in the afternoon, yipping and shouting to announce the success of their mission. The grandson of the chief was back where he belonged at last. Right away, the women of the village began to cook, because there would be great feasting as well as dancing. By this time, in fact, Viktor had eaten so much that he was beginning to feel stuffed.

Wolverine leaned over toward him and said, "We have a surprise for you."

Viktor chuckled. "The past weeks have held many surprises, many of them not very good. What is one more?"

"I do not know if you will like this one," Wolverine said. "No longer will we call you white man. Now you will have a Blackfoot name, like your woman Flame Hair."

"Did you hear that, Viktor?" Alena asked, excited in spite of herself. "Your own name in Blackfoot!"

"I heard," Viktor said. "What will you call me?"

Wolverine gestured toward Buffalo's Back Fat. "That is for our chief to decide."

Clearly, Buffalo's Back Fat had been waiting for this moment. He stood up, uncoiling easily from his cross-legged position despite his years. The others followed his example. The singing and drumming and dancing continued as Buffalo's Back Fat came to stand in front of Viktor.

The chief rested his hands on Viktor's shoulders. "You are responsible for the safe return of my grandson. You have killed many of our enemies, the Crows. You are one of us now, and we will call you Three Ponies."

Viktor took a deep breath, struggling with the emotions coursing through him. This impromptu naming ceremony meant as much to him as anything that had ever happened to him. "I am honored, Buffalo's Back Fat," he managed to say after a moment. "But I have only one pony, the dun I call Saber."

Wolverine spoke up. "This is true, but you are as *big* as three ponies, my friend!"

Everyone laughed, even Buffalo's Back Fat, and with a grin, Viktor said, "I will wear the name with pride."

"And from now on," Alena said, "I will be the woman of Three Ponies."

Viktor tried to look sternly at her, but his glance of disapproval was quickly transformed into another grin.

With the bestowing of his new name out of the way, the celebration continued. Viktor had no idea what time it was when he and Alena finally left for their lodge. All he knew was that after battling the giant Crow warrior to the death, riding most of two days back to the Blackfoot village, and eating and drinking much more than he should have, he was exhausted. He was half-asleep by the time he rolled into his buffalo robes.

But he came awake when he felt Alena stealing close to him and sliding her arms around him. Her breath was warm against his bearded cheek as she leaned over him in the darkness and whispered, "Three Ponies?"

"What do you want, Alena?"

"I am not Alena. I am Flame Hair, the woman of Three Ponies, the mighty Blackfoot warrior. I want you to love me, Three Ponies."

Viktor took a deep breath and rolled over, forcing her to pull back slightly from him. The fire in the center of the lodge was only embers now, and it gave off such a faint light that he could barely see her face. But the words she had spoken and the boldness with which her hands had played over his body when she embraced him were more than enough to tell him what she was feeling.

He sat up and put his hands on her shoulders to keep her from hugging him again. "I do love you, Alena," he said huskily. "You are my princess, my little one . . . my friend. But that is all there can ever be between us."

She strained against his hands. "Why?" she asked, her voice anguished now. "Why must that be all, Viktor? Our homeland and everyone we know are on the other side of the world! Here there is only the two of us. We are . . . all that we have. Unless—" She caught her breath. "Unless you have found a Blackfoot woman you wish to make your mate."

With an effort, he kept from laughing. "No," he said.

"Flame Hair is the only Blackfoot woman I could ever want."

"Then you do desire me!" she exclaimed. "And I am yours, Viktor. Why do you not take me?"

In truth, it would be all too easy to give in to what she wanted. She was lovely, and what she had said about everyone else they had ever known being on the other side of the world in Russia was also true. If they were going to stay here among the Blackfeet, then the natural thing to do would be to make her his woman, fully and completely.

But he knew she still longed to return to her home, and she could never go back to Russia after she had given herself to a Cossack. Even if she was not with child, she would know what had happened—and so would he. Nothing could ever be the same. . . .

"Some things are not meant to be," he said gently, hoping she would at least try to understand. *He* was not rejecting her; it was the culture in which they had both grown up that stood between them and always would. She had called him hidebound and rigid once before, and she was right. He could not go against the code of honor that made him what he was.

She sighed. "You are the most exasperating man! You still see me as the aristocrat, the noblewoman. Well, what if I *order* you to make love to me?"

"Then you would be Alena again, not Flame Hair, and the Blackfoot warrior Three Ponies would not have to obey you."

"Oh! You—"

In the shadows of the lodge, Viktor found her mouth and laid a finger on it, silencing her. "Good night, little one," he said. "Sleep well."

Then he turned away and rolled himself in his robes once more. For a moment Alena did not move, then he heard her sigh again and return to her own side of the lodge. Exhaustion claimed Viktor yet again, and he felt himself sliding into slumber.

But not before he heard Alena mutter, "Sleep well? Not likely . . . !"

Alena behaved quite coolly toward him the next day, and Wolverine noticed as much when the warrior came to the lodge to fetch Viktor.

"Flame Hair is unhappy," the warrior said, watching as Alena walked out of the lodge with a flip of her long hair.

"True," Viktor admitted, setting aside his empty bowl. Alena had brought him breakfast, as was expected of her, but she had said nothing as she delivered it, nor had she spoken while he was eating.

"You should keep your woman happy, Three Ponies."

"Sometimes that is an impossible task, my friend," Viktor said, uncomfortable with this entire conversation. He wished Wolverine would get on to whatever had brought him here this morning.

Thankfully, Wolverine did just that. "Buffalo's Back Fat has sent me to bring you to his lodge. He would speak with you."

"I am his to command," Viktor said with a nod. He followed Wolverine out of the lodge, and they started through the village toward the dwelling of Buffalo's Back Fat. Viktor had heard the drums and the chanting all night, and they continued this morning, although with far fewer participants. The celebration would soon be coming to an end.

He saw Alena sitting with Crystal Stone and some of the other women mending buckskins near the chief's lodge. Always, the work went on, in peace and war, in times of triumph and times of tragedy.

Inside the lodge, Buffalo's Back Fat greeted Viktor warmly and motioned for him to sit down. As Viktor did so, Alena and Crystal Stone entered the lodge as well, Alena looking puzzled. Viktor was surprised, too, but obviously Buffalo's Back Fat had told his wife to bring the young woman in. Crystal Stone went to sit beside her husband, and Buffalo's Back Fat gestured for Alena to take her place next to Viktor.

Reluctantly, Alena complied. If Buffalo's Back Fat noticed her hesitation, he ignored it. Instead, he began solemnly, "Eeh-nis-kin and I have decided that our grandson can no longer live with us. As long as he is here, he will be in danger from the Crows and our other enemies."

That announcement surprised Viktor. After everything they had all gone through to return the child to the village, he expected that nothing would ever pry the boy away from Buffalo's Back Fat again. And yet, what the chief said made sense. The boy's situation as the heir of Buffalo's Back Fat placed him in constant danger.

"What will you do with him?" Viktor asked.

"The one called M'Kenzie, at the white man's fort, offered to care for the boy once before, after the second time the Crows stole him. Now I will accept M'Kenzie's offer. The boy will live at the fort until he comes of age to be chief and take my place."

"You are going to Fort Union?" Viktor asked quickly.

Buffalo's Back Fat nodded. "We will leave in the morning."

Alena could not keep the excitement out of her voice as she said, "Then you can take us with you."

"If this is what you and Three Ponies wish," Buffalo's Back Fat said slowly.

"Oh, yes!"

Viktor felt the eyes of Buffalo's Back Fat and Wolverine and Crystal Stone. The chief said, "We had hoped you might decide to remain among us. But I have promised that you would go free if you returned my grandson to me, and you have done this thing, Three Ponies."

Viktor took a deep breath, finding it much more difficult than it should have been to say, "We should return to our own people. It is our way to be with them."

Buffalo's Back Fat nodded. "Then it shall be done."

Alena threw her arms around Viktor, her earlier anger

forgotten. "Oh, Viktor," she cried, "we are going home! We are going back to Russia!"

"Yes, little one," he said, and he hoped the hollowness he felt inside was not reflected in his voice.

25

By THE NEXT MORNING Alena was still just as excited about going back to Fort Union and, ultimately, to Russia. Some of her enthusiasm had even worn off on Viktor, who was getting the dun ready to ride when she came up to him.

"Viktor . . ." she said, and her voice was so pensive that he looked at her in surprise.

"What is it, Princess?" he asked, worried that something might be wrong.

"Do you really want to do this?"

He frowned. "Do what?"

"Go back to the fort."

"What else can we do?" he asked. "Now that the Blackfeet are willing to let us go, would you have us stay here with them?"

A shudder ran through Alena before she said, "No. They have treated us fairly decently, I suppose, but I can never forget that they killed my aunt and Frederick and poor Sasha and all of our friends."

"I know," Viktor said as he put a hand on her shoulder and squeezed lightly. "Wolverine is a good comrade-in-arms, but for all I know, he is the one who killed Zephaniah. They believe they were justified in attacking us because of that young man Frederick shot, but I cannot forget what they did."

She stepped closer to him and rested her hands on his chest, but there was nothing seductive in the gesture this time. "I'm glad you want to go back, too. I know you've been happy here, and I . . . I didn't want you doing it just because of me."

Viktor cupped her chin and chuckled. "For you, Princess, I would *swim* back to Russia!"

She laughed and said, "I believe you would, Viktor Alexandrovitch. I believe you would. . . ."

The party that prepared to leave the Blackfoot village to journey to Fort Union was fairly small. Buffalo's Back Fat and his grandson would accompany the two Russians, along with Wolverine and several warriors, just in case they ran into any enemies of the Blackfeet during the trip.

When they were ready to depart, Viktor helped Alena onto one of the Blackfoot ponies, a paint with a shaggy mane and a prancing gait. The horse suited her. Viktor was mounted on Saber, of course, and before he left the village, he reined the dun to a halt and looked back. To some, this place of hide lodges would be nothing but a squalid outpost in a barren, dangerous wilderness, but to Viktor it had been home for several weeks. He had formed some good friendships here, fought some good battles on behalf of these people. There was a chance he would never see them again, although he had not yet decided exactly what he would do when he and Alena reached Fort Union. He could not help feeling a pang of melancholy.

"Farewell, Eeh-nis-kin," he said to Crystal Stone. "Thank you for your kindness."

"Good-bye . . . Three Ponies," the chief's wife said in her laborious English. She switched to Blackfoot and said something else, and Buffalo's Back Fat translated, "She asks the spirits to watch over you and Flame Hair."

Viktor smiled and nodded at Crystal Stone. Alena reached down from her pony and caught hold of the older woman's hand, squeezing it tightly for a moment. Crystal

Stone was the closest thing to a friend that she had here among the Blackfoot, and Viktor was not sure she would have survived if the older woman had not looked after her.

Viktor said his farewells to several other warriors whose acquaintance he had made, then the party rode out of the village, heading southeast. Several days' ride would take them to Fort Union, where the steamships that plied the waters of the Missouri River made regular stops. In a few weeks he and Alena could be back in St. Louis, Viktor thought, and from there they could travel down the Mississippi to New Orleans, where they could board a ship that would take them to Vladivostok. It was a long overland journey from that port city to Moscow, but Viktor knew that by the end of summer, he and Alena might well be home once more.

If he decided to go with her all the way to Moscow . . .

And that was a decision he had not yet reached.

The journey passed without any trouble. The grandson of Buffalo's Back Fat had brought along the balalaika, and while they were camped at night, Alena taught him several Russian folk songs. The boy had a natural talent, Alena declared, and he was already much better with it than she had been after months of practice.

"You should have been my aunt Zora's pupil," Viktor heard her telling the boy one night, and he heard the catch in her voice as she spoke her aunt's name. "She tried so hard to teach me, but I was never very good."

The boy just smiled at her, not understanding the words she had spoken. Viktor went over to Alena and put a hand on her shoulder, hoping she would not start crying. Then he would have to explain to Buffalo's Back Fat and Wolverine and the others what was wrong. But she merely smiled bravely at him, and though tears glistened in her eyes for a moment, none rolled down her smooth cheeks.

A couple of days later, in the middle of the afternoon, the group of riders topped a small hill, and Buffalo's Back Fat reined in. As the others halted, the chief lifted an arm and pointed at something in the distance. Viktor recognized it as the stockade fence around Fort Union.

The grandson of Buffalo's Back Fat sat his horse between Viktor and Alena, the balalaika slung on his back. Wolverine was next to Viktor, and Buffalo's Back Fat was slightly in advance of the rest of the party. The chief turned his horse and said to Viktor, "There is the fort, Three Ponies. No one will stop you and Flame Hair from riding there."

"You are not going?" Viktor asked, remembering the friendship that seemed to exist between Buffalo's Back Fat and Kenneth McKenzie, who ran the trading post. George Catlin, the artist, might still be at the fort, too.

Buffalo's Back Fat shook his head. "The white man's army may want to make war on the Blackfeet for things that have been done. We will not go into the fort."

Viktor knew what the chief meant. Doubtless when the Russian expedition had failed to return, Captain Davis had sent out a search party to look for them. The soldiers would have found the bodies of the slain aristocrats and their Cossack and cavalry trooper escorts. To the American soldiers, it would look like the evidence of an Indian massacre, nothing more. It was indeed possible that a battle might result if the Blackfeet appeared near the fort.

"There is something I would ask you to do," Buffalo's Back Fat went on. "Will you take my grandson to the one called M'Kenzie, Three Ponies?"

"I will," Viktor promised.

"Then you have my thanks, and the thanks of my people."

Buffalo's Back Fat turned to the boy and spoke to him in the Blackfoot tongue. The youngster was obviously making an effort to be brave, even though he was going to be separated from his grandparents and the rest of his people for an undetermined amount of time. He replied to Buffalo's Back Fat with a great deal of dignity for his age.

Wolverine moved his horse closer to Viktor's mount. "Come back to our village someday, Three Ponies," he said, "and we will kill many Crows together. Their women will weep in their lodges for many days."

"Someday, my friend," Viktor said, and he hoped he would be able to keep that pledge.

"Do not forget, Climbs High is waiting to kill you."

"The Crow will have to be patient," Viktor said.

Wolverine laughed and reached out to clasp Viktor's wrist. Viktor returned the gesture, holding tightly to his friend for a long moment.

Then, without looking back, he and Alena started down the hill toward the fort, the boy riding between them.

A young soldier stood on the parapet inside the walls of Fort Union, staring off into the distance and looking bored and tired. Excitement was rare out here on the frontier, and when it came it wasn't always welcome, since it was usually in the form of Indian trouble, and that meant blood and death and horror. But some days, even the prospect of an attack didn't sound too bad; at least it would break the monotony, the trooper thought as he leaned on the butt of his rifle and hoped the sergeant of the guard didn't see him.

That was when he spotted the three distant figures riding toward the fort.

The young soldier straightened, frowning. Little more than black dots at first, the figures came steadily closer until the sentry could tell that they were three people on horseback. One of them seemed to be a big fella, mighty big, and then there was one that was middle-sized, and finally a little one in between. For a second the trooper remembered a story his ma used to tell him about a little girl and three bears, then he shook his head and put that thought out of his mind. Those weren't bears riding toward the fort, they were people, and they were wearing buckskins. Indians, sure enough—but since when did Indians have long red hair, which was what the middle-sized figure seemed to have on its head?

When faced with a situation this confusing, there was only one thing to do, the soldier knew.

He turned his head and yelled, "Sergeant! Riders comin'

in, Sarge!" Under his breath, he muttered, "And you ain't goin' to believe who they look like."

A few minutes later, in the headquarters building of the fort, an excited sergeant of the guard was shown into Captain Davis's office. The sergeant snapped a brisk salute and said, "Beggin' yer pardon, sir, but I thought you'd like to know that three riders are comin' in."

"Indians?" Davis said, not really paying much attention.

"Well, they're wearin' buckskins, but at least one of 'em ain't no Injun. Not with that red hair."

That was enough to make Davis look up. "Red hair?" he repeated.

"Yes, sir. Just like that Russian gal had."

Davis put aside the pen he had been using to write his monthly report for the War Department. The body of Alena Galovnin was one of two that had never been found following the slaughter of the Russian hunting party. No one held out any serious hope that she or the big Cossack called Dorochenko were still alive. But stranger things had happened out here in the West, Davis supposed.

" 'Twas Private Benton who spotted 'em first," the sergeant went on. "He called me over, and when I got a good look at 'em, I came straight here to tell you. Thought maybe you'd like to take a spyglass up on the wall and have a look for yerself, Cap'n."

"Thank you, Sergeant," Davis said as he stood up. "I'll do that." He reached for his hat and said to his adjutant, "Come on, Lieutenant Wayne, and bring my spyglass."

Followed by the sergeant and the adjutant, Davis emerged from the headquarters building and strode briskly to a set of stairs that led up to the parapet built along the inside of the stockade wall. The private who had first reported the strangers approaching was waiting there, a look of excitement on his young face. "I saw 'em, Cap'n!" he said. "I was the first one."

"Good work, Private," Davis told the trooper. He turned to his adjutant and held out his hand. Lieutenant Wayne gave him the spyglass.

Davis lifted the instrument to his right eye, squinting the

left one shut. The three riders in the distance instantly sprang into sharp focus. One of them was only a boy, and definitely an Indian. The other two . . .

Well, Private Benton and the sergeant had been right about the red hair, Davis thought. There was no mistaking it, just as there was no mistaking that its owner was a woman. The tight buckskin dress left no doubt of that, but Davis was a married man, so he quickly turned his attention to the third rider.

"My God," the captain murmured.

No Indian ever possessed shoulders that broad or sat so tall on the back of a horse. And no Indian ever sported a fierce black beard, either. Whether he was wearing buckskins or not, that man was the Russian Cossack, Viktor Dorochenko.

Slowly, Davis lowered the telescope. "Private, I think you're right." He turned to the adjutant. "Lieutenant, let our guests know about this right away."

Wayne snapped a salute. "Right away, sir." He hurried down the stairs and headed toward the officers' quarters.

The sergeant of the guard said, "I sure never expected to see those folks again, Cap'n. What do you think happened to 'em? Where have they been all this time? And who's that Injun kid with 'em?"

"I don't know, Sergeant, but I imagine the answers to those questions will be quite interesting. And we should know them soon enough." Davis turned his head and called down, "Open the gates!"

26

V IKTOR SAW THE GATES OF
the fort slowly swing open and knew that their approach to
the fort had not gone unnoticed. On the other side of the
grandson of Buffalo's Back Fat, Alena had seen the same
thing, and she cried out excitedly, "Look, Viktor! They
know we're coming!"

"I hope they do not mistake us for a war party," Viktor
said jokingly, but Alena took him seriously and turned a
wide-eyed face toward him.

"You don't think they will shoot at us, do you?" she
asked anxiously.

Viktor could not keep from laughing. "I do not think so,
Princess," he said. "Not with that red hair of yours announcing to the world that you are not an Indian."

Alena heaved a sigh of relief. "Do not worry me like that
again," she scolded in a mock-serious voice.

Between them, the boy looked back and forth, not understanding a word. They might as well have been speaking Russian, although they had gotten out of the habit of
doing that in recent weeks, first because of their American
escorts and then later because English was the only language they had in common with any of their Blackfoot
captors.

As they neared the fort, Viktor could see soldiers lined up on the parapet. The Americans held their rifles at the ready, even though the little group of three riders obviously represented no threat. The fort's commanding officer—Davis, that was his name, Viktor recalled—was taking no chances, however. In case the visitors represented some sort of trick, he was going to be ready for trouble.

Now only a hundred yards separated them from the fort. Viktor slowed the dun's pace and looked back over his shoulder at the distant hill where they had taken their leave of Buffalo's Back Fat, Wolverine, and the other warriors. The Blackfeet had vanished, of course; they might still be watching from a distance, but as Zephaniah had pointed out, they were masters of seeing without being seen.

In his mind's eye, Viktor saw them still, Buffalo's Back Fat and Wolverine sitting their horses atop the ridge, tall and proud. He saw them raise their lances over their heads in farewell to the white man who had become one of them . . . and then the vision slowly faded away.

Viktor took a deep breath and turned his eyes toward the fort. He had to deal with this now.

Side by side, the three of them rode through the open gates.

Inside the fort, the commotion had drawn the attention of everyone in the trading post, including Kenneth McKenzie and George Catlin. The trader and the artist stepped onto the porch of the long building and stared in amazement at the figures riding through the gate.

"Good Lord!" McKenzie exclaimed. "Is it really them, George?"

"Appears to be," Catlin answered laconically. "And that's the grandson of Buffalo's Back Fat with them."

"Come on," McKenzie said. He and Catlin started toward the group gathering around the newcomers on the parade ground.

Nearby, on the porch of the officers' quarters, Lieutenant Wayne came hurrying out of the building, calling over his shoulder, "The Captain sent me to fetch you, sir, because he knew you'd want to see this."

Viktor swung down from the dun's back, recalling that the horse had originally been a cavalry mount. Was Saber glad to be home, too? He wondered. He turned to help Alena down from the paint, then lifted the boy from the third pony and placed him on the ground.

By that time, the tall, slender American captain who commanded this fort stood before them. He said briskly, "You're Dorochenko the Cossack, aren't you?"

"Yes, sir," Viktor said, turning to face the officer.

"And Miss Galovnin," Davis said to Alena. "You're all right?"

"I am fine, Captain," she told him with a smile. "Viktor saw to—"

"Alena! Alena!"

The voice stunned both Viktor and Alena, and they turned quickly to see Sasha Orlov running toward them. The young man burst through the ring of soldiers and dashed up to Alena, sweeping her into his arms and hugging her so hard that her feet came up off the ground. Alena looked as surprised to see him alive as he was to see her.

Viktor was shocked, too, but his mind was already leaping ahead with possibilities. If Sasha was still alive, then . . .

Viktor looked past the soldiers and saw Count Frederick Orlov walking toward them with one of the fort's officers, his pace much slower than his impetuous younger brother's, his features as cold and unreadable as the distant mountains.

"I thought I would never see you again!" Sasha was saying as he whirled Alena around and around until she was dizzy. She put her hands on his chest and pushed until he stopped.

"Is it really you, Sasha?" she asked. "We thought the Indians had killed you."

"And we thought you were dead! It is a miracle!"

Once again the soldiers parted, and Frederick strode up

to join the group. "Hardly a miracle," he said. "But certainly good fortune." He smiled icily at Alena, who was still in Sasha's arms, then turned his gaze to Viktor. "I see that you are alive, too, Dorochenko."

"Alive and well, Count," Viktor said. There had been a time when he would have been happy to see that his fellow Russian had survived the Blackfoot attack. Now he wasn't so sure.

"Put her down, Sasha," Frederick said sharply to his brother. "She is not *your* fiancée."

Flushing with embarrassment, Sasha lowered Alena to the ground and stepped back. Frederick marched up to her, put his hands on her shoulders, and leaned over to give her a quick, perfunctory kiss on the lips. "Welcome back, my dear," he said. "You certainly gave us all quite a scare. It is good to see you again."

"Thank you, Frederick," Alena murmured.

That was a passionless greeting on both sides if he had ever seen one, Viktor thought.

"Where have you been all this time?" Frederick asked.

"We . . . we thought you had been killed in the fighting. Viktor and I thought we were the only ones who had survived."

Frederick turned to look at the Cossack again, no more friendly than he had been before. "Is this true, Dorochenko?" he demanded.

"It was surprising enough that we were still alive, Count," Viktor said, controlling his distaste. "We had no idea that anyone else had lived through the attack."

"So that led you to believe you could take the woman to whom I am betrothed and hold her prisoner in the wilderness for weeks?"

The harshness of the words lashed at Viktor and clearly surprised Sasha, Captain Davis, and the other American soldiers. With an effort, Viktor reined in the anger that was welling up inside him and said, "We were only trying to survive. Alena was not my prisoner."

"This is ridiculous, Frederick!" Alena said. "If not for

Viktor, I would be dead. How dare you accuse him of such a thing?"

"I know these Cossacks," Frederick snapped. "They are little more than savages, not much better than those red-skinned murderers who populate this land. I am sure that after spending so many nights on the prairie with this man, you and he have—" He broke off his tirade and drew a deep breath. The others looked at him in shocked silence. After a moment he went on, "No. I will speak no more of it. What is done is done, and the marriage between us is arranged. I will still have you for my wife, whether you are pure or not."

Alena was openmouthed, clearly unable to comprehend the depth of Frederick's arrogance. Sasha frowned darkly, displeased at his brother's arrogant and unfounded accusations, and the American officers watched with a mixture of anger and embarrassment. Viktor's face flushed darkly with outrage.

"You should not say these things, Count," he said, his voice tightly controlled. "I was charged with protecting Alena and I have done so. I have not laid one hand on her."

"It's true, Frederick," Alena insisted. "Anyway, we weren't alone out there on the prairie. We've been staying with the Blackfeet."

Frederick's eyebrows rose. "Indeed? That's even worse. Did those savages take turns with you?"

Alena could do nothing but gape at Frederick in mortification. But Viktor knew he had to act.

He let out a roar of rage and lunged toward Frederick, his fist lashing out. The blow caught the count solidly on the jaw and sent him sprawling on his back.

"Viktor, no!" Alena cried. Sasha stood beside her, hands balled into fists, and looked as if he wished *he* had been the one to land a haymaker on his brother.

Frederick pushed himself into a sitting position and pointed a trembling finger at Viktor. "Captain! I want that man arrested! Now!"

"You can't have him arrested!" Alena protested. "This is America, not Russia. These men are not serfs on your estate!"

Frederick ignored her. "Captain Davis, I said I wanted this man arrested. You have been ordered—"

"I was ordered to extend every reasonable courtesy to you, Count," Davis interrupted coolly. "I don't see that arresting the man who probably saved Miss Galovnin's life is very reasonable."

Seething at this display of insolence, Frederick turned to his brother. "Sasha! Help me up."

With a shake of his head, Sasha said slowly, "I don't think so, Frederick."

"What?" Frederick looked as if this new outrage was going to make him explode. "How dare you!"

"You should not have spoken so of Alena. You should have respected her." Sasha turned to her and took her arm. "Come, Alena. I'll move my things from my quarters, and you can stay there."

Alena looked at Viktor, who nodded. Then she smiled at the young man and said, "Thank you, Sasha." Arm in arm, they started toward the officers' quarters.

Viktor stood nearby, rubbing his right hand. The knuckles were already swollen, and it would be stiff and sore by the next day. But so would the jaw of Count Frederick Orlov, and by God, that was a trade Viktor would make any day!

"You will regret this, Dorochenko," Frederick said as he pushed himself to his feet, his voice shaking with anger.

"Not as much as I regret some of the other things I have done in my life—such as serving you."

Captain Davis moved between the two Russians. "Viktor, isn't it?" he said in a friendly tone. "Come on, Viktor. I want to hear about those Blackfeet who held you and Miss Galovnin prisoner."

"Of course," the big man said. "But there is one thing I must do first."

Throughout the argument and the flurry of violence, Buffalo's Back Fat's grandson had remained silent, observing. He had understood none of the words, of course, nor the behavior of adults, but he had enjoyed the spectacle of Viktor knocking Frederick down. Now Viktor, who had spotted

McKenzie and Catlin in the crowd, put his hand on the boy's shoulder and led him over to them.

"Mr. McKenzie, Buffalo's Back Fat, chief of the Piegan Blackfeet, requests that you do him the honor of caring for his grandson until the boy is old enough to assume his position as the new chief of the Blackfeet."

McKenzie nodded without hesitation. "I've offered to do that before, and the offer still stands," he said. Smiling, he knelt in front of the boy and spoke in Blackfoot. The boy nodded eagerly, and McKenzie looked up at Viktor. "We're good friends, this lad and I."

"I imagine you must have had quite an adventure out there, Mr. Dorochenko," George Catlin said. "You're going to have to tell us all about it."

McKenzie stood up and rested a hand on the boy's shoulder. "Over a glass or two of whiskey from my trading post," he said to Viktor. "Sorry I don't have any of that Russian vodka you're fond of."

Remembering Zephaniah and Titus, Viktor nodded. "Some who-hit-John will be fine, sir."

McKenzie laughed and shook his head, then he and Catlin led the grandson of Buffalo's Back Fat toward the trading post. Viktor watched them go, then turned his head as he sensed someone beside him.

Captain Davis stood there, a worried frown on his narrow face. "There's something I have to know right off, Viktor. The Blackfeet who held you and Miss Galovnin prisoner . . . were they the same bunch that attacked Count Orlov's hunting party?"

Viktor had been expecting that question, and he had thought about all the implications of his answer. Without hesitation, he shook his head.

"No, that was a different band. Buffalo's Back Fat and his people were very friendly to us. They saved our lives."

And that much, at least, was true.

27

ALENA HELD TIGHTLY TO Sasha's arm as they climbed the small hill near the fort. She wished Viktor was with her, but he was talking to Captain Davis and Mr. McKenzie and Catlin, the artist. Anyway, she told herself sternly, the Cossack was no longer the only friend she had. Sasha was here, and he had been very attentive to her ever since her arrival the day before.

She had postponed this task for as long as she felt she could, but it was time to pay her respects. As she looked up the hill at the small cemetery, her fingers tightened on the stems of the bouquet of wildflowers she had gathered. Her breath caught in her throat.

"Are you all right?" Sasha asked, sensing that something was troubling her.

"I will be fine," she told him. "This is something I must do."

He led her to one of the recently dug graves. There were all too many of them. Grass was beginning to grow on the mound of earth. By the end of summer, Alena knew, it would be completely covered.

At the head of the grave was a plain white cross. Letters in the Russian alphabet had been carved into the wood. Alena read the name engraved there, and tears ran down her cheeks, although she managed not to sob aloud. She stepped to the grave and knelt to place the flowers at the base of the cross.

"Poor Aunt Zora," she murmured. "She did not want to come here. Now she will never go home."

Sasha hesitated, clearly unsure whether he should speak or not. Then he said, "I would like to think that she *is* home. I am sorry about her death, Alena."

Alena nodded, knelt there a moment longer, then straightened and moved to stand beside Sasha. He lifted his arm, put it down, then raised it again and tentatively placed it around her shoulders.

After a few minutes of silence she asked, "How . . . how did you and Frederick escape?" They had not talked of the battle until now, because Alena had difficulty bringing herself to think of that day. It was time to face the memories and put them behind her, she told herself.

"It was none of our doing," Sasha said. "Fortune smiled on us. The horses ran away, taking the carriage with them."

"I remember," Alena said. "Actually, I don't, but Viktor told me about it. I had been thrown out, and I was lying senseless on the prairie then."

"Yes." Sasha's voice caught as he struggled with his own memories of that bloody day. "I . . . I did not know what to do. I could not reach you . . . so I followed the carriage, trying to get to Frederick. The Indians must have lost sight of us in the confusion, because they did not pursue us. When the carriage horses finally stopped, we were a long way from the battle. I thought we should go back, but Frederick insisted we try to reach the fort. I was wounded, so I . . . I finally agreed."

"Were you hurt badly?"

Sasha shrugged. "Some scratches. Nothing more."

Alena thought he probably underestimated the seriousness of his injuries. She remembered seeing the bloodstains on his clothes before she was thrown from the careening carriage and knocked unconscious.

"You are very brave."

"No," he said, his voice catching. "I ran away. I should have stayed to protect you . . . like Viktor."

"That was Viktor's job," Alena said gently. "It was not yours."

He let go of her and turned away. "I should have done it anyway."

Alena reached out toward him. "You would have only been killed."

"It would have been worth it . . . to save you."

She put her hand on his arm, turning him back to face her. Firmly, she said, "Sasha, that is sweet of you. But you should not feel this way. You did the right thing."

He took a deep breath. The wind that swept almost constantly over the rolling Montana landscape ruffled his hair as he asked, "Are you still going to marry my brother?"

"I . . . I do not want to," Alena answered honestly. Her voice strengthened as she went on, "I will not marry him."

"Frederick will be very angry."

Alena pushed back her hair. "I no longer care. I don't care if he will be angry . . . and I don't care for Frederick. Not at all."

"I imagine . . . after being with Viktor . . . noblemen seem too . . . too soft for you."

She frowned at him and said impatiently, "I was not *with* Viktor, not like that. Does everyone think that?"

"I'm sorry, Alena," Sasha said quickly, looking down at the ground. "I did not mean to offend you. I just meant that . . . since you have seen what a real man is like—"

"You are as real as any Cossack, Sasha Mikhailovitch Orlov."

His head lifted, and an expression much like hope appeared on his face. Before he could say anything, the strains of balalaika music drifted to their ears. Alena and Sasha both turned and looked down the hill toward the fort. The grandson of Buffalo's Back Fat was standing just outside the walls, carefully playing a tune on the instrument. The boy's entire concentration was focused on the task, and he did not even glance up at the cemetery. Alena suspected that he was oblivious to her and Sasha's presence.

"Did you teach him that?" Sasha asked quietly.

Alena recognized the melody of a Russian folk song she had taught the boy. It had been one of her Aunt Zora's favorites, she recalled, and one of the few tunes Alena had truly mastered.

"He learns quickly," she said. "He has a talent for the balalaika. He should have been Aunt Zora's student, not me. I told him so, but of course he did not understand."

"He understands the music," Sasha said. "Perhaps your aunt hears it even now."

Alena smiled, feeling new tears in her eyes. "I would like to think so. . . ."

Viktor was sitting on the porch of the headquarters building with McKenzie, Catlin, and Captain Davis when Alena and Sasha strolled by a little later. All four of the men came to their feet, and McKenzie, Catlin, and Davis touched the brims of their hats. Viktor still wore the buckskins Alena had made and his head was bare, the long black hair falling almost to his shoulders.

Davis said, "Miss Galovnin, would you do us the honor of having dinner with us tonight? And you, too, of course, Mr. Orlov?"

Alena smiled. "Certainly, Captain. I would be glad to."

"Thank you, sir," Sasha added.

"In my quarters, then, about six o'clock," Davis said.

He entered the building, and McKenzie and Catlin started toward the trading post. Viktor stepped down from the porch to join Alena and Sasha. He knew they had been up to the cemetery overlooking the fort so that Alena could visit her aunt's grave. He thought he saw traces of tears in Alena's eyes, and that was probably a good thing. She needed to grieve before she could put that terrible part of her life behind her.

At the moment, though, Viktor needed to discuss something of equal importance with her. He said, "Princess, I must speak with you privately for a few moments, if you please."

"Of course," she said. "Sasha, do you mind . . . ?"

Sasha frowned a little at the thought of leaving Alena alone with Viktor, but then shrugged and nodded. "I will see you later in the captain's quarters." He turned and walked toward the trading post, his back stiff.

"What is wrong with him?" Viktor asked.

Alena gave a little laugh. "He is jealous."

"Jealous? But why?"

"He thinks I am in love with you." Alena looked intently at Viktor. "And perhaps he is right . . . just a little."

"Princess!" Viktor said with a frown of his own. "You should not say such things."

"Why not? You are a man and I am a woman. You saved my life and risked yours for mine many times in the past weeks. How could I not feel—"

"We have talked about this," he broke in. "I have told you the way it must be."

Alena sighed. "Yes, you are right, of course. You are too often right. The gulf between us is too wide. . . . But why did you want to talk to me?"

Viktor was glad she had changed the subject. Lowering his voice so that no one could overhear, he said, "The captain does not know that it was the band of Buffalo's Back Fat which attacked the hunting party. I told him it was a different band, perhaps not even Blackfeet at all. He has talked of this much since we got here yesterday, and he believes what I have told him. Only you and I know the truth."

"Why did you lie, Viktor? That is not like you."

"In the eyes of the Blackfeet, the attack was justified," he said. "The Count killed one of their young men, murdered him in cold blood. I know that the soldiers who were killed, both the Americans and my Cossacks, were not to blame for Cloud Caller's death, and neither were your aunt or any of the others. But if the American army seeks vengeance on the people of Buffalo's Back Fat, then even more innocents will die. It may sound strange for a bloody-handed Cossack to say this, but . . . I would see an end to the killing."

He took a deep breath. That had been a very long speech for him, and if he had not thought it all out ahead of time, he'd have become tongue-tied. He hoped Alena agreed with him. She had listened intently throughout his speech.

Solemnly, she put a hand on his arm. "Viktor, I . . . I feel the same way. It would not bring my aunt back if Crystal Stone were to die. That would be just one more useless death."

"We are agreed, then. We will say nothing more about the Blackfeet."

"Agreed." She rose up on tiptoe to brush a kiss across his cheek. "And as for the other . . . what is between the two of us . . . we will say no more about *that,* either."

"Thank you, little one," Viktor said fervently, relieved at her willingness to do as he asked.

"You will be at dinner with the captain this evening?"

"Of course."

She smiled. "Then I will see you there."

The table in the captain's quarters was set for dinner when Viktor arrived. The captain's wife, an attractive blond woman who had evidently resigned herself to making the best of her life in this isolated fort, greeted him. Viktor had taken off the buckskins and was wearing a suit borrowed from one of the enlisted men, a private who was almost as large as he was. The trousers were a bit short, as were the sleeves of the coat. Viktor thought the Indian garb would have been inappropriate for an occasion like this, however, so he was making the best of the situation, too.

He saw that he was the last to arrive. Alena, Sasha, Captain Davis, McKenzie, and Catlin were gathered around the table. There was no sign of the two Davis children or the grandson of Buffalo's Back Fat, so Viktor assumed the youngsters were together somewhere, probably under the supervision of a junior officer.

The captain came over to Viktor and extended his hand. "Welcome to my home, Mr. Dorochenko," he said formally.

Viktor shook Davis's hand. "You do me an honor by inviting me, sir." He looked at the man's wife. "And my compliments to you as well, madam."

"Thank you," she said. "Please sit down, Mr. Dorochenko. All of you, please be seated."

They took their places at the table, and an orderly began to serve the food. Being waited on like this made Viktor feel slightly uncomfortable. In fact, even being in the captain's quarters felt somehow wrong. He should have been in the barracks with the enlisted men. Putting a smile on his face, he resolved to get through this evening and then try to avoid such circumstances in the future.

Captain Davis sat at the head of the table, facing his wife. Viktor was to the captain's right, Alena beside him, the Sasha on her other side. McKenzie and Catlin were across the table from them. The place settings were strictly utilitarian, nothing fancy about them, as befitted a frontier outpost. But the windows had lacy white curtains, a touch of femininity and civilization, and the table was covered by a white linen cloth. Mrs. Davis was at least trying to bring some warmth to the place.

The food was simple, beef and potatoes, biscuits and gravy. That suited Viktor just fine. He ate hungrily, washing down the food with chilled buttermilk from a large pitcher. The meal was good, and he felt himself begin to relax.

That was when the door of the captain's quarters opened and Count Frederick Orlov strode into the room.

"I see that I was not invited to dinner, but this Cossack was," Frederick said with his customary sneer. "This is an insult I will be sure to report to your State Department when I get back to Washington, Captain."

"Sorry, Count," Davis replied, but it was clear that offending Frederick meant nothing to him. "I didn't figure you'd want to join us."

"You are right. I would not sit down with commoners. And neither should my brother or my betrothed. Sasha! Alena!" Frederick glared at them. "Come with me."

"No, Frederick," Alena said without hesitation. "I have no desire to go anywhere with you. And I am no longer your betrothed."

The count's eyes widened in surprise and anger. "What? How dare you—"

"You heard the lady, Count," Kenneth McKenzie said harshly. "I'm getting mighty tired of you, mister. We all are. Maybe it's not that way in Russia, but out here on the frontier, we treat decent women with respect."

"I care nothing for what you do on your barbaric frontier!" Frederick snapped. "This woman is to be my wife, and she will do as I say!"

Sasha sprang to his feet, and Viktor watched with great interest as the young man said, "No, Frederick. Things have changed. Neither Alena nor I will allow you to . . . to . . ."

"Boss you around?" Catlin suggested with a grin.

"That is it!" Sasha pointed a finger at his brother. "You will no longer boss us around, Frederick. We are not in Russia now."

Frederick's mouth was a taut line, and his eyes were narrow with menace. "Perhaps not," he said, "but we will be again, one day, and you will regret your insolence, Sasha. Very deeply." He crossed his arms and snorted in disgust. "I should not have expected any more from this country. Any place where nobles are set upon and slaughtered for no reason—"

"There was a reason."

The words were out of Viktor's mouth before he realized it. A part of him wished he had not spoken, wished he had kept his knowledge to himself. But it was too late now.

Frederick glowered at him. "Be silent, Dorochenko!"

"A man's got a right to speak his mind if he wants to," George Catlin said. "At least around here he does. What were you saying, Viktor?"

Now that he had started this, he had no choice but to go on, Viktor realized. With a glance of regret at the uneaten food on his plate, he pushed himself to his feet, faced Frederick, and said, "What have you told these people about the attack on our party, Count?"

"The truth! That we were attacked for no reason other than that bloodthirsty savages saw an opportunity to slaughter some innocent whites." Frederick glared defiantly at Viktor, as if daring him to claim otherwise.

Instead it was Alena who contradicted him. "That's not true," she said. She turned to Sasha. "Sasha, did you not tell them?"

"Tell us what, ma'am?" Captain Davis asked, leaning forward with an expression of great interest on his face.

"I . . . I am sorry," Sasha said. He flushed with shame. "I should have told the truth, but Frederick made me swear—"

"Silence!" Frederick bellowed. "Not another word, Sasha!"

"No!" Sasha shot back at him. "I have been silent for too long already." He looked at the others grouped around the table. "The Indians attacked us because my brother shot one of them first. A young man. Frederick killed him."

"That is a lie!"

"No," Viktor said. "It is the truth. And all here know it now."

Sasha stepped over to Frederick, taking his brother by surprise. He reached into the pocket of Frederick's coat and pulled out the medicine bag the count had taken from the slain Blackfoot youth. With a Russian oath, Frederick snatched it back, but he was too late.

"I reckon we all know it, all right," Captain Davis said. "That's a Blackfoot medicine bag. No doubt about it."

Frederick sputtered, "I will report these insults—"

"Go right ahead," Davis told him. "Your threats don't mean any more to me now than they did before, Count. I intend to report your attempts to stir up Indian trouble during your visit here."

Unable to control his fury, Frederick turned on his heel and started to stalk out of the room.

"Hold on there!" Davis's sharp tone stopped Frederick. "One more thing, mister. There'll be a riverboat docking here in a few days before heading back down the Missouri. I suggest that you leave with it."

Over his shoulder, Frederick gritted, "If you think I would stay one second longer than necessary in this place,

Captain, you are more than sadly mistaken. You are insane!"

With that, he bolted from the room, slamming the door behind him.

After a moment of awkward silence, McKenzie said, "I don't know about you folks, but I can't say that I'll be sorry to see that fella go."

"Neither will I," Catlin put in.

"We take no offense, gentlemen," Sasha told them. "Do we, Alena?"

She shook her head. "None. I think we have all learned a great deal on this journey."

"This country may not be very old," McKenzie said, "but it's got a way of opening people's eyes to a lot of things."

"Are the rest of you accompanying the count on the riverboat?" Davis asked.

Sasha sighed. "I suppose we must. Alena should return to her family as soon as possible."

"Well, the boat won't be here for a few days yet," the captain's wife put in. "There's no reason why we can't enjoy the rest of this dinner."

"None at all, madam," Sasha said with a smile. Now that he was speaking for himself, he seemed to gain confidence. Viktor was glad to see that. Sasha might be able to look after Alena on the long journey back to Moscow.

Because as for himself, Viktor was not at all sure he would be leaving Fort Union when that riverboat headed back down the Missouri.

28

VIKTOR STOOD STIFFLY ON the trading-post porch in a new set of buckskins. The clothes were heavily fringed but were not decorated with painting and beadwork, unlike the ones Alena had crafted. This outfit resembled the ones worn by the white mountain men who trapped beaver and other animals in this untamed territory, right down to the coonskin cap on his head. Viktor held a flintlock rifle and had a powder horn slung over his shoulder. A hunting knife was sheathed on his belt, and he still carried the broken saber, too, behind the broad leather belt. His hair had been trimmed, as had his beard. His face bore a solemn, almost stern expression.

"Just a few more minutes, Viktor," George Catlin said from behind the easel that was set up on the porch.

"It cannot be too soon for me, Mr. Catlin," Viktor said from the corner of his tight-set mouth. Posing for this portrait had been even more difficult than he had expected. But he had needed some occupation while waiting for the riverboat to arrive at Fort Union, and Catlin had been persuasive.

The brush moved with sure, practiced strokes from palette to canvas and back again as Catlin completed the last details of the painting. Finally, after what seemed like an hour to Viktor, the artist stepped back and announced, "There! It's done."

Alena and Sasha, who were sitting nearby on the porch in cane-bottomed chairs, stood up to look at the portrait, and Alena exclaimed, "Come see, Viktor! It looks just like you."

When Viktor carried the flintlock over to the easel and looked at the canvas, he had to admit that the painting was true to life. There he stood, in buckskins and coonskin cap, looking for all the world like one of the American fur trappers, although the broken saber thrust behind his belt lent an exotic touch. Viktor looked at the portrait for a moment and felt more than a little embarrassed.

"It is very good," he said to Catlin. "Thank you."

"No, thank *you*, Viktor, for being such an excellent subject. And for staying so still while I was painting you."

Viktor shrugged. "Sometimes it is necessary to be still when hunting so that the game will not know you are there. This is no different."

That was also true when it came to hunting men, Viktor thought, but he kept it to himself.

McKenzie strolled onto the porch, trailed by the grandson of Buffalo's Back Fat. Both of them had to look at the painting, too, and McKenzie praised both Catlin's skill and Viktor's imposing presence on canvas. "You look like you could've tramped this prairie with Lewis and Clark or old John Colter."

"I would have enjoyed being among the first to explore this land," Viktor admitted. "They must have been very thrilled by what they saw on their journeys."

McKenzie grinned. "You'll cut quite a figure in that outfit when you get back to Moscow."

"But these are not my clothes," Viktor said with a frown. "And this rifle, as well, came from your trading post."

McKenzie waved off the objections. "Keep 'em. The clothes, the rifle, the powder horn, the whole outfit's yours now, Viktor, with my compliments." The trader rubbed his jaw in thought, then added, "Maybe that Czar Nicholas fella will decide to outfit all his troops like this."

"I do not think so," Sasha said with a laugh. "But I'm sure Viktor will cause quite a stir at court."

"Perhaps I should not do this. . . ." Viktor began uncertainly.

"Nonsense!" McKenzie told him. "You go right ahead."

"Yes, Viktor," Alena said. "You look just like an American frontiersman."

"Well . . ." Viktor nodded. "All right. I will keep the clothes and the rifle."

The sound of a boat's whistle, high and shrill, made them all direct their gazes toward the river landing through the open gates of the fort. "That'll be the *President Jefferson*," McKenzie said. "Right on time. Reckon you folks'll be started home pretty soon."

"Home," Viktor echoed hollowly. "Yes."

Sasha turned to Alena. "Shall we go down to the river to watch the boat dock?"

Alena was looking at Viktor. Distractedly, she said to Sasha, "You go ahead. Perhaps I will be there shortly."

The young man seemed a bit crestfallen. "Are you sure?"

"Yes." Alena turned her head to smile at him. "Go ahead, Sasha. I will catch up."

The dazzling brilliance of her smile made him forget his concerns. "All right," he said. "Don't wait too long."

"I won't," Alena promised. She remained behind with Viktor as Sasha, McKenzie, Catlin, and the grandson of Buffalo's Back Fat joined the soldiers who were moving out of the fort to greet the riverboat.

"You should go with them," Viktor said. "The boat will be here soon."

"I have seen riverboats dock before."

"There was a time not long ago when we both thought we would never see such a sight again," Viktor pointed out.

Alena nodded. "True. I thought I would die before I ever

saw civilization again. But you saved me, Viktor. You brought me back here."

"It was my duty to protect you," he said stiffly.

"And it is my duty now, as your friend, to tell you that you do not have to go back to Russia with me."

That very possibility had been much on Viktor's mind since their return to Fort Union, but automatically he said, "Of course I must go with you. I must watch over you—"

"Sasha can do that."

Without trying to sound too harsh, Viktor said, "Sasha is little more than a boy."

"But he has grown a great deal in the past days. You have seen the way he stood up to Frederick. Did you ever think he would do such a thing?"

Viktor had to shrug. "I hoped that sooner or later he would."

"So you see, I will be safe on the journey home. You can stay here in America if you want."

It *was* what he wanted; he was sure of it. But now, as always, his ingrained sense of honor stubbornly insisted on intruding itself.

"There may still be danger downriver," he said. "I must go with you at least as far as St. Louis."

Alena looked as if she was going to argue the point, but then the sound of the riverboat's whistle cut through the air once more. Just as he knew sometimes when persuading her was futile, she must have sensed that she was not going to shake his resolve in this matter.

"All right," she said with a nod. "You go with us as far as you like, Viktor. As always, I will be glad to have you with me."

"Thank you, Princess. Now, that riverboat is just about here, and Sasha is waiting."

"Yes," Alena said, looking toward the Missouri. "Yes, he is."

The *President Jefferson* was not scheduled to make a long stop at Fort Union. Kenneth McKenzie had a load of furs to ship downriver to St. Louis, to the headquarters of the

American Fur Company. Several of the company's employees who worked for McKenzie at the trading post began carrying the furs to the river landing in wagons as soon as the boat had docked. It would take an hour or so to load all of them, Viktor estimated as he watched.

The four Russians were the only passengers boarding here. They had little in the way of luggage, mostly some spare clothes McKenzie had provided for them.

The fur-company factor stepped up to the porch of the trading post and nodded to Viktor, who was leaning on the railing and watching through the open gates of the fort as the riverboat was loaded. "We'll miss you around here, Viktor," McKenzie said. "That Indian boy especially will. He's about half-convinced you're some sort of spirit warrior sent here to look after him."

"He is a good boy, very brave," Viktor said. "I would like to know what name he chooses when the time comes for him to take one."

"I could write to you and let you know," McKenzie offered.

"It would be difficult to get a message to me." Viktor had said nothing to anyone except Alena about his dilemma.

"Well, I don't mind trying." McKenzie hesitated, then asked, "Is the count going to be able to cause trouble for you once you get back to Russia?"

McKenzie could believe what he wanted to about whether or not he was returning to Russia, Viktor decided. "Perhaps. No matter what he says about what happened during our journey, he will be believed."

"Even if Miss Galovnin and that young fella Sasha tell a different story?"

"The count is a nobleman," Viktor said. "He will be believed."

"That's just not right." McKenzie stuck his hands in his trouser pockets and looked intently at Viktor. "Say, have you given any thought to just staying here? Let the others go back by themselves."

"I could not," Viktor said quickly and firmly. He did not

want McKenzie trying to convince him to stay, not as ambivalent about the matter as he already was.

"Well, I'd think about it if I was you."

At that moment Frederick emerged from the officers' quarters and walked toward the wagon on which the Russians' few belongings had been loaded. Ever since the confrontation in the captain's quarters, he had made himself scarce, taking his meals in the temporary quarters he had been given. Now, as stiff and haughty as ever, he strode toward the wagon, obviously expecting to ride down to the landing instead of walking.

Alena and Sasha exited the officers' quarters, too, but they started toward the trading post, and Viktor was glad to see that they were walking arm in arm. He had hopes that Sasha would turn out to be a good man, and would make a better husband for Alena. Better than a Cossack, too, Viktor thought with a wry smile.

Just as Alena and Sasha reached the trading post and stepped up onto the porch, a commotion broke out at the fort's open gates. Viktor looked in that direction and was surprised to see a buckskin-clad man push his way past the knot of soldiers. Viktor recognized him immediately as Titus, Zephaniah's former partner and his friend from the early days of the expedition.

Titus was carrying his rifle, and his face was dark with anger. Even across the parade ground, Viktor heard him demand harshly, "Where is he? I heard that crazy Rooshan count was here. He's the one who got ol' Zeph killed!"

Frederick was standing nearby, and he and Titus saw each other at the same time. Frederick turned pale as Titus's face turned even more livid.

"There you are!" Titus bellowed as he started toward Frederick. "I got a score to settle with you, mister!"

The count looked around wildly, obviously frightened. His gaze fell on Viktor standing on the porch of the trading post with Alena, Sasha, and McKenzie, and he called out nervously, "Dorochenko, you must deal with this man. He is a lunatic!"

Viktor stepped down from the porch, but he went no

closer to the gate. "I no longer follow your orders, Count," he said. "You will have to handle this yourself."

Frederick turned toward the headquarters building. "Captain!" he shouted. "Captain Davis! Someone help me!" A shrill note of panic had crept into his voice.

Titus came to a stop about ten feet from Frederick and shook his rifle. "You had to go and shoot that Injun boy!" he accused. "None of the rest of it would've happened if you hadn't done that. You're to blame for Zeph and all them other folks bein' dead!"

"Stay away from me," Frederick warned as he began to back away from Titus. Once again he looked toward Viktor. "Dorochenko!"

For the first time Titus seemed to absorb what Frederick was saying. He swung his baleful gaze toward Viktor, and his expression changed into one of shocked recognition. "Viktor? Is that you, boy? I heard you was dead!"

"I am alive, friend Titus," the Cossack said, walking toward the mountain man. "Are you well?"

The glare came back on the mountain man's face. "As well as I'm goin' to be until I settle the score for Zeph and them others with this here so-called nobleman." He snorted in contempt as he looked again at Frederick. "You're about as noble as a polecat, mister."

Captain Davis finally emerged from the headquarters building, looking puzzled and concerned. "What's all the shouting about?" he asked, then his eyes fell on the buckskinned newcomer. "Oh, it's you, Titus. I heard you were back in these parts."

"And I heard this Rooshan fella was here, too," Titus said. "He's got a lot to answer for, Cap'n, in case you don't know the whole story."

"We know what happened," Davis said, keeping his voice calm. "Viktor and Miss Galovnin and the count's brother told us the whole story."

"And what're you doin' about it?"

The captain shook his head. "Unfortunately, there's not much we *can* do. Count Orlov is a Russian citizen and a guest of our government. In fact, he's about to leave Fort Union and start his journey home."

Titus stared at the commanding officer in disbelief, unable to speak for a moment. Finally, he said, "You mean there ain't goin' to be anything done to him? He's responsible for all them folks bein' dead. The rest o' them Rooshans, and all those American soldier boys, and all of Viktor's Cossack pards . . . and ol' Zeph, the best friend I ever had in this world." Titus's voice shook. "And you're tellin' me he's goin' to get away with it?"

"We may not like it, Titus," Captain Davis said quietly, "but that's the way things have to be."

"Not hardly!" Titus roared. He brought his rifle up, cocking the flintlock.

Frederick cringed against the side of the wagon and cried, "My God, no!"

Without trying to think too much about what he was doing, Viktor suddenly lunged toward Titus. His fingers closed around the barrel of the flintlock and jerked it up just as the furious mountain man fired. The blast of black powder was nearly deafening as the heavy lead ball whizzed several feet over Frederick's head. Viktor wrenched the rifle out of Titus's hands while several of the nearby soldiers lifted and aimed their own weapons.

"Hold your fire!" Captain Davis shouted. "That's enough shooting, blast it!"

Still pressing his body tightly against the wagon, Frederick shouted, "I demand that you protect me from that madman, Captain!"

"You're mighty free with your demands, Count," Davis snapped, "especially since you consider us nothing but barbarians." He took a deep breath to settle his own anger before continuing. "But you're still a guest of the United States government, and I won't have you shot down like a dog." He added under his breath, but loud enough for all of them to hear it, "Whether you deserve it or not." Davis turned to the soldiers. "Take Titus and lock him in the smokehouse until he cools down."

"I got a right!" Titus yelled as a couple of troopers

stepped up and took hold of his arms. "Me and Zeph was partners! I got a right to settle the score!"

"I may agree with you, but there's nothing else I can do." Davis gestured for the soldiers to take Titus away.

As they tugged the unwilling mountain man toward the sturdy log smokehouse, Captain Davis took a watch from his pocket and checked the time.

"That riverboat will be leaving in half an hour, Count. I suggest even more strongly than before that you be on it. And don't even think about ever coming back to Montana Territory."

Now his life was no longer threatened, Frederick had regained some of his composure. He straightened his jacket and said, "I think that is so unlikely as to be impossible, Captain. Once I am back in Mother Russia, I will never set foot in your uncivilized country again."

Kenneth McKenzie said, "We may be uncivilized in your eyes, Count, but we know how to git when the gittin's good. I'd head for that riverboat if I was you."

With a sniff of contempt, Frederick climbed onto the seat of the wagon. Davis motioned for one of the troopers to handle the vehicle, and the young private climbed onto the seat beside Frederick. Flicking the reins against the backs of the mule team, he got the wagon rolling through the gates, heading toward the landing and the *President Jefferson*.

Turning to Viktor, Captain Davis extended his hand. "I'm surprised you saved the count's life," he said, "although I'm glad you did. My superiors back in Washington City might not have taken it too kindly if I'd let him get himself killed."

"That is one reason I did it," Viktor said as he returned the officer's handshake. "And . . . old habits are difficult to break."

"That they are. Come back to see us sometime, Viktor. And if you ever want to enlist in another army . . ."

"I think I have had enough of armies, at least for the time being." The big Cossack's normally grim countenance creased in a smile.

Davis shook hands with Alena and Sasha as well. "I hope you have a pleasant journey home, Miss Galovnin," he told Alena. "And good luck once you get there."

"Thank you, Captain," she said. "I think I will almost miss this Montana Territory of yours. Almost."

Davis returned her smile and then said to the young man beside her, "Sasha, you'll be welcome back here anytime. Just don't bring that brother of yours."

"I do not think that any of us need concern ourselves with that, Captain. Farewell."

George Catlin and Buffalo's Back Fat's grandson had slipped out of the trading post and joined the little group without the others noticing. The boy spoke up now, addressing a long speech in the Blackfoot tongue to Viktor, then repeating it to Sasha.

"That goes for me, too," Catlin said with a grin, not bothering to translate. "So long, folks. Have a safe trip."

The grandson of Buffalo's Back Fat walked over to Alena, and suddenly the solemn expression on his face threatened to disappear. His bottom lip quivered for a moment, and tears glistened in his eyes. But then he pulled himself together and gave Alena a grave nod. She returned it. Abruptly, the boy threw his arms around her waist and hugged her tightly. Alena bent to return the embrace. When he let go of her, the youngster stepped back, trying hard to be as dignified as his position required.

McKenzie shook hands all around, then with waves for these people who had become good friends, Viktor, Alena, and Sasha walked out of the fort, heading toward the riverboat. The now-empty wagon that had taken their belongings—and Count Frederick Orlov—to the boat rattled past them on its return trip. Viktor's eyes scanned the decks of the *President Jefferson*. He saw no sign of Frederick. The count must have gone below immediately to his assigned quarters.

That was fine with Viktor. If he never had to see Frederick again, it would have been all right with him. That seemed unlikely, however, even if Viktor accompanied the party only as far as St. Louis. And if he wound up going all the way back to Russia—

He paused and looked back at the fort, wishing he'd had a chance to say good-bye to Titus. Beside him, Alena and Sasha stopped as well, and Alena asked, "Will you ever come back to this place, Viktor?"

"I would like to someday," he said with a nod. "It is a hard land, but a good one. In many ways, it reminds me of Russia."

Then, without looking back again, the three of them walked on toward the landing and the riverboat that would start them on their journey home.

29

THE STEAM ENGINE OF THE
President Jefferson rumbled and chugged as the riverboat
made its way downstream. The huge paddle wheel on its
stern turned steadily, churning the waters of the Missouri
and leaving a muddy froth in its wake. Billows of grayish-
white smoke rose from the tall stacks that led down to the
boiler room. The pace set by the captain of the *President
Jefferson* was slow but steady . . . slow enough to avoid the
sandbars and the snags that dotted the broad sandy
riverbed, steady enough to have the passengers back in St.
Louis in about a week's time.

Viktor stood at the forward railing on one of the decks
and watched the rugged landscape move past. On both
sides of the Missouri were towering rocky bluffs that were
gradually becoming more gentle. As Viktor recalled the terrain from the trip upstream, they would soon be reaching an
area marked by shorter banks and rolling hills. It was there,
in fact, that Frederick and the others had hunted antelope.

Slowly, Viktor shook his head. About two months had
passed, but it seemed much longer. So much had changed.

With those thoughts occupying his mind, he did not even
hear Sasha come up beside him until the young man said, "I
seem to remember this place."

Viktor grunted in surprise and looked over at him. "You should," he said. "The river has changed but little in the time since you saw it first."

"Rivers change slowly," Sasha said, "but people do not. They can be transformed so quickly. . . ."

Viktor frowned. Had the young man somehow been privy to his thoughts of a few moments earlier? Impossible, of course. Sasha simply recognized some of the same truths that had occurred to Viktor.

Viktor changed the subject. "Where is Alena?"

"She said she was going to lie down in her cabin," Sasha replied. "She was tired, and I think she was upset about what almost happened at the fort, too."

"Perhaps she was afraid that Frederick would be killed. Even though she is no longer willing to marry him, she may still have some feelings for him."

Sasha shook his head. "I don't think so. I believe she was more worried about you." For a moment the big Cossack thought Sasha was jealous again, but the young man went on, "You are her best friend. She looks up to you as she would her father."

"Well . . . good," Viktor said. "That is how she should feel."

Sasha hesitated. "Viktor . . . I want to ask you something."

"All right."

"And I am relying on your honor as a Cossack to be truthful in your answer."

Viktor had to grin a little at the seriousness of Sasha's tone. "Perhaps you overestimate our sense of honor, but I will still answer you truthfully."

"Alena says there is nothing between the two of you but friendship. This . . . this is right?"

Viktor nodded, no longer grinning. Sasha deserved a serious answer. "You said it yourself," he pointed out. "She thinks of me as a father. She is the daughter of my old commander. There could never be anything else between us, even if . . . one of us wished it were otherwise."

"You do not have to say anything else," Sasha said. "I understand."

Viktor sensed that Sasha had something more on his mind. "Was there anything else?" he asked.

Again Sasha hesitated. "I was wondering . . . now that Alena is no longer betrothed to my brother . . ."

"If there might be something between the two of you?" Viktor finished for him.

Sasha sighed in relief, probably because he himself had not had to put the matter into words. "Yes."

"That is up to the princess," Viktor said. "But I will say this, if I may be so bold—"

"Please."

"You are not the same boy who left Moscow. Do not misunderstand me. You are still a boy . . . but not as much of one. I can see the man within you now."

Sasha's fingers gripped the railing eagerly. "Then you think that perhaps someday, Alena and I—"

"As I said, that is up to the princess. But you must tell her how you feel, otherwise she may never know for sure."

Sasha looked down at the deck, seemingly stricken by that thought. "I cannot," he said in a quiet, wretched voice.

"Men can do what they believe they can do."

Silence fell while Sasha thought about these words. Finally, he nodded slowly. "I will try," he said.

Viktor put a hand on his shoulder. "That is all any of us can do. Good luck . . . my friend."

In his office at Fort Union, Captain Davis pushed his chair back from the desk and reached into his jacket for a watch. He opened the timepiece, nodded, snapped the cover closed. "That riverboat's had plenty of time to get a long way downriver by now," he said to his adjutant. "Have the sergeant of the guard let Titus out of the smokehouse, Lieutenant Wayne."

The adjutant, a short, fussy-looking officer with a neatly trimmed black beard, asked, "Are you certain that's wise, Captain? I hate to agree with Count Orlov, but that mountain man strikes me as something of a lunatic."

"We can't always play it safe, Wayne," Davis said. "Titus is bound to have calmed down some by now. Have him brought here, like I said. I'll have a talk with him."

The lieutenant nodded. "Yes, sir." He hurried to obey the order, and a few minutes later the sergeant of the guard and another trooper ushered Titus into the office. The mountain man's face was creased in a furious frown.

Davis stood up and gestured toward the chair in front of the desk. "Have a seat, Titus," he invited. "I thought we'd have a little talk."

"Don't want to talk to nobody," Titus said. "Just give me my guns back and I'll be gettin' out of here."

"Not so fast. There are a few things I want to say to you first."

Titus ignored the chair and took a step closer to the desk. Behind him, the soldiers tensed, but Davis motioned for them to relax.

"You can't do a thing to me," Titus snapped. "I ain't in the army, so you ain't got no, what do you call it, jurisdiction. I don't take orders from you."

"That's where you're wrong, Titus," Davis said, his voice growing cold as he clasped his hands behind his back. "As long as you're within the walls of this fort, you're under my command, civilian or not. And I'm not going to allow you to leave until I'm convinced that you don't intend to cause any more trouble."

"I got a score to settle—" Titus began hotly.

"Some scores *can't* be settled," Davis cut in. "If you kill Count Orlov, will it bring back your friend Zephaniah? Or any of the other innocent people who were massacred?"

Titus glared across the desk. "Maybe they'd rest a mite easier knowin' that crazy Rooshan was dead," he muttered.

"There's no way of knowing that, though, is there?"

Titus drew a deep breath and looked down at the floor. "I reckon not," he said.

"Sit down," Davis suggested again. "Have a drink with me."

That offer caught Titus's interest. "A drink?" he repeated.

"Lieutenant Wayne, break out that brandy I've been saving," Davis ordered.

The adjutant leaped to obey, heading for a cabinet that was positioned beneath a map of Montana Territory. "Yes, sir!"

Reluctantly, Titus sat down in front of the desk, and Davis settled into the chair behind it. With less reluctance, the mountain man took the cup of brandy Lieutenant Wayne poured for him. Lifting the cup to his lips, Titus downed a healthy slug of the liquor. He smacked his lips and said, "I reckon that'll make a man see things a mite clearer."

"I was hoping it would," Davis said. He sipped from his own cup. "I can have you taken back to the smokehouse and locked up for the next week, you know. That would give the *President Jefferson* time enough to get to St. Louis."

Titus looked a little sheepish. "I know you could, Cap'n," he said. "But there ain't no need."

"You're not going to try to settle the score with Count Orlov?"

"Like you said, it wouldn't bring back Zeph or any of the others," Titus said with a sigh. "There's nothin' I can do for 'em now."

Davis leaned back in his chair. He wanted to keep Titus talking for a while longer. "What have you been doing with yourself since you left the Russian expedition?"

"Trappin', mostly. That's all I know, 'cept for guidin' folks like those Rooshans. I heard from a bunch of friendly Injuns 'bout how the Blackfeet jumped the expedition and wiped 'em all out. Made me pure sick, but there wasn't nothin' I could do about it. I figgered ever'body was dead. Didn't find out until later, from some different Injuns, that the count and his brother had made it back here."

"It wasn't the Blackfeet who attacked the party, according to Viktor Dorochenko and Miss Galovnin," Davis said.

Titus snorted. "Sure it was. I seen the boy that blasted count shot, and he was a Blackfoot, all right. Ain't no mistakin' those markin's on his clothes and moccasins."

Davis frowned in thought. "You're probably right. The medicine bag Count Orlov was carrying as a trophy was definitely Blackfoot in design, according to Mr. Catlin, and he knows those people as well as anyone." The captain shook his head. "For some reason, Viktor and Miss Galovnin want us to believe it was another band who massacred the members of the Russian expedition."

Titus stared at him. "Why would Viktor and that little Rooshan gal want that?"

"I don't know," Davis answered honestly. "Perhaps they grew fond of the Blackfeet during their captivity. I've heard of such things happening. They may feel that they owe their lives to old Buffalo's Back Fat and his people. In a way, I can understand. I've always been fond of the chief myself. He hasn't caused nearly as much trouble for the army as he could have."

"But now that he's on the warpath, you're goin' after him?"

Davis sipped his brandy again. "We have no proof of anything, other than that medicine bag," he said. "And with the testimony of Viktor and Miss Galovnin that another band was responsible for the attack, there's not much I can do. The War Department wouldn't like it if I rushed off to attack the Blackfeet based on what we know now."

Titus drained the rest of his cup and put it down hard on the captain's desk. "So the redskins get off scot-free, just like that Count fella," he said disgustedly. "Zeph and all them other folks die, and nobody pays the price for it. Where's the justice in that?"

Captain Davis laughed quietly. "This is the frontier, Titus. We have to be concerned first of all with survival. Justice, when it comes, is usually in the hands of a higher power."

30

NIGHT HAD FALLEN OVER the gentle, grassy slopes as the riverboat reached the area of rolling hills. Viktor, Alena, and Sasha had eaten supper in the officers' mess with Captain Fulton and the other officers. Frederick had dined alone in his room, which was a good decision, Alena thought. None of them wanted to spend any more time with him than was absolutely necessary.

Captain Thaddeus Fulton was a short, stout man with a bushy salt-and-pepper beard, through which he habitually stroked his blunt fingers, and a shock of hair that seemed equally divided between streaks of coal black and pure white. After dinner, he invited Viktor and Sasha to join him for a drink. Viktor accepted readily, but Sasha hesitated until Alena said, "I'll be going back to my quarters now." She stood up, prompting the men around the table to stand as well.

"I will escort you," Sasha offered quickly, but Alena shook her head.

"I can find my way with no trouble," she said. "Your riverboat is impressive, Captain Fulton, but hardly so large that one could easily get lost."

"You seem to know your way around, ma'am," Fulton

said. "But I can have one of my men accompany you, if you like."

"Thank you, but it is not necessary."

Fulton shrugged in acceptance and Alena said her good nights, leaving the men to sit around the table and smoke and drink and tell bawdy stories—or whatever it was that men did in these situations. A part of her was curious and wished she could stay, but she knew her companions would not behave as they normally would if she was there.

She tightened a shawl given to her by Captain Davis's wife across her shoulders as she started toward her cabin. The night was silent, but after listening to the roar and thump of the boat's engine all afternoon, that silence seemed somehow deafening. The *President Jefferson* had come to a stop for the night, since trying to negotiate the river's treacherous bed in the darkness was too dangerous. They would resume their journey bright and early the next morning, Captain Fulton had assured them at dinner.

Despite the fact that spring was almost over, the nights were still cool this far north, something else about Montana Territory that reminded Alena of Mother Russia. She was glad she was wearing the shawl to ward off the chill, and hastened to get out of the night air.

Out of the thick shadows that danced along the inside of the deck next to the wall, a figure suddenly emerged, startling a frightened gasp out of Alena. She stepped back, her hands tightening on the shawl. She thought the looming figure was probably one of the boat's crewmen, but she said, "Who . . . ?"

"Good evening, my dear," came the voice of Count Orlov, and Alena relaxed. She disliked Frederick intensely and wished she had never been betrothed to him. But she did not fear him as she would have feared one of those rough American boatmen.

Frederick moved into the faint light from the stars and a quarter moon. Alena could see his face now. He wore his usual arrogant expression, the same smirk he had displayed ever since she had known him.

Had he learned *nothing* from all his experiences here on

the frontier? How could he still be the same man who had come here? Alena wondered. She was certainly not the same woman.

"You've been at dinner, I take it?" he said.

"Yes, with the captain and with . . . with Viktor and Sasha."

"Ah, yes, the Cossack and my brother. Traitors, both of them."

Alena stiffened. She did not want to hear anything Frederick had to say, especially any lies he had made up about Viktor and Sasha. "Excuse me," she said, her voice as cool as the night air, as she started to step past him.

Frederick moved smoothly to block her path. "You no longer enjoy my company?" he said.

"You know I do not. That is one reason I said I would not marry you."

"You may change your mind when we return to Russia. I am a rich man, you know. I have money as well as my title."

She stared at him in contempt and amazement. Once, perhaps, such things might have had meaning to her, but she was not fully convinced even of that. She had agreed to marry Frederick because of her family, not because of his wealth and status.

"My brother has nothing, you know," Frederick continued. "He has a place to live on my estate only because of my generosity. As for Dorochenko . . . what can he offer you? He is only a Cossack, and they are known for their poverty, as well as their barbaric, uncivilized ways. But still, I am curious . . . has he offered to do the honorable thing and marry you?"

"Viktor is incapable of doing anything *dis*honorable," Alena gritted through clenched teeth. "Unlike some people I know! But he has not asked me to marry him, because he has no reason to. He has always behaved as a perfect gentleman."

Frederick laughed scornfully, clearly incredulous.

"And as for Sasha," Alena went on, her words growing more heated and angry, "he is a good man, better than you will ever be, Frederick Orlov! He does not need your . . . your charity!"

"Oh, yes," Frederick said, "I can just see the two of you, struggling to survive in Moscow, never having enough to eat or to feed the multitude of squalling brats you would probably breed." He stepped closer, and his voice dropped to a purr. "Or you could still be with me in my *dacha* on the Black Sea, eating the finest food, sleeping on silken sheets, never running out of wood in the winter. . . ." Abruptly, his hands shot out and grasped her arms, making her gasp again. "The two of us should be together, Alena! You cannot turn your back on me. I want you—"

"But I do not want you," she said, struggling to pull away from him.

"You will," he said. "I swear that you will."

He jerked her against him then and brought his mouth down hard on hers.

Alena did not hesitate. Her knee drove upward into his groin with all the strength she could manage in her awkward position. Frederick cried out in pain and shoved her away as he doubled over, clutching himself. Russian curses tumbled out of his mouth, but Alena paid no attention to the vile names he was calling her. She was almost overcome with the rush of satisfaction going through her. What she had just done had been long overdue.

Frederick lifted his head. "You have . . . grown very bold," he said through gritted teeth. "I am surprised you did not . . . did not scream for Dorochenko or my brother."

"They would have killed you," Alena said, "and you are not worth getting blood on the hands of either Viktor or Sasha."

With that, she pushed past him, and he made no move to stop her. But as she strode toward her cabin, he called out softly, "You will be sorry for this, Alena. I can make you suffer in ways that you never imagined!"

Alena kept walking, even though she felt the cold touch of fear. Frederick might be right; he *was* still a powerful man in Russia, no matter what had happened here in America.

But whatever form his revenge on her took, it might be worth it to have finally—*finally!*—struck a blow in her own defense.

That, she thought with a faint smile and a nod, had really felt good.

Viktor and Sasha spent a pleasant hour with Captain Fulton and the other men, talking and smoking and drinking. Sasha, especially, seemed to enjoy himself. For the first time he had been accepted into a circle of men on his own merits, rather than simply because he was Count Frederick Orlov's brother. He was having such a good time, in fact, that Viktor told him to stay even though he himself was ready to turn in.

"Are you sure, Viktor?" Sasha asked.

"There is no reason for you to leave just because I am growing old and tired, my friend," Viktor told him. "Good night, Sasha. Good night, gentlemen."

Fulton extended a hand. "Good night, Mr. Dorochenko. It's been a pleasure to share the evening with you, and I'm happy to have you as a passenger on my boat."

Viktor shook hands with the captain, then left the rest of the men to their talk and their pipes and their cups of liquor. When he stepped out onto the deck and closed the door behind him, he drew a deep breath of the cold, clean air. It invigorated him, making him less tired, but he knew the effect would be fleeting. While it lasted, he strode to the railing and gazed out over the darkened prairie, looking far into the west.

This would be a good night, he thought, to roll into a buffalo robe next to the embers of a cooking fire. An even better night to do that with a woman in his arms . . .

"Good evening, Dorochenko."

The voice, smooth and cultured but full of hate, came from behind him, startling him. He really was getting old and inattentive, Viktor thought disgustedly as he turned around. Sasha had come up on him unawares earlier, and now so had Frederick.

"Are you enjoying the voyage so far?" the aristocrat asked mockingly.

"I will enjoy it more when we are back in Russia," Viktor snapped. That was not really true, but he *was* looking forward to seeing Alena truly safe once more. If that meant having to return to Russia, he would go willingly.

"Really?" Frederick murmured. "I do not think you will enjoy your return to our motherland at all, Dorochenko. Do you know why?"

Viktor did not answer. He glared at Frederick in silence.

"I shall tell you, then," the count went on after a moment. "When we get back to Moscow, I intend to ask the czar to have you executed as a traitor."

"That is a lie," Viktor said.

Frederick continued as if he had not heard Viktor's statement. "I shall tell Nicholas how you betrayed those you were supposed to protect, how you kidnapped Alena after letting all the others be massacred, and how you became little better than the red savages with whom you lived."

"None of that is true. I betrayed no one. I kidnapped no one. And the Blackfeet are no better or worse than anyone else—including those at the court of the czar."

"You see," Frederick said smugly. "You convict yourself with your own words. I am certain Nicholas will agree with me. Shall I ask him to have you hanged . . . or shot . . . or perhaps beheaded?"

"The czar will not believe you—" Viktor began.

"He *will*. We both know it, Dorochenko. You are doomed. You never should have humiliated me and cost me the woman I intended to marry."

"So that is what this is about," Viktor breathed. "You never really wanted her. She was simply another adornment for you."

"Nevertheless, I was meant to have her. I still intend to have her, once you are dead and she has gotten over her foolish infatuation with my brother. I plan to send Sasha so far away that Alena will never see him again. Soon she will forget about him and turn once more to me."

"You *are* insane," Viktor growled as he pushed roughly

past Frederick and started on down the deck toward his quarters. Behind him, the count laughed.

"Go on, run, Dorochenko," he called after Viktor. "You cannot escape your fate. Your days are numbered, and each one brings you that much closer to death."

Viktor kept walking, but his steps were heavy with the knowledge that Frederick might well be right.

The sound of galloping hoofbeats grew and swelled over the prairie. A rider was pushing his mount hard, a dangerous practice on such a dark night. All sorts of unseen dangers lurked about. A man riding that fast in the dark was either a fool—or one who had a mighty strong purpose.

Titus figured he had such a purpose. Captain Davis had given him back his rifle and pistol and allowed him to leave the fort late in the afternoon, believing that the riverboat was too far downstream for Titus to catch up to it.

That wasn't the case, not if he rode hard all night. That was exactly what Titus intended to do. He was leaning eagerly over his mount's neck, the long-barreled flintlock held across the saddle in front of him.

"If that cap'n thinks I'm goin' to forget who's to blame for Zeph gettin' killed," Titus muttered to himself as he pushed his horse on to greater speed, "he sure as blazes better think again!"

31

AROUND THE MIDDLE OF the next day, Captain Fulton ordered the *President Jefferson* brought to shore. "Wood's scarce most places out here," he explained to Viktor as several of the riverboat's crewmen leaped ashore with axes and began felling the trees in a small stand. "Anytime we get a chance to take on some fuel for the boilers, we do it."

Viktor nodded, a frown furrowing his forehead under the coonskin cap. He was wearing the buckskins as well, and had the broken saber tucked behind his broad black belt. "You must not waste an opportunity," he said. "You must act while you still have the chance."

"That's right," Fulton said. "Been times I've had to bust up furniture from the cabins just to have something to throw in the woodbox. It ain't a good feelin'."

Viktor could understand that. Desperate situations sometimes called for desperate remedies. How well he knew that!

He looked toward the rear of the vessel and saw Count Frederick Orlov standing near the railing, arms folded, a disinterested look on his patrician face. The count had left his cabin to see why the boat was stopping, Viktor assumed, and he was now perhaps enjoying the warm midday sunshine.

Alena and Sasha were doing the same thing, but they were at the front of the boat, standing at the railing and watching the crewmen fell trees. The sharp sounds of ax blades striking wood filled the air.

Captain Fulton bustled off to tend to some other chore, and Viktor walked toward the bow of the riverboat, the flintlock rifle Kenneth McKenzie had given him cradled in his arms.

Sasha pointed out something to Alena, and Viktor heard her laugh softly as he approached. Sasha smiled at her.

They looked good together, Viktor thought. Too good to allow their future happiness to be ruined by someone like Frederick.

"There is something I must tell you," the big Cossack said bluntly as he stepped up behind the two of them. They both turned, looking surprised.

"What is it, Viktor?" Alena asked.

"I have decided that I am not going back to Russia with you." There, he had said it. He almost sighed in relief, so glad was he to have reached a decision once and for all. Part of a decision, at any rate . . .

"What?" Sasha exclaimed.

Alena was not as startled. She and Viktor had discussed this very possibility. She said quietly, "You are sure this is what you want?"

Viktor had to smile as he gestured at the rolling plains and the snowcapped mountains still visible in the distance. "Why not? This is a big land. Big enough for one Cossack."

"But Russia is your home," Sasha protested.

"No more. I have no family waiting for me there. Perhaps here it will be different."

Alena reached out and rested a hand on his arm. "I feel like I am part of your family, Viktor."

"Leaving you is the hardest thing of all, little one," Viktor said, carefully keeping his voice under control. It would not be proper for a Cossack to display a feeling of loss or sorrow too openly. "But now I know you will be all right. Sasha will look after you."

"Me?" Sasha said, his voice squeaking a little. "I mean—of course I will look after—it will be my honor, my privilege—Alena, I —"

"I know what you are trying to say, Sasha," she told him. "I feel the same way." She turned back to Viktor. "Will you never return to Russia, even for a visit?"

"I cannot," he said heavily. "Nothing awaits me in Russia but death. The count has promised that he will see to that. He is going to ask the czar to have me executed." Viktor said nothing of the other promise Frederick had made, the vow to ruin Sasha and Alena's relationship by sending Sasha far away from Moscow.

"Frederick cannot do such a thing!" Sasha said angrily. "Alena and I both know you did nothing wrong. We will tell the czar—"

Viktor shook his head. "But who will the czar believe?" He paused. "Nicholas will believe what your brother tells him, because Frederick is a nobleman and I am only a Cossack. Nor will he believe either of you. Even if he did, he would have no choice but to publicly accept the count's story. My only chance to live is here in this land, where I can make a new start."

"Oh, Viktor," Alena said, her voice suddenly trembling, "I know you are right, but I can hardly bear the thought of being parted from you forever!"

She threw herself into his arms. Viktor embraced her and awkwardly patted her hair, feeling as uncomfortable as he always did during these demonstrations of affection.

As he held Alena, however, he knew that he had reached the right decision. He had not told her and Sasha all the truth. His life *would* be in great danger if he ever returned to Russia, but not because of any lies Frederick might tell the czar. Frederick would never have that chance, just as he would never have the chance to send Sasha away and ruin two young lives that were so full of promise.

Before he left the riverboat, Viktor intended to make sure that Frederick Orlov was dead. He was willing to make himself a murderer, if it meant happiness for Alena and Sasha.

"A very touching scene indeed."

Viktor turned slowly to face Frederick, who had come up behind them. He had heard the count's footsteps this time, but was unwilling to turn away from Alena and Sasha until Frederick spoke. He was not surprised that the count had been unable to resist the temptation to taunt them with his plans.

But Viktor *was* surprised at the sight of the pistol in Frederick's hand. Frederick's arm hung loosely at his side, so that the barrel of the gun pointed toward the deck, but there was still an aura of menace about him.

"What was that I just heard you saying, Dorochenko?" Frederick went on. "That you intend to leave us?"

"I will not go back to Russia," Viktor said bluntly. There was no longer any point in denying it.

"You are still a member of the czar's army, Dorochenko," Frederick snapped. "You must follow my orders. If you do not—" His right hand came up, bringing the pistol with it. "I will be justified in shooting you down like the dog you are."

Alena cried, "Frederick, no!" and would have stepped forward, but Sasha caught hold of her arm, tugging her closer to him.

"Put the gun down, Frederick. Please." Sasha's voice was still a little tentative, Viktor thought, but there was strength there. Strength that would grow, if it was ever given a chance.

Without looking at them, Frederick said harshly, "Be quiet, both of you. The time for talking is past." His gaze was fastened on Viktor, and a strange light burned in his eyes. "Well, Dorochenko, what is it to be? Will you return to Russia and face your fate there . . . or do you die here and now?"

Viktor moved slightly, putting more space between him and Alena and Sasha. He did not want anything happening to them, even by accident. "I will not go back," he said.

The count smiled. That was obviously the answer he had wanted to hear. "Very well," he said. The pistol was leveled at the Cossack, and Frederick's finger began to tighten on the trigger. . . .

Viktor suddenly lunged toward the count, lashing out with the flintlock rifle. The long barrel struck Frederick's wrist and knocked his arm aside just as he jerked the trigger of the pistol. The gun blasted, but the shot went wild. The next instant Viktor crashed into him, and both of them went down in a tangled sprawl on the deck.

"Viktor!" Alena screamed.

"Frederick, stop it!" Sasha shouted.

Viktor heard the exclamations of his young friends, but he had no time to even glance in their direction. He had his hands full with Frederick, who was struggling desperately. The count's strength was surprising, but not when one remembered that he was a military hero as well as a nobleman. Viktor pinned him to the deck momentarily by pressing the flintlock across his chest, then he let go of the rifle and reached for Frederick's throat.

The sound of running footsteps came vaguely to Viktor's ears as he closed his fingers around Frederick's neck. That would be Captain Fulton and other members of the riverboat's crew, their attention drawn by the shot and the shouting. They would be hurrying to see what the trouble was.

None of them would interfere, Viktor thought as he tightened his grip. This was between the two of them, and the Americans would not want to become involved.

Americans solved their own problems and were quick to let others do the same. And he was an American now, Viktor thought, more American than Russian.

Nearby, Alena grabbed the arm of one of the crewmen who had rushed up to see what was going on. "You must stop them!" she said anxiously to the brawny riverboatman.

"No offense, lady," the man replied with a grin, "but they look like they're doin' just fine. Out here, we don't get mixed up in a personal scrap 'tween two men."

Frantically, Alena turned to Sasha, who was just as upset as she was. "Sasha, do something!"

He shook his head regretfully as he watched Viktor and

Frederick rolling around the deck, each trying to gain the upper hand. "I cannot," Sasha said. "This is between Viktor and Frederick, and both of them would hate me if I tried to stop them. The trouble between them has gone on long enough. There must be an ending."

Alena moaned in frustration, but her eyes never left the two thrashing figures.

Frederick lashed out with the empty pistol he was still holding, smashing it against Viktor's head. The blow made Viktor loosen his grip on the count's throat. Frederick heaved his body upward, throwing Viktor off to the side.

Frederick rolled the other way and came up onto his knees. His hand went to his bruised throat, and he knelt there holding it for a moment while he drew great heaving breaths of air. When he had recovered enough to speak, he grated, "I . . . I will kill you for that, Dorochenko! You are not the only one who fought against the mad Frenchman!"

Viktor was still stunned from the blow to his head. It had knocked the coonskin cap off, and his hair fell down over his eyes. He shook it back and looked up at Frederick. The count might not know it, but he had played right into Viktor's hands. The Cossack had been prepared to kill him in cold blood if necessary, to protect Alena and Sasha, but now that would not be necessary.

This fight was a fair one, and it would be to the death.

Frederick surged to his feet before Viktor was ready. The Cossack tried to get up as well, but the count was faster. Frederick's booted foot caught him in the side in a vicious kick, sending him rolling across the deck again. Frederick reached down and snatched up the rifle Viktor had dropped. He lifted it, ready to slam the butt down on Viktor's head.

"Viktor, look out!" Alena cried.

Viktor had just come to a stop after rolling away from Frederick's kick. He moved again, throwing himself to the side as the butt of the flintlock slammed down onto the deck where his head had been an instant earlier. Viktor reached up and caught hold of Frederick's coat. With a grunt of effort, he slung him to the deck and sent the rifle clattering away across the wooden surface.

That gave Viktor a few seconds respite, and they were precious seconds indeed. Viktor scuttled to one side, putting a little more distance between them, then heaved himself to his feet. Frederick began to do the same thing. Unlike the count, however, Viktor did not try to strike while his opponent was still getting up. He stood, fists clenched, waiting.

Captain Fulton and his men were ranged across the deck, watching the battle. Fulton called out, "You want me to put a stop to this, Dorochenko?" He rested his hand on the butt of the pistol tucked behind his belt.

Viktor shook his head, partially in response to Fulton's question and partially to clear away some of the cobwebs in his brain. "We will finish this, the Count and I," he said.

"*I* will finish it!" Frederick roared. "I will kill you, Cossack!"

Viktor lifted his hands and motioned with them. "Come on, Count," he said, scorn and contempt dripping from his voice.

With an incoherent shout, Frederick charged. Viktor was ready for him. For a long moment the two men stood toe-to-toe, slugging it out, each of them landing punch after punch, seemingly to no effect. Viktor was caught up in such a desperate rage that he was able to shrug off the blows, and he suspected Frederick felt the same way.

Eventually, though, one of Frederick's punches missed, throwing him off balance. Viktor took advantage of the opportunity to bury his fist in his opponent's midsection, doubling over the nobleman. Viktor raised his arms and clubbed his hands together, intending to bring the linked fists down on the back of Frederick's neck and end the fight.

But before he could do so, Frederick drove forward, butting him in the stomach and knocking him backward. Viktor tried to stay on his feet, but Frederick's maneuver had taken him by surprise. He felt himself falling, and an instant later he crashed onto the deck again, this time with Frederick on top of him.

Frederick's right hand closed on Viktor's throat with

crushing force, cutting off his air. Viktor reached up and caught hold of Frederick's throat, using the muscles in his arm and back to force the count to the side. They went rolling across the deck again, locked in the life-and-death combat.

Suddenly Viktor felt Frederick's free hand groping at his waist, and too late he realized what Frederick was after. Frederick ripped the broken saber free from behind Victor's belt, and Viktor felt the icy bite of the blade as Frederick stabbed him in the side.

"Frederick, no!" Alena screamed, and Viktor barely heard her.

"Damn you, Frederick!" That was Sasha. His footsteps rang on the deck quite close to the struggling men, and Viktor knew he was going to try to stop Frederick from using the broken saber again. As caught up in a killing frenzy as Frederick was, he might turn on Sasha with the saber if the young man interfered. Viktor could not let that happen.

Ignoring the pain in his side and the sudden wetness that was soaking the buckskin shirt, Viktor reached inside himself and found the last of his strength. With a roar, he rose from the deck, lifting Frederick with him. The muscles in his arms and shoulders bunched as he straightened and flung Frederick away from him. Frederick slammed to the deck and lay motionless as Viktor stood there several feet away, swaying, pressing a hand to the wound in his side.

Too late, Viktor saw that he had thrown Frederick right next to the flintlock rifle. . . .

Frederick's eyes cleared, and he seized the rifle before anyone could stop him. His thumb looped around the hammer of the flintlock and pulled it back as he sat up, training the barrel on Viktor's unsteady form.

"Stop it, Frederick!" Sasha said, again starting forward.

Viktor waved him away with his free hand. "Stay back!" he ordered. "He is a madman!"

Frederick was climbing awkwardly to his feet, keeping the rifle pointed toward Viktor as he did so. "A madman, am I?" he said hoarsely. "Perhaps. But I have won this fight, Dorochenko, and you have lost."

"For God's sake, Frederick," Alena said in a strangled voice, "if you ever loved me—"

"Love is for lesser men," Frederick snapped. "I desired you, and I still do. You will be mine, Alena. I will send Sasha away so that you will never see him again. And as for Dorochenko . . . he will be dead." The barrel of the rifle steadied as Frederick lined the sights on Viktor's face. "Now, in the name of the czar and the Russian people, I execute this traitor."

"Do not lie," Viktor said calmly, still holding his left hand to the wound in his side. "You kill me only because we all know there is nothing noble about you."

"Either way, Cossack," Frederick hissed between clenched teeth, "you are still dead. . . ."

Viktor stared at him, defiant and unafraid to the end, as a gunshot rang out.

Frederick's head jerked back, his body stiffening. The rifle slipped from his suddenly nerveless fingers and fell to the deck, unfired. A trickle of blood welled from the black hole in the center of his forehead, and then he crumpled to the deck.

Alena let out a scream, and Sasha pulled her tightly against him. He swallowed hard as he stared at the lifeless body of his brother.

Slowly, Viktor looked around, searching for the source of the shot that had killed Frederick. For an instant he thought that Fulton or one of the crewmen from the *President Jefferson* had gunned down the count, but then he realized that the sound of the shot had come from too far away for that to be true. The next moment his keen eyes spotted the figure standing on a ridge a hundred yards from the river. Even at that distance, Viktor recognized him.

Titus still had his flintlock rifle pressed to his shoulder. Smoke curled from the muzzle of the long barrel. He lowered the rifle, waved down at the people on the riverboat, then turned to his horse. Viktor watched as Titus mounted up and rode away, vanishing over the crest of the hill.

"That man," Sasha said in a hollow voice. "He saved your life, Viktor."

"And settled a score," Viktor said quietly. "Farewell, Titus. Perhaps we will meet again someday."

Captain Fulton stepped forward. "Looked to me like a justifiable killing, and that's what I'll tell anybody who asks me about it," he said.

"Thank you," Viktor said solemnly. "I would not have trouble following Titus because he acted to save my life."

Fulton pointed at the bloodstain that was spreading on Viktor's side. "Speaking of saving your life, we'd better get that patched up before you bleed to death all over my boat. And there's the matter of burying this fella, too."

"I will bury him," Viktor said. "It is my responsibility. Then I will leave."

"But you're hurt!" Alena exclaimed. "And you don't have to go now. Frederick is dead. You can go back to Russia."

Viktor shook his head. "The count was not the only reason I wished to stay in this land. And this wound . . . it is nothing. A mere scratch."

"That is the Cossack in you talking," Sasha said.

"Perhaps. I am sorry about your brother."

Sasha sighed. "Frederick brought his fate on himself."

Viktor turned and looked toward the west, toward the hill where Titus had disappeared. "As do we all . . ." he murmured.

32

LATER THEY STOOD ON THE bank of the river, next to the mound of freshly turned earth. Viktor held his coonskin cap in one hand, the flintlock that had almost taken his life in the other. Beside him, Sasha put his arm around Alena's shoulders. Both of the younger people were crying silently, but they were not mourning Count Frederick Orlov.

Viktor put his cap on and turned away from the grave, moving a little stiffly due to the bandages around his midsection. Captain Fulton had suggested that he accompany them as far as the next settlement, at least, so that a doctor could look at the wound in his side. Viktor had declined. The first mate of the *President Jefferson,* who seemed to have some medical knowledge, had done a good job of cleaning and dressing the wound. Viktor thought it would heal without much trouble, but if it did begin to fester, he was fairly certain he could find some of the moss that old Stands with a Stick used to heal the earlier wound in his shoulder. No, it was better that he be moving on, Viktor thought.

Captain Fulton and several of the crewmen were standing a respectful distance away. He could depend on them to deliver Alena and Sasha safely to St. Louis, Viktor knew.

He reached inside the pouch that was slung over his shoulder along with his powder horn and brought out the medicine bag Frederick had taken from the body of the young Blackfoot warrior.

"Do you have to go?" Alena asked from behind him.

"There is much to see in this land," Viktor replied without turning to look at her. He kept his gaze fixed on the rolling prairie and the distant mountains. "I would see all of it that I can."

"Will you go back to Buffalo's Back Fat and his people?"

"I must return this medicine bag to the family of Cloud Caller. After that, who knows?" Viktor tucked the bag away, then steeled himself to turn and look at them. To Sasha, he said, "You will take good care of the princess. I expect much of you, my friend."

"I give you my word," Sasha said, his voice thick with emotion. He looked down at Alena as his arm tightened around her shoulders. "I will watch over her and . . . and love her."

"Sasha . . . ?" she said, looking up at him and smiling through her tears.

Viktor shouldered his rifle and turned toward the west. "Farewell, my friends. Perhaps one day we will all meet again." He began walking.

"But, Viktor," Alena called after him, "you don't even have a horse."

He looked back at her and smiled. "I am Three Ponies, remember? I do not need a horse."

He turned again and strode toward the far-off mountains. His long-legged strides carried him away quickly, and his figure began to dwindle in the distance as Alena and Sasha watched him go. Alena lifted her hand and waved. "Good-bye, Viktor!" she called, not knowing if he could still hear her or not. "Good-bye, Three Ponies!"

Viktor did not look back again. He walked on, moving steadily toward the mountains, and soon he was gone from sight.

AUTHOR'S NOTE

Some of the events in *Cossack Three Ponies* are loosely based on historical incidents. The Blackfoot chief Stu-mick-o-sucks (Buffalo's Back Fat), his wife Eeh-nis-kin (Crystal Stone), and their grandson actually existed, and the boy was stolen by the Crows, traditional enemies of the Blackfeet, several times. The artist George Catlin and the trader Kenneth McKenzie are also historical figures, and McKenzie took care of the grandson of Buffalo's Back Fat at Fort Union, as mentioned in the novel. Several parties of Russian noblemen traveled to the American frontier to hunt buffalo and visit the Indians, but the Russian expedition in this novel is fictitious, as are all the other characters and incidents.

J. L. REASONER

AUTHOR OF *RIVERS OF GOLD*

__*Healer's Calling*   0-425-15487-4/$5.99

On the bloody battlefields of the Civil War, Sara Black had proven her courage and skill as a medic. Now, the war had ended, but she had found her true calling: to become one of America's first woman doctors.

__*The Healer's Road*   0-515-11762-5/$5.99

When his parents died because of a lack of proper medicine, Thomas Black vowed to become a doctor and better people's lives. Now, with the advent of war, he is challenged to provide better care than ever before–in a fraction of the time. During the savage conflict of the Civil War, Thomas Black, and his two children who follow in his footsteps, will embody the true nobility of the American spirit.